"Somehow I don't get the feeling you're a man who asks for kisses all that often."

Was that her voice? Those seductive, breathy tones that sounded like they came from the deepest part of her?

"I can't remember ever wanting one more."

He hesitated for the briefest moment, those vivid blue eyes sparking with fire, before pressing his lips to hers. Where she thought the awkward angle of their airplane seats would make it difficult to enjoy his kiss, it did the opposite. The barrier actually made the kiss sweeter, a subtle reminder they needed to work for what they wanted.

Or reach out and take it.

The thought hovered in the back of her mind as she laid her hands on Liam's shoulders. If their kiss in the elevator that morning had been a surprise assault on the senses, this was a lush invitation.

Dear Reader,

Welcome back to the House of Steele! I've had a wonderful time writing about the Steele siblings—Liam, Campbell, Kensington and Rowan—and the high-end security firm they founded as a family. And oh, boy, have I been looking forward to writing Liam's story.

In *The Manhattan Encounter* the elusive, play-by-his-own-rules Liam finally falls into a situation he can't brush off, walk away from or ignore. Pressed by his wily grandfather, Liam reluctantly takes on the case of a family acquaintance who has fallen into a spot of trouble.

Dr. Isabella Magnini, a quiet scientist, has discovered an incredible breakthrough in DNA research. But when that breakthrough leads some unpleasant people to her door, she goes to the House of Steele for help.

One of the things I most love about being an author is when a book takes me places I never expected. *The Manhattan Encounter* was one of those special books. When I started out, this was a fun, suspenseful romp putting two polar opposites on the run from the bad guys. What came out was an exploration of the importance of family, of self and of the deep importance of giving yourself—heart and soul—to another.

I hope you enjoy Liam and Isabella's story!

Best,

Addison Fox

THE MANHATTAN
ENCOUNTER

—

Addison Fox

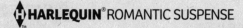

Recycling programs
for this product may
not exist in your area.

ISBN-13: 978-0-373-27880-0

THE MANHATTAN ENCOUNTER

Printed in U.S.A.

H HARLEQUIN®
www.Harlequin.com

ADDISON FOX

is a Philadelphia girl transplanted to Dallas, Texas. Although her similarities to Grace Kelly stop at sharing the same place of birth, she's often dreamed of marrying a prince and living along the Mediterranean.

In the meantime, she's more than happy penning romance novels about two strong-willed and exciting people who deserve their happy ever after—after she makes them work so hard for it, of course. When she's not writing, she can be found spending time with family and friends, reading or enjoying a glass of wine.

Find out more about Addison or contact her at her website—www.addisonfox.com—or catch up with her on Facebook (addisonfoxauthor) and Twitter (@addisonfox).

For Jan

Dearest friend, trusted confidant, word ninja, sounding board and wine enabler. For all these reasons and so many, many more, I am so blessed you are a part of my life.

Chapter 1

London, Today

"You can't be a damn playboy all your life."

Liam Steele stared down his grandfather and ignored the fact the man's rheumy blue eyes held more mischief than censure. "Fascinating advice coming from a man who narrowly avoided an arranged marriage to a princess because the urge to sow wild oats remained too strong."

"I was waiting for the right woman. She wasn't it."

"Maybe I am, too."

Alexander Steele's snort was loud and about as subtle as the whistle of an oncoming freight train. "Could have fooled me."

A light sigh floated over the top of Liam's head before a gentle hand cupped his shoulder. "Alex. For the love of God and all that's holy, would you please leave the man alone? Even I'm sick of listening to you."

Liam stood and took his grandmother's hand, helping her into the chair. "Nice save, Grandmother."

"A necessary one." She settled her hands in her lap, her gaze focused on her husband. "He's been going on and on and I'm done listening to him. You'll settle down when you're damn well ready to and not a moment sooner. Just because your father married at twenty doesn't mean that's the right path for you."

"Now, Penelope." His grandfather started in with the tone Liam and his sister Kensington had dubbed the "Parliament Address." "Marriage is good enough for Campbell, Rowan and Kenzi."

"Because they found the right partners. Liam's still looking for the woman who makes his heart sing."

Liam shook his now-empty glass, the whiskey-tinged ice cubes making a satisfying sound to echo the end of Round 1. "I'm actually standing right here, you know."

"Yes, dear." His grandmother patted the hand he'd left on her shoulder. "But sadly, the argument rages on whether you're here or not. Your grandfather has wedding fever."

Which, to his grandmother's earlier point, his siblings had done an admirable job of feeding. Three relationships in less than a year—good, solid relationships that were destined to stand the tests of time—had only increased his grandfather's focus.

His grandfather's *maniacal* focus.

"In the event it's escaped anyone's notice, I date plenty."

"Plenty being the operative word," Alexander Steele grumbled. "You date a series of vapid models who are convinced a piece of chewing gum will make them fat. Real women eat."

Liam had learned long ago to let the opinions of others—even those he loved as dearly as he did his family—

roll off his back. He lived his life as he chose and couldn't muster up much concern about what anyone else thought.

So why was the urge to simply leave so overwhelming?

"I'm only in London overnight. Any chance we can discuss something a bit more interesting?"

"What's more interesting than the rest of your life?"

"Living it." He set the leaded glass down with a thud on his grandmother's antique end table. Whatever either of his grandparents had been about to say faded on their lips as they both stared at him, silence descending on the room like a thick roll of fog.

Isabella Magnini dug the piece of paper out of her pocket once more to double-check she'd come to the right address. Rain beat down on her umbrella, sluicing off in a curtain of water that made the front door hard to see, and she squinted to make out the gold numbers partially hidden by wet ivy. At least she'd found the place.

The bottom of her slacks was a soupy wash of wool against her ankles, striking evidence that the Tube ride that had begun her evening was a monumentally bad idea.

Like coming here.

She fought the thought and marched the rest of the way toward the door. No backing out now. No turning around. No wishing her actions away. She needed help and if the increasing threats finding their way to her office, her home and her car were any indication, she needed it now.

The London townhome rose several impressive stories above her as she lifted the heavy knocker. A small porch cover shielded her from the rain and she turned to shake off her umbrella as she waited for the door to open. A heavy clap of thunder startled her—just like everything else these days—and she jumped, water flying off her umbrella like a wet dog shaking out its fur.

"Hey!"

A dark voice behind her added to the surprise and she whirled around, the motion flinging more heavy drops of water toward the doorway.

A man filled the portal, his thick dark—almost black—hair brushed back except for a few errant curls that formed artful waves over his forehead. Broad shoulders filled the breadth of a white button-down shirt that tapered into a narrow waist clad in black slacks. The water she'd inadvertently slung at him stained the white in heavy drops and he wiped water from his eyes before turning a narrow gaze on her.

"Sorry. I'm so sorry." She reached forward in a vague attempt to wipe the water off his shirt but stopped with her arm outstretched as the man took a decided step back.

Oh no. She'd written the address down wrong, that had to be it. Another mindless mistake, one of the many she made in her daily life as her head filled with the abstract thoughts of her work. Thoughts that took up so much room she edged out all the smaller details others had no problem recalling with ease.

She shook her head and dropped her outstretched arm, the heavy pour of rain at her back misting against her nape. She had the wrong house. Alexander Steele was eighty-five if he was a day and the man who answered the door most definitely did not have the look of hired help. This part of London was known for its high-end homes, an increasing number filled by eligible bachelors who worked the stock market or billed exorbitant rates at the city's most well-heeled law firms. She'd clearly found her way to the front door of one of them.

"I'm so sorry. I must have the wrong house."

The smallest spark of warmth filled his shockingly blue

eyes before he reached out a hand and gestured her closer. "Where are you headed?"

She glanced at the crumpled paper, now nearly transparent with rain, but didn't move from her spot. "Three twenty-five."

"You've found it."

"But I'm looking for Mr. Steele."

"I'm his grandson, Liam." Cultured tones lit up his voice—not quite British under the American but obviously influenced—before he reached out and snatched the umbrella, then took her firmly in hand. "You must be this evening's entertainment."

Entertainment? "I'm just here to see your grandfather, Mr. Steele. I won't take up much of his time."

A small smile lit up his face and the transformation was so shocking she simply stopped in the center of the large foyer to stare for a moment. A large glass chandelier hung from the ceiling, lighting the entryway in a soft glow and the warm light bounced off the rich locks of his hair.

The smile changed his face—warmed it considerably—and in some small, nonsensical portion of her brain she had the distinct thought the man smiled rarely, if ever. The stoic figure who stood in the doorway had looked like a formidable opponent. But the smiling man before her was a devastating one.

Sleek as a shark and likely as lethal, with a smile that begged you to come closer.

"Who are you?"

The words were as effective as the rain at dousing her fancies and she pulled herself from her drifting thoughts. "Isabella Magnini."

"*Dr.* Magnini?"

"Yes."

"The Dr. Magnini who presented at Davos last year?"

"One and the same."

Liam shook his head once more, his muttered words nearly undetectable as another clap of thunder echoed off the marble entryway. "Wily old bastard."

"Excuse me?"

"Please, let me take your coat. My grandparents are in their sitting room enjoying a cocktail."

"I'm so sorry to intrude on your family's personal time."

The smile fell, that stoic facade concealing all expression on his face. The slightest lines bracketed his eyes and mouth—faint, yet evident enough to add character—and whatever sarcasm she'd sensed vanished when he finally spoke. "No intrusion at all as I've no doubt you were invited this evening."

"Your grandfather suggested I come. He's been—" She broke off, not sure how to explain the conversations she'd had to date with Alexander Steele about the strange happenings in her life.

How did one explain the subtle sense of being watched? Or the odd feeling that someone had rifled through your things, even when your clothing and papers and bookshelves remained in perfect order?

Or the very real sense someone had been inside your home?

She fought the shiver that threatened to roll down her spine and focused on the man before her, willing her nerves to calm. "Your grandfather believes he has the resources to help me with a…small matter."

If he had any question about her hesitation he gave no indication. "May I take your coat?"

Isabella glanced down at the rain-soaked front of her jacket—how had she forgotten it?—and slipped from the garment. The endless days of spring rain had greeted her the moment she'd arrived in London the previous week from New York and she had moments where she'd wondered if she'd ever get dry.

His fingers brushed hers when she passed over her coat and she forced herself to maintain simple, even breaths despite the flare of heat that skittered up her arm. Humans touched. Their bodies came into contact all the time. It was normal. Common, even.

And certainly nothing to dwell on.

She was dimly aware of his gaze before he turned to settle her coat on a hallway stand. That same rush of heat that had run up her arm kept up its assault, crossing her chest before settling in her stomach. With a precision born of long years of practice, she counted off the periodic elements in her head and willed her pulse to calm.

Hydrogen. Helium. Lithium. Bery—

"Let's go introduce you to my grandparents, then."

With a soft sigh she followed behind him, the elements fading away like smoke, replaced with decidedly more *well-formed* thoughts. Like how strong and safe and solid and *reassuring* those broad shoulders looked under his rain-flecked shirt. And how enticing it would be to simply reach out and touch him.

Stick with the elements, girl.

Men who looked like Liam Steele didn't look twice at women with wild hair and curvy figures and, in the rare instances where they did, her profession typically ran them off before they could take a third glance.

Or any action at all.

Wily old bastard.

The thought had run through his mind on a loop since Dr. Isabella Magnini arrived, soaked to the skin, a half hour ago. Liam hadn't touched the second whiskey his grandfather had poured for him while he'd gone to answer the door, preferring to keep his wits fully about him. The choice was a smart one as it hadn't taken Alexander Steele long to dive into the matter at hand.

"You need to protect the girl, Liam."

"Of course we will, Grandfather. That's what the House of Steele does." He and his siblings had formed the House of Steele about four years before, their diverse interests and skills a match for a surprising number of in-need individuals and companies. From basic protection to digital forensics to active investigation, he and his siblings had the tools and the talent to fix problems.

While Liam ran the firm with his siblings, there was no mistaking his grandfather's continued use of the word "you" had a distinctly singular ring to it.

Although it was clear the rain-soaked doctor needed their help, he'd yet to fully understand what her problem was, and his grandfather's pleading eyes and continued insistence on protection weren't getting him any closer to figuring it out.

"Why don't you explain the problem for me, Dr. Magnini?" He'd kept his attitude casual, unwilling to play into Alexander's hands, but Liam had to admit his gaze had strayed toward the woman a few more times than was comfortable. He had no idea why, but something in her demeanor had drawn his attention.

It certainly wasn't her clothes.

Her sweater—a rich cashmere that looked like it had been stretched and worried over at the waist until it lost all shape—didn't do much for her figure, and the wool pants that clung to the bottom of her legs like wet shackles were about as fashionable as a potato sack, but...

His thoughts tapered off as her gaze collided with his.

Those large green eyes blinked in surprise, before she nodded and looked away. "I've tried to explain it to your grandfather and not very successfully, I'm afraid. Something's wrong, even if I can't define exactly why."

"Wrong how?"

"Someone's rifled through my things at work. And I know my notes have been tampered with." She took a small sip of the water his grandmother had foisted on her earlier before delicately resetting the glass on a small end table. "And I believe someone broke into my home last week when I was at work late."

"Your home?" Anger coated his throat with raw fire and he suddenly wished for the whiskey he'd spent the last half hour avoiding. "What do you think this person's after?"

Her slender fingers bunched in the waist of her sweater and Liam saw why the piece of clothing had no shape. "My work. My research."

"Which revolves around what, exactly?"

"Genetics."

Liam knew science had its champions and its critics across all branches, but what could she have possibly gotten herself involved with? And when did run-of-the-mill scientists become the object of something dangerous enough to have them seeking help?

"Enough talk for the moment. Let's go into the dining room and eat. Poor Isabella looks famished."

Penelope Steele's words received no argument and he helped his grandmother to her feet. He was startled to see Isabella follow suit with his grandfather, making a show of giving over her arm when Liam knew good and well the motion really helped to steady the older man.

"She's lovely, isn't she?" Penelope wasted no time on the observation, her comment uttered the moment the two of them were out of earshot.

He shot his grandmother a sideways eye. "You're in on this, too?"

"The woman needs help, Liam."

"No doubt, but the timing of her arrival and Grandfather's evening lecture were rather curious, don't you think?"

His grandmother made a show of dusting some nonexistent lint from her sweater. "I'm sure I don't know what you mean."

"Of course you don't. You're the innocent here instead of a ready foil for Grandfather's machinations."

"She needs you."

Liam stared down from where he towered over his petite grandmother in height. There was an urgency underlying her words, but it was the bleak look that creased the tissue-thin skin of her face that pulled him up short.

"We'll help her, Grandmother. I promise."

Penelope nodded, then disengaged their arms as Liam pulled out her chair. Her quick glance at the empty doorway had her continuing. "Isabella's a tough girl. A shockingly brilliant one, too. She spent her late teens with her grandfather after her father was tried as a British traitor about fifteen years ago."

"Tried for what?"

"He was convicted as a traitor of selling dirty bombs to third-world rebels."

"And her mother?"

Penelope's lips pursed tightly together and Liam knew that look didn't bode well. "She had a mental breakdown after the news of her husband's activities. She's spent years in a private facility."

Isabella and his grandfather came through the door and he ignored the small spear of sympathy attempting to burrow under his breastbone as his gaze took in the pair. He knew what it was like to lose a parent. To lose both parents.

And while death wasn't fair, there was a certain mercy in knowing the loss wasn't by choice.

"Thank you, dear." His grandmother patted his arm as she settled her napkin in her lap.

The small gesture was enough to pull him from his strange musings and he moved around the table to help Isabella. A subtle confusion filled her gaze when he pulled her chair back before she readily accepted with a small nod. "Thank you."

"My pleasure."

Her light scent—a subtle mix of roses and the lingering scent of the rain—sent a quick shot of adrenaline through his system as he pushed in her chair. His stomach clenched on the sensation and he tightened his grip on the back rail to stop the slight trembling in his fingers.

If that madness wasn't enough, he almost reached for one of the dark, heavy curls that flowed down her back before he caught himself.

The knowing smile on his grandmother's face was the effective dousing he needed and he stepped away quickly and took his own seat.

The same, self-righteous anger that had carried him through the earlier portion of the evening rose up once again to tighten his throat. He loved his grandparents—knew their bond was closer than most, especially with their hand in raising and caring for him and his siblings after their parents' unexpected deaths—but that didn't give them the right to meddle in his life.

He got along just fine by himself. Absolutely fine. And no amount of interference from his family was going to change his mind.

Satisfied he'd worked through that moment of ridiculous fancy that had gripped him, Liam refocused on Isabella through clear eyes. The good doctor was in trouble, she had a heap of baggage—both current and past—bogging her down and she dressed like a woman who attempted to hide herself. None of those things, however, were reason to assume she'd be the target of some sort of attack.

He waited until their first course of soup had been laid down and his grandparents' cook, Seamus, had returned to the kitchen before pressing the issue. "Why do you think someone's after your research?"

"Because she's the best in her field." His grandfather's resounding retort came barreling across the table.

"I'm acquainted with Dr. Magnini's reputation, Grandfather, but that doesn't explain why someone would want to hurt her or break into her home. Last time I checked, scientists weren't very visible targets."

"My research is somewhat controversial." Isabella laid down her soup spoon, a small spark flaring to life in the depths of her moss-green gaze. "And it's very visible to those who are interested in what I do for a living."

Aha, so the good doctor did have a backbone. And a stubborn streak of pride to boot.

Liam warmed to the evidence of both as he leaned forward. "Then tell me what it is about this specific research that would put you in the crosshairs."

"My work is about remapping aspects of the human genome."

Liam didn't miss the contrast of her stiff shoulders with the lush, almost wild hair that ran down her back or the steady flame that still lit her gaze. Dr. Magnini was a study in contrasts and he suspected there was more heat and passion underneath that oversize sweater and shapeless slacks than even she knew herself. "The field's grown and expanded for several years. Why is your research any different?"

"Because if my sequencing efforts are correct, I've found the genes that affect aggression, reason and logic."

"Sound research, to be sure, but I still don't understand why that puts you in harm's way."

Her shoulders grew even stiffer, if that were possible, and her voice lowered to a breathy whisper. "Because if what I've uncovered is correct, we now have the power to create a race of super soldiers. Indefatigable instruments of war."

Chapter 2

Isabella waited for some response, the silence around the table even more intimidating than the entire exercise of coming to Alexander Steele's home.

Why had she come here?

And why had she exposed herself to the censure and dismay that would inevitably come once these kind people understood to what she'd devoted her life?

She hadn't intended her work to go so far—or to have such far-reaching global implications. All she'd wanted to do was understand where she came from. A father with no moral center and a mother who was functionally unable to handle what life dished out.

And then there was her own questionable life, Isabella thought ruefully. She had a sound mind and moral certitude in spades, yet still she pushed herself and her research each and every day until her eyes blurred. Pressing herself on, desperate for the answer to one simple question.

Why?

Why had her father used his gifts for ill? Why was her mother unable to care for her? And why had she been given this driving need to answer those questions?

The joke was on her, Isabella now knew.

In her rush for answers, she'd never fully grasped what her research might suggest to others. Those without any moral certitude who, instead, believed that "might was right" and the ability to win at all costs was all that mattered.

That was why she had to bring her research to life in her own way. She needed to go on record and state why her work shouldn't be abused. Why humans shouldn't become guinea pigs for someone else's soulless ambitions.

"How would you propose to do that, dear?" Penelope's gaze had remained warm and kind—an altogether unexpected response at the evidence she had the scientific equivalent of Dr. Frankenstein at her dining room table—and Isabella stayed still for a moment, caught up in the warmth.

Had another nurturing female ever looked at her that way? Even when her mother was functioning, she'd always had a vapid sense of responsibility.

If she wanted an extra cookie, her mother never even offered up a token protest. If she wanted to stay up reading until three, with the clear consequence of being unable to stay awake the next day, no one was there to argue with her. And if she even attempted to discuss what had happened at school—from a perfect grade to a bullying incident in the lunchroom—her mother simply dismissed it all with a wave of her hand.

"The original purpose of my research was to understand our psychological functioning better."

"Nature versus nurture?" Penelope's gaze remained steady and warm.

"Yes, but more. There are those who are simply unable to handle the stresses of the world around them. I thought—" she broke off, knowing the truth was much too close to the surface. "Well, let's say I've been searching for the key that can unlock the pain far too many live with."

When no one offered any further comment, Isabella tried to further defend her actions. "I recognize the same challenges I'm looking to eradicate are the very tools others could use to turn individuals into soulless agents on their behalf. It's why I've been working through a solution to manage my work responsibly."

"Why not simply stop the research?" Liam's gaze was intent on hers across the table. "When you understood the depths of what you had, why not simply stop? That sounds like a damn effective solution to me."

"I didn't know what I had. Not as a weapon, at least. I thought my research would help us better understand those humans who choose to live outside the fringes. It's—" She broke off, the excuse flimsy and rather useless. She was responsible for her own actions—her own research—and blaming others for the potential they saw in it was equally flimsy and useless.

"I didn't intend my research to be applied in this fashion, but now that I've received clear feedback that will be its intent, I have a responsibility to press for responsible use. I've already published my preliminary research."

"Isn't that standard in your field?" Liam's vivid blue gaze never wavered.

"Presenting research is, yes. It's expected, even. But I was perhaps a bit too—" she broke off, struggling for the right words. "I was hasty in my speed to publish. So now I've got a second article in development with the same journal. The publisher has made arrangements to cross-publish the implications of my findings with the *New York Times*. The public needs to know what I'm sitting on."

"And you had no idea it would come to this?" Liam's gaze stayed direct, but she saw something behind those magnetic blue eyes—whether it was censure or understanding she had no idea—but there was something behind his words.

"Why would she know that?" Alexander demanded, his loud voice and hard fist to the table effectively ending the moment. "You know as well as I do no one has a crystal ball."

"I understand that, Grandfather." Liam's words were measured and, although directed toward Alexander, his gaze never left her own. "What I'd like to understand is if Dr. Magnini really thinks this little exercise of cleansing her guilt with the press will stop her from later selling her research to the highest bidder."

"Of course I don't think this absolves me of guilt. But I do believe it's the right thing to do."

His voice dropped, the tone velvety smooth. "Or perhaps, Isabella, you're biding your time before simply selling it to your employer?"

She shook her head, fighting the rising indignation that had her feet itching to race for the door. Liam's questions—no matter how directly asked—were nothing compared to what she'd receive from the press and public so she'd better learn to handle it. "I own all my research. I'm not beholden to anyone."

His eyebrows shot up at that one, the first look of genuine surprise she'd seen. "How'd you swing that?"

"I had a benefactor."

"And they don't want a piece of the action?"

"Dr. Stephenson is dead. He was my professor—mentor really—in graduate school. The funding was his final gift to me."

Isabella knew she was beyond fortunate for the gift Daniel had bestowed on her. His research had contributed heavily to the field and his own personal wealth had funded much of what he'd worked on. He'd believed in her and believed she'd carry on his legacy, advancing the science to new heights.

And how had she repaid him?

By publishing her results to the entire scientific community.

Her vanity had brought the wolf to her door. And she hoped like hell Liam Steele would know how to keep him at bay.

Liam swirled the whiskey in his glass, the late hour ensuring he'd be escorting Dr. Isabella Magnini home in a taxi. A steady layer of ire had coated his throat since dinner and no amount of coffee or the stronger nightcap could do anything to assuage it.

What the hell was she thinking?

And even as the judgmental thoughts crowded his mind he pulled himself back.

He was the last person who should judge. His choices—misguided and full of his own foolish vanity—had resulted in far more heartache and pain than he could have ever imagined.

His phone buzzed in his pocket and he pulled it out, his sister's name on the readout. "Kenzi. Prompt and efficient as always."

"Excellent. I can see by your nasty and condescending tone Grandfather convinced you to take on Dr. Magnini's situation."

"You knew damn well he would."

"And you knew damn well you would, too."

He sighed, the stiff set of his shoulders relaxing slightly. Whatever else she was—and royal pain in the ass frequently sat on the top of the list—his sister had his back. She also understood him, likely better than any other member of his family. "She's in deep, Kenz."

The tart lemons faded from her voice and underneath the professionalism he heard the camaraderie they'd shared since they were small. "Grandfather knows she needs help and I'd wager he didn't have all the specifics when he not so gently encouraged us to take this job."

"Or more likely chose not to share them." He caught her up quickly on what he'd gleaned at dinner—both the information Isabella shared as well as his overarching suspicions about her situation—before going in for the kill. "She's got some serious research on her side. Thinks that's the reason people are after her."

"You think she's legit? Grandfather's got an eagle eye but even he can get rusty from time to time." Kensington broke off, the line going quiet, before she continued. "I looked into her background."

Liam knew the circumstances of her father's downfall would have pinged for Kensington almost immediately so it was some surprise when a ready defense leapt to his lips. "She shared her background with us already and made no attempt to hide who her father was."

"He's a nasty piece of work." The sound of light tapping on her keyboard had a small smile curving his lips. Whatever else she was—nearly all of it good—his sister was a dog with a bone when it came to information. "I'm sending you what I've found. Check your email."

"Aye aye." The faint beep alerted him the message had arrived.

"Liam—"

His sister hesitated, very un-Kenzi-like. That silence did more to catch his attention than the loudest shout. "What is it?"

"This isn't a joke. She's going to have problems. Serious ones, if her father's any indication. Add on how she's chosen to build her career and you've got someone whose choices are very personal."

"Isn't that the very definition of the choices we make for ourselves?" Liam wasn't sure why—first his grandparents and now his sister—but where he normally let things slide off, something in her words lodged in his gut. So the good doctor had something of an ax to grind in her rush to get over her past. Until she'd made the monumental mistake of making the information public, she was well within her rights to figure out where she came from however the hell she pleased.

"Just be careful of her motivations."

"You can stop your worrying. She appears normal enough, for a poorly dressed scientist who seems somewhat oblivious to the world around her."

An image of the woman standing on his grandparents' front stoop leaped into his thoughts, a slightly manic look in her eyes as she spun toward him with her wet umbrella. The mania that filled the deep green of her eyes did battle with what could only be described as an absent-minded quirk of her eyebrows.

"You sure did notice a lot for an hour's visit."

The impression in his mind of those vivid green eyes faded as he keyed back into all the things Kensington *wasn't* saying. "That's my job."

"And I'm doing mine. Look at the file and let me know your impressions. Anything else you want me to dig into, just let me know."

"Got it."

"Give Grandfather and Grandmother a kiss for me. I'll talk to Grandfather in the morning."

"You always do." An image of her sister's daily conversation over oatmeal and blueberries with Alexander filled his thoughts and he sought to lighten the mood he'd managed to weigh down. "Maybe you can break with tradition tomorrow and toss a few raspberries in your oatmeal. You know. Shake it up a little."

"I'll take it under advisement." He didn't quite get a laugh, but he did hear the smile through the three thousand miles that separated them.

They disconnected and Liam took a few minutes to skim through Kenzi's email. He'd spend more time with it later, but the base facts matched what he'd gleaned at dinner.

She's going to have problems. Serious ones, if her father's any indication.

Liam read through the list of her father's grievances—spying and treason the least of his offenses—and fought another roll of judgment as he imagined the power of Isabella's research.

And the danger that would be unleashed if it got into the wrong hands.

He had to help her. It's what they did with the House of Steele.

And maybe, just maybe, if he found a way to fix Dr. Magnini's problems he might gain some salvation from his own.

Penelope Steele patted the foil into place around some of Seamus's famous chocolate chip cookies. They were her grandson Campbell's favorite, but the rest of her grandchildren had eaten more than their fair share through the years. She'd tried repeatedly to replicate the recipe, but had never found a way to get the proper mixture of gooey chocolate chips and rich, vanilla-tinged dough.

So she'd left Seamus to his expertise and had honed hers to a sharp point.

"You don't need to do this, Mrs. Steele. Dinner was a feast."

"Nonsense. A little sweet after the interrogation you received this evening is only fair."

"Your family's taking on my…circumstances. They deserve to have their questions answered."

"Yes, well, my grandchildren sometimes need to realize when a job is more than a job. I know you don't know us, Isabella, or have any reason to trust us. But Alex and I have known your grandparents for years. We want what's best for you."

The young woman blinked, the words an obvious surprise. "Thank you."

"I mean it. Your grandfather has kept us updated on your work through the years. He's so proud of what you've accomplished." Penelope laid it on with a trowel, pleased to see Isabella's stiff, stoic demeanor fade as talk shifted to her grandfather.

"He's been so supportive. So understanding."

Penelope heard the "but" underneath Isabella's words, but stayed silent, allowing her to work it through. It was the single biggest difference between her and Alexander. Her husband wanted to bully the answer out of people and she was content to wait and let it come.

And if she'd read Isabella Magnini correctly, the dam was near to cracking straight down the center.

"I didn't mean—" Isabella broke off on a hard exhale. "I didn't mean for it to come to this. To create work that others could abuse."

Penelope smoothed a corner of the foil-wrapped cookies and waited. She'd sensed a fire and spirit inside the girl—knew it was there from her grandfather's description—and knew the moment her patience was rewarded.

"It's groundbreaking work. Amazing work that can help us with all sorts of illnesses." Passion flared in Isabella's voice, blazing through the kitchen in a rush. "We can fix people. Help them. Heal the pain they're born with to keep them from hurting others."

Ah, there it is, Penelope mused. "That's what makes your work different. Special. Worthwhile."

"Not if it's abused as I've come to realize it will be."

"You want to heal." She laid a hand over Isabella's. "Don't ever forget that."

"But what if I've created the ability to destroy instead. Then I'd be no better than my father."

"You were better than your father the moment you decided the course of your work was to help others, not profit from them."

"I used to believe that. Wanted to believe that. But now I don't know."

Penelope squeezed the stiff fingers beneath hers. "The fact you can ask that question is reason enough to believe."

Isabella stared at the rain-slicked streets from the protection of the cab and watched London pass by. Penelope Steele's kind words had gone a long way toward offering a port in the storm, but she still couldn't fully escape her thoughts. Or the ready belief she was completely responsible for the circumstances she found herself in.

Pushing it into a mental corner for further reflection later, she focused on what she could control. She'd already packed for her flight in the morning and had given Liam the details he'd need to contact her once they were both back in the United States. All she really needed to do was follow his directions and all would be well.

It had to be.

He shifted and although there was space between them on the cab's back bench seat, she couldn't shake how overwhelming it was to sit next to him.

He was a tall man—well over six feet—and his frame was larger than he appeared on first inspection. He had a trim litheness to him that belied how solid he was and her gaze kept straying to his profile, highlighted by the glow of his phone.

Like a loop she couldn't break herself out of, her gaze traveled, first over the solid planes of his face, along the length of his jaw and over his Adam's apple, then over the fine cut of his raincoat. She followed the lines of the material, then along the black slacks stretched taut over his thighs. She stopped there—lingered, really—and her thoughts turned to more interesting dimensions every time she imagined what lay beneath that fine cut of material.

He had a refined, sexy masculinity that made her fingers itch to explore the skin underneath. And as a woman who'd spent her life around men who placed more value on what was inside their head than the capability of their bodies, she couldn't hold back the sheer feminine appreciation for Liam Steele's form.

Focus, Isabella. Keep your focus.

Of course, keeping focus meant she had to think about the very reason why she was sitting in the back of a cab, driving through the rain-soaked London streets next to Liam Steele. Focus meant she had to think about flying alone back to New York and revisiting her Chelsea apartment. What was once her haven had become tainted with the very real stain of fear.

And focus meant she had to spend some time consid-

ering her options. The next few weeks would take all her
energy, but after the fervor of her work was made public,
she had to decide what to do with the rest of her life.

She wanted to continue her research—wanted to continue learning about the scientific mysteries that lived
inside her own skin—but the implications of what she'd
discovered had weighed heavily.

Too heavily, at times.

"My sister has arranged for an escort for you from the
airport to your apartment. I'm taking you to Heathrow
myself."

A protest sprang to her lips but Liam cut her off before
she could say much. "Your escort is ex-military and armed
to the teeth. He'll make sure your apartment is safe and
will also check for bugs."

"It can't be that bad." Even if she'd lain awake for the
last three nights in her London hotel room worried that it
was, in fact, that bad.

Liam's subtle frown was all she got in reaction before
he shoved his phone into an inside pocket of his coat and
turned his full attention on her. "How much research do
you keep at home?"

Isabella fought the jitters that leaped through her stomach like hummingbirds as those liquid blue eyes—clearly
visible even in the darkness of the cab—lasered in on her.
"Minimal. More notes than anything else. Everything of
value is on small drives in various safe deposit boxes and
my computer that's always on me."

"I haven't seen a computer."

She smiled—her first easy one since climbing into the
cab. "You've somehow missed my oversize purse that
could carry a set of triplets?"

"I've got sisters." A sweet little twinkle lit up that gaze

and she took her first easy breath. "To be honest, I assumed it was simply a purse that could carry a set of triplets."

"Yes, well, the only triplets I carry are my laptop and two tablets." She patted the large leather purse on her lap. "They're heavy enough."

"My brother's going to light up like Christmas when he hears that."

"I'm sorry?"

The smile hovered but his tone changed—grew more conversational and, well, *human*—when he spoke. "My brother, Campbell, is our family computer wiz. It's also what he does for the business. Other than his wife and the other computer geeks he occasionally spends time with, I'm not sure he knows anyone who is that well-outfitted with technology."

"Occupational hazard. Plus, it keeps—" The words faded as she realized what she was about to admit. A man like Liam Steele likely had no idea what it was like to sit alone for hours on end, thoughts raging through your mind like a firestorm with no one to share them with and no way to quiet the melee. One tablet kept her research and the other was purely for entertainment.

"It keeps what?"

"Oh, nothing, really. Just a silly thing."

"You sure? Because I thought you were about to tell me you cracked the code on the latest version of Jewel Crush in which case, I'd be honor-bound to kidnap you and drag you to the House of Steele all on my own."

How'd he know that? And why did a decidedly naughty lick of heat just whip through her belly at the image of being thrown over Liam Steele's shoulder like a pirate's spoils? "Why would you want to do that?"

"Because you're likely the only person who can beat my sister Rowan and if she knew there was someone who had the secret to the next level she'd never stop hounding me if I didn't produce them. I swear, she's obsessed."

"I enjoy games as a diversion. They let me relax and allow whatever problem I'm working on to float to the back of my subconscious for a while."

"Nothing wrong with that."

The ready acceptance before he shifted his attention toward their driver, directing the man toward the turn-off for her hotel, gave her the few moments she needed to collect her thoughts.

For years, she'd heard so many things about Alexander Steele's grandchildren through her grandfather that Isabella realized she'd begun to think of them in near-mythic proportions.

But maybe they were just regular people.

She'd almost convinced herself until Liam turned toward her, those blue eyes blazing once more. "You coming?"

"Of…of course." She hated the stammer but quickly slid across the seat. The rain had died down to a gentle mist and it coated her immediately, a cooling balm to her heated skin.

She followed him toward the revolving doors of the hotel and nearly stumbled into him when he stopped to gesture her ahead. "Steady, Isabella." His hand snaked out and steadied her, holding her still for a moment.

"I'm fine."

"All evidence to the contrary."

Again, she fought the tug of those deep blue eyes and wondered how he did it. Liam Steele was just a man, nothing more. Yet he somehow managed to make her forget herself.

Made her wish for things she couldn't have.

With that thought foremost in her mind, she stepped

through the revolving door, using the few precious seconds as she walked through to center herself. He didn't need to see her to her room. He hadn't needed to even see her this far.

"Thanks for seeing me back. I'll be fine the rest of the way."

"Orders are orders. You're under my watch now and I'll see you upstairs."

"It's not necessary."

His large hand settled at the base of her spine as he guided her toward the elevators. "If you won't humor me, please humor my grandfather. I'd hate to have to call him and tell him you're being uncooperative."

"I'm no such thing!" She lowered her voice, the ricochet of her protest still echoing off the mirrored walls of their elevator car. "I'm just trying to save you a trip. I'm perfectly fine. This is a nice hotel and I left the Do Not Disturb sign up."

That sly smile curved his firm lips and she couldn't stop the sensation—yet again—of feeling as off-kilter as a brand new colt. "Then I'm sure you have nothing to worry about. This is simply a routine check so my mind can be at ease."

"You're not funny."

He tilted his head as the elevator pinged for their floor. "And you are. Sweetly so. I didn't expect that."

"I'm—" She broke off as a couple greeted them from the other side of the doors. She could argue with Liam Steele later. Or, Isabella knew, not at all now that she had time to reconsider her actions.

The man had the upper hand, that's all there was to it. If she was going to retain any sense of sanity she'd do well to accept that and go along for the ride.

Her room was a short distance from the elevator and

she had her key out, the lock turning green in mere seconds. It was only when she pushed through the door, intent on saying goodbye to Liam as quickly as possible that she stopped, a cold wash of awareness slithering across her skin.

"What is it?" Liam flipped on the light.

She glanced around the room, the soft light doing nothing to assuage her panic. Instead, she only felt it ratchet up another notch as she carefully ticked off the various quadrants of the room.

Bed. Dresser. End table.

All appeared to be in order, nothing out of place.

But even as her vision filled with the signs that nothing had been disturbed, she knew better.

"Someone's been here. Inside my room."

Chapter 3

"Here?"

Liam reached for Isabella, pulling her toward him as the blood drained from her face, leaving nothing but a milky white pallor over her skin. A subtle shake gripped her, the vibration of her body evident even through her layers of clothing.

Although he didn't doubt her, the small room was empty now, the limited space leaving nowhere to hide. Whoever had been here was long gone. Wrapping an arm around her shoulders, Liam pulled her forward toward one of the two double beds and settled her on the thick duvet. "Sit here. I'm going to do a quick sweep."

He crossed to the entry of the bathroom, the small cubicle obviously empty, but he flipped on the lights all the same and checked behind the shower curtain. "All clear."

The words were clearly of little solace as he caught sight of her huddled form when he stepped back into the room. Her eyes were bright orbs of green that took up almost half her face and that ghostly pallor still tinged her cheeks. "No one's here."

"They were here."

Liam fought the protest that sprang to his lips and searched the room himself. The neat, military smoothness of the covers appeared undisturbed. A small stack of leather-bound folios sat on the desk, perpendicular to the edge and layered one on top of the other with neat efficiency. Even the TV remote edged the end table with a precise lay-down against the lamp. Nothing looked disturbed.

"Why do you think someone was here?"

"I know it."

"Housekeeping."

She shook her head. "No. They'd already come and gone before I left for your grandparents."

"I'm sorry but I need a bit more. What set you off?"

He sat down next to Isabella, trying to make sense of her reaction. The woman appeared stable—and his grandfather's endorsement of the same went a long way toward keeping Liam from second-guessing her—but the room looked as if no one had touched it since housekeeping. Was she imagining the threat against her?

"The curtains are off."

"Where?" He crossed to the hanging drapes, the city visible through a veil of rain outside the window. He saw the London Eye in the distance, the lights of its bright wheel like diamonds in the wet mist, and wondered what Isabella could possibly be seeing.

"There. Where the edge hangs open. It was flush against my suitcase when I left."

Liam didn't touch the curtain, instead taking in her description. "And before?"

She got off the bed, her pallor fading as she took stock

of her surroundings. She pointed toward her small black suitcase before brushing her fingers over the handle. "When I left, I settled my luggage against the wall, the edge lined up to the curtain. Look at it now. The drape hangs over the edge of my bag."

Liam crouched down, and saw how the curtain hung over the edge of her small suitcase. "You're sure?"

"Of course." A small sigh drifted from her lips before she crouched down next to him, her fingers brushing the edge of the curtain. "I'm precise that way. I like things to line up. I know how I left it and that's not how it is now."

"Anything else?"

She got back to her feet and pointed toward the top of the suitcase. "The zippers aren't lined up. I always put them in the center. Those are off. I'm—"

"You're what."

"I like order. It's silly, I know, but they're small things that comfort me."

He knew about order. And the desperate need for it that formed from the midst of chaos. Her light scent filled his nose once more, that subtle blend of roses wafting from her skin, and Liam tried desperately to keep his wits about him.

Roses were for women his grandmother's age. Women who perfumed themselves in tepid fragrances that were safe and watered down.

So why did the scent seem exotic and highly erotic as it drifted from her heated skin?

Liam ignored that subtle tug of attraction and got to his feet, pulling out his phone. His brother's voice filled his ear a few moments later. "Twice in one night. First Kenzi and now me. What's going on, O Silent One?"

"I need you to hack into a few video cameras for me."

Campbell snorted. "Sure. Cuz it's that easy."

"For you it is." Liam gave his brother a quick rundown of what they'd discovered upon their arrival and Isabella's conviction someone had been in her room.

"That's a nice hotel. It's not like anyone can walk up and sneak into a room. It's a pretty locked-down environment."

"Which is why you're going to hack it." Liam knew barely enough to be dangerous when it came to computers but his brother, on the other hand...

Liam had learned long ago to leverage Campbell's skills and not ask questions.

"What time do you think it happened?"

"Between six and ten tonight."

The light tapping of keys along with a few muttered curse words gave Liam the confidence to end the call. "Be quick. If you work through dinner Abby'll have my ass."

"Then it's lucky for you I'm damn good at what I do."

"You're in already?"

"No, but close. Leave there and take her to the grandparents. I'll call you later."

"I can't take her there. They're worried enough."

"Then take her to that new, fancy flat you bought."

Liam held back the shocked "Hell no" and instead opted for something a bit more diplomatic. "I don't think that's a good idea."

Campbell let out a long, low whistle. "She must be something special if you're afraid to take her home."

"I'm not afraid."

"Keep telling yourself that, Big Brother. Keep telling yourself that."

Isabella glanced around the impressive apartment and marveled that Liam Steele lived here. She'd understood him to be New York-based so the fact that he kept a London flat—and *flat* really was too simple a word for the floor-to-ceiling windows and what had to be about two thousand square feet—but she chalked it up to family money and success in a highly paid profession.

"I thought you lived in New York."

"I do. I just live here, too. I bought the place in January. I spend a lot of time here in London and it seemed wiser than throwing my money away on hotels."

"I'm sure your grandparents would love to have you."

Despite the lingering fear that hadn't fully left her since leaving her hotel, she couldn't hold back the smile at the mixture of shock and—if she weren't mistaken, subtle horror—that tensed Liam's jaw.

Keeping her amusement to herself, her gaze drifted back to the view, the depth of the Steele wealth not lost on her. She knew she was fortunate—she paid her bills and still afforded a nice apartment by New York standards—but none of it changed the fact she lived in the human equivalent of a nice shoe box and he…didn't.

Isabella saw Liam move closer through the reflection in the glass. "Do you want a drink?"

"No, thank you. I had enough at dinner."

"Something hot, then? Tea?"

The traditionally British offering felt like the right thing and she turned away from the window. "That sounds nice."

The tea *was* nice and ten minutes later, when he placed a mug in front of her and settled another for himself, she couldn't hold back the subtle surprise. "I didn't take you for the tea type."

"And I didn't take you for the type to gather the interest of some very nasty people. We're all full of surprises."

"I suppose we are."

Her hands fumbled in the waistband of her sweater and she worried the cashmere between her fingers. The gesture was silly—and far from comforting—but she kept up anyway.

"You can relax here. No one's going to hurt you."

"That's what I thought about the hotel."

"They're not going to hurt you here."

His tone brooked no argument and she reached for her tea once more, warming her hands on the mug. "I never thought it would come to this."

He hesitated, which was another surprise as she sat there, taking in the solid lines of his face. Whatever else Liam Steele might be, he seemed to have no issue with being direct. The fact that hard jaw stayed closed added another layer of tension to the discussion.

"Come out with it. You can't insult me."

"How couldn't you think it would come to this? You've discovered something of deep value."

"To me, yes."

"To everyone." His blue eyes glittered under the overhead light of the kitchen, alive with a subtle fire. "Everyone wants to understand where they come from. How they're wired. Usually because they'd like to change it. That opportunity has always been walled off—locked up as it were—yet you've found the key. How can you honestly sit there and think no one else would care?"

His words were like an ice pick at her conscience, stabbing at the guilt that already consumed her.

"I didn't know."

"You do now."

The small penlight swept side to side through the apartment, highlighting stacks of books, overflowing bookshelves and a neat—and empty—fish tank. She'd told him once she kept the empty fish tank as a reminder not to get any fish because she was so absent-minded she'd likely forget to feed them. He'd laughed at the time and they'd traded stories about living inside their heads, but he couldn't help but see the irony of it now.

Science was all they had. Their only companion when even having fish was too much effort.

A stack of file folders on a credenza caught his attention and he followed the small stream of light to the neat, but towering, stack of manila folders. With careful precision, he flipped through them, taking in her scrawled handwriting as he went.

If the handwriting was an impatient mess, the notes were the antithesis. Page after meticulous page detailed her findings. Her successes and failures. All her learnings from the lab.

His gaze caught on a set of notes in the tenth file he flipped through. The date matched the basic time frame of her discovery and detailed the gene sequence she'd isolated for further investigation.

He took a seat at her desk and flipped through the rest of the notes, the lab findings reading like a symphony in his mind. Cellular research. Dissection of tissue samples. Gene sequencing. It was all there, detail after detail of what she'd uncovered. Questions littered the margins and the increasing scrawl of the notes indicated her excitement as clearly as if he were standing next to her.

She'd done it. Figured out the secret to what made humans tick. And with that knowledge, had figured out how to augment that to gain a specific result.

A wash of pride flashed through him, flushing his skin with heat. He was so proud of her and what she'd accomplished. He'd always known her gifts—the brilliant mind, the active curiosity and the tenacity to keep working a puzzle until she solved it—but this was more than he could have ever hoped for.

His gaze skimmed the last set of papers in the file, stopping on a small note at the bottom of the page. It was a name and a phone number he recognized—the editor of one of the most respected scientific journals in the world. Along with the name there was a quick notation:

Confirm Bradley's understanding on gene sequence and his impressions of the work.

The article she'd ultimately published had held back a few details, promising further articulation in an upcoming issue.

He'd suspected she'd shared the details—or was going to—and now he had the proof. The details he and his partner were committed to keeping from the world were in the hands of the reporter.

No matter how much it pained him to consider snuffing out such a bright talent, they couldn't stop now.

With efficient movements—something that would never grow old—he reordered the files, securing them in the neat stack she preferred, then slipped back through the oversize room and out into the hall.

A hard-won lesson clamored through his mind, his partner's voice echoing like church bells.

If you want to make an omelet, you've got to break some eggs.

He understood. He'd made a commitment to his goal. And, like Isabella, science was all he had.

And if a sharp pain speared his heart as he walked away from her apartment, well, he'd have to live with that as his penance.

Isabella stared out the wall of windows in Liam's apartment, her gaze captivated by the rain-washed city. She'd always loved London and now wondered why she hadn't spent more time here. More time with her grandfather. More time living life outside of a laboratory.

She hadn't allowed herself to dwell on such fanciful thoughts before, but now? They seemed more present. More *urgent*.

Especially when she might not get the chance again.

A hard sob caught in her throat as she thought of her grandfather. The urge to call him was great, but she had held back, taking the Steeles' advice. Both Liam and Alexander had assured her repeatedly the night before that her grandfather was safe—ensconced on Steele property in the wilds of England at the insistent invitation of Liam's grandmother—but they also had warned her not to give him too many indicators of what was going on.

No use worrying him.

He already worried enough, she well knew. It wasn't only her life that had changed with her father's betrayal. Roberto Magnini had also borne the pain of watching his son's disgrace.

How horrified he'd be, then, when he discovered the implications of her work. The risks she'd brought to their door and the potential horrors she'd unleashed on the world.

It was funny, she mused, how even though her intentions were better, the outcome wasn't that far off from her father's.

"It's late."

The deep voice called to her across the large living room and Isabella turned from the windows, her maudlin thoughts dissipating like smoke.

She thought she was prepared for the sight of Liam by now. The broad shoulders, trim waist and magnetic blue eyes had captivated her from the first but she thought she could deal with them. How humbling, then, to find out that she was just as devastated as before.

And just as curious to know what it would be like to run her palms over those broad shoulders. To drift a lazy finger over the hard lines of his jaw. To press her body against his and feel all that power and strength wrap around her.

Possess her.

"I couldn't sleep."

Her words sounded strained to her own ears but there was nothing to be done for it. She could only hope he mistook the slightly strangled tones of her vocal chords for fear instead of bone-deep arousal.

"I was unduly harsh earlier."

"You were honest. There's a difference."

He cocked his head and she had the subtle impression he weighed his words. "Most women aren't so quick to release a grudge."

"You're assuming I was holding one."

"What else had the pensive stare out the window?"

"I was thinking about my grandfather."

He moved forward at that, coming to stop before her. "I promise you we have him safe. I had the security arranged myself and my grandparents are joining him for the weekend to keep him company. You don't need to worry about him. Not on top of everything else."

Although his promises couldn't change the reality of how little of her adult life she'd spent with her grandfather, they did go a long way toward assuaging her concern. "Thank you. He'll enjoy that. He still misses my grandmother terribly and the company will be good for him."

The moments drifted from quiet to awkward as they both stood there. "Your home is beautiful."

"I haven't been in it that long. I'm still trying to get over the sense that it's temporary."

"The occupational hazards of being a rolling stone." She meant the statement as a joke but knew immediately her words had fallen flat.

"You sound like every other woman in my life."

"I didn't mean it was a bad thing. You have a life and are living it. I'm no one to judge."

"My grandmother and sisters don't feel quite the same way."

Since standing in the middle of his living room had passed awkward and had moved right on to deeply uncomfortable, she took a seat. Two overstuffed leather club chairs formed a conversation circle with an equally large and overstuffed leather couch and she was grateful for the thick cushions and a soft place to land.

Their conversation might be painfully awkward but at least she'd be physically comfortable while having it.

"So have a seat on the couch and tell me all about it."

The joke was just enough to lighten the mood and she didn't miss Liam's rueful smile as he took a seat—fully upright—on the couch. "I thought your degree was in scientific matters, Dr. Magnini."

"I've spent enough of my life with shrinks to know a few tricks or two."

Damn it. Why had she mentioned psychiatrists?

It would be too easy to blame the simple camaraderie and warmth of the moment but she suspected her motives went deeper. For reasons she couldn't define, she felt the need to expose who she was to Liam Steele. Was it so he could reject her outright?

Or so she could prove to herself—once and for all—a man like Liam Steele would never be a part of her life?

* * *

Liam knew he was a heartless bastard about a lot of things, but he'd always believed himself open and honest about the challenges of life.

So why did that light flush that colored Isabella's cheeks suggest she was embarrassed by seeking professional help?

"I've spent some time on the doctor's couch, myself."

"You have?"

"All my siblings did. Our grandparents insisted on it after we lost my parents." When skepticism continued to hover behind the moss green of her eyes he pushed a bit harder. "You look like you don't believe me."

"You don't seem the type."

"And what's the type?" He couldn't resist poking her a bit at her ready attempts to stereotype. Even if he had more than a few of his own.

He'd already painted her as the geeky scientist in his mind and it was increasingly difficult to keep that stereotype front and center in his thoughts as he stared at her lush, pouty lips and the thick fall of hair around her shoulders.

"I don't know. You just seem so solid. Powerful."

That flush deepened and he leaned forward, his gaze unwavering on hers. "Being strong doesn't mean you have no vulnerabilities. It simply means you understand how to work around them. Live with them and accept they're a part of you."

"You make it sound easy."

He sat back at that, half-serious and half-amused at their 2:00 a.m. philosophy session. "Some days. The good days. Other times? Not so much."

"You really expect me to believe you're a mere mortal?"

Liam knew her words for the light tease they were, but couldn't fully quell the slight itch at the base of his neck. Without warning, memories of a conversation with his sister, Rowan, a few months before, prickled his subconscious.

At the time, Rowan had suggested he hadn't understood how hard it had been for her to deal with the loss of their parents. As if her age or sex somehow made the pain more difficult for her to bear.

He'd shrugged it off—thought he'd fully forgotten it—so it was a surprise to realize yet again that the impression he created in others was so far from how he saw himself.

He knew he kept others at arm's length—a lifelong trait, not one initiated by the loss of his parents. He'd simply honed it to a fine point after they were gone.

None of it meant he didn't feel. Or care. Or live with loss.

"I'm as human as the next person. I suggest you remember that."

"I'll try."

Whatever tender moments they'd shared vanished as he stood. "I'll see you in the morning."

He was across the room before she spoke. "Liam, I am sorry."

Curious, he turned. She stood in the middle of his home, the ambient glow of London haloing around her. "For what?"

"For dragging you into this."

"It's what I do."

"You protect people who deserve it. I know you believe I don't based on what I've done, but I hope you'll come to understand I never meant for any of this to happen."

He took a few steps toward her before he stopped. He knew she was scared—knew it from the first moment he saw her on the other side of his grandparents' front door—

yet he couldn't quite get past his irritation at the situation she found herself in.

"Actions and consequences, Dr. Magnini. That's what we're dealing with."

Without waiting for her reply, he continued on to his room.

Liam slammed his clothes into his overnight case with all the finesse of a grizzly bear searching for breakfast. He'd slept little, that bleak expression that rode Isabella's face like a sad mask haunting him through the night.

He had no right to judge her.

No right at all.

She was scared and she hadn't acted deliberately. So why had he been so resolute in keeping her at arm's length? And why was he so determined to make her feel the pain of her choices?

The packing done, he dragged on the last zipper and heaved the suitcase off his bed. It was time to go eat a rather large plate of crow.

He walked into the main living room and heard the pop of the toaster and smelled the coffee as he settled his suitcase by the door. "That smells good."

"I hope you don't mind." Isabella shrugged from behind the large island that dominated his kitchen. "I'm not one to skip meals."

"Of course I don't mind. I'm glad you found something."

The stilted conversation stuck in his throat and he walked to the single-brew coffee machine and set up an extra dark roast he hoped would do something for his mood.

"What happens once we get back to New York?"

Her words were quiet but there was no mistaking the

apprehension laced underneath. That fact was even more evident as Liam turned toward her and caught sight of her shaking hand as she buttered her toast.

"We'll protect you."

"It's not that simple. Whoever's behind this has proven how stealthy they are. Do you have the resources to go up against someone with black ops training? Special forces training?"

The immediate reaction had him cocking his head. "You think a government's behind this."

"It's a very real possibility."

"What about the possibility it's someone closer to you? The threats and intrusions have been very personal in nature."

"Not possible."

"Why not? To your point, someone in special ops knows how to take out a target." The words were out before he could snatch them back and Liam knew how insensitive he sounded. Although it was another point in the "Liam's a bastard" column, he refused to mince words with her.

He and his siblings had decided long ago that they wouldn't keep clients ignorant of the danger that surrounded them. It was at best unfair and at worst, perilous to keep them in the dark.

"You're saying if I were their intended target, I'd have been dealt with by now."

"Yes."

"It's still not someone I know."

"Why won't you consider that possibility?"

She laid down the knife, her eyes wide. "I don't have anyone in my life, friend or enemy. There's no one who can hurt me."

With precise movements she began wrapping the cord around the toaster and cleaning crumbs off the counter.

Liam wanted to say something else—*anything* else—but he held back. He'd already been insensitive enough. What else could he say?

He moved into the living room and made a show of puttering with his suitcase and checking his bags. The sooner they got on their way, the better. When he heard the final sounds of the toaster being put away and running water in the sink he walked back in. "I have a service. You can leave those."

"It's just a few dishes."

He'd have argued but she was already halfway through washing and had the plate and cup put up in minutes. The small motions fascinated him and he was forced to admit the women he usually brought here were all too happy to leave a mess behind, allowing someone else to take care of it.

Hell, he was all too content to leave a mess behind, paying someone to handle it.

And you're getting weird over a plate and a cup, Steele.

Isabella grabbed her suitcase and headed for the door, the faintest smile playing at the corners of her mouth. "Ready when you are."

The ride to the lobby was quiet, the early morning hour ensuring very few were up and about. His doorman wasn't at his post, which struck the back of his thoughts mere moments before the sight of a stranger sitting on one of the leather couches in the lobby caught his attention.

Where was Henri? And why was there someone in the lobby without supervision?

Isabella was still behind him, not yet visible until she stepped through the elevator. "Are we hailing a—"

Without thinking through the implications, he dragged Isabella into his arms and back toward the elevator doors. The car they were in had already closed and he stabbed the button with his free hand while pulling her close with the other.

"I'm thinking we can be late, darling." His words echoed through the lobby, loud enough for anyone in earshot.

Without giving Isabella a chance to respond, he pressed his mouth to hers and prayed like hell the guy hadn't seen her face.

Chapter 4

Her mind finally caught up with her actions and Isabella came to the abrupt realization she was kissing Liam Steele. *Kissing him!*

Her lips opened on an "O" of surprise and he simply used the gesture as an opportunity to slide his tongue fully against hers.

It was madness.

It was bliss.

The subtle ping of the elevator door went off behind her and she abstractly felt herself being walked backward into a waiting car. Rationally, her mind knew what was happening but she couldn't seem to hold on to a single thought as insistent bursts of need buffeted her like winds battering a ship at high sea.

On some odd dimension of her brain, her scientific mind registered what was happening. The accelerated heart rate that slammed into her chest. The tightening of her skin, resulting in aching nipples. The rush of liquid heat at her core.

But the woman who'd been denied those reactions for far too long felt something entirely different.

The hard flex of his muscles where her hands lay over his shoulders. The tension of his tongue thrusting between her lips in an erotic dance that had stars exploding before her closed eyes. And the warm, rich scent that filled her senses with an earthy heat she couldn't quite define. Cedar? Tobacco? Fresh grass?

Nothing fit, even as she catalogued each of those earthy scents before discarding them.

He was Liam and the power she'd sensed in him was nothing compared to the experience of having him pressed against every inch of her body.

That tantalizing scent continued to swirl around her senses before she was jerked from the moment—

"I'm sorry."

Sorry? "What?"

Her stomach curdled as if filled with sour milk as he put distance between the two of them, moving to the far side of the elevator car.

"I don't know why my doorman isn't at his post and I didn't like the look of the man in the lobby."

"You think—" she broke off, not trusting herself to speak. That pervasive sense of danger returned—blessedly absent for those few brief moments in his arms—and along with it, she now had the embarrassment of extreme naïveté. "You think it's the same threat from the hotel."

"We can't rule it out." The elevators swung open on his floor and Liam stepped through the door, his outstretched hand keeping her in place in the elevator. She waited as he did a sweep of the hall, then saw his head nod. "Come on."

She followed him, her suitcase heavy against her hand, as they retraced their steps to his apartment.

A ruse.

The kiss was nothing but a ruse to fool this mystery man in the lobby that set Liam's antennae off. Empirically she knew her reaction was not only silly but immature, but the lingering feel of Liam's lips on hers was a haunting reminder of things she hadn't felt in far too long.

Or ever, her conscience taunted.

Pushing it down, she walked past him into his apartment.

He was protecting her and obviously thought a kiss was the most expedient way to keep her hidden from a threat. That thought was only punctuated when he began barking out orders from his cell phone.

"Henri? Where were you?"

Isabella only caught Liam's side of the conversation but it wasn't hard to piece together what had happened. The man had obviously been summoned by a call and felt he could take it at such an early hour. No one had been in the lobby when he left his post, nor had anyone been there when he returned.

"Damn it." Liam muttered the curse and looked up from his phone. "Henri didn't see him."

"What did he look like?"

"Someone who didn't belong." Liam's words were swift before his fingers flew once more over his phone. He was equally direct with whomever answered. "It's me. What did you find?"

Isabella walked toward the windows that rimmed the far side of the room. Once again, Liam snarled out a series of orders and questions, varying them up based on whatever response he received.

As she stared out over the London skyline, Isabella

knew she was in capable hands. Liam Steele had taken on full responsibility for her safety and security.

So why did that thought leave her feeling so bleak?

Liam allowed his gaze to travel over Isabella's taut form, silhouetted against the light from the window, before forcing himself to focus on his brother's words.

"I can say it again and I can say it louder, but it's not going to change the results, Liam. I found nothing on the hotel video feed that suggested someone went in or out of her room yesterday."

"And you don't think it was tampered with?"

"Not that I could tell."

"Check again."

"Damn it. I checked it twice and so did T-Bone. There's nothing there." Campbell spit out a few more expletives and Liam knew his pushing was only exacerbating an already tense situation.

"Do you believe she's right about this?" Campbell softened his words. "I get she's a scientist and precise and all that, but we're talking about a few millimeters of space on a suitcase. Hell, she could have kicked it with her foot and moved it. Or the curtain could have been bunched up and it fell down."

"That's not it."

He believed Isabella. Recognized something in her prescriptive attention to details.

And just when had he gotten so fanciful?

Liam knew his brother had a point. He also knew Campbell and the computer expert he kept on his team, T-Bone, knew what they were doing.

"Fine. We'll keep digging. What has you upset now? You said something about a problem this morning."

"I need you to check the video feed in my lobby. My

doorman left his post and never saw a man come in and out of the lobby, but the guy was there when Isabella and I got off the elevator. I don't like it."

Campbell made quick work of the request, the cameras in all of their buildings already connected to his security feeds. Liam knew it wasn't a common luxury afforded to all residents of his building, but when he'd demanded the additional access—and sweetened the deal with an incremental payment—the building's ownership had been surprisingly willing to negotiate.

Add on the reduced surveillance services the House of Steele had readily negotiated for said building owners and they had a rather nice arrangement going.

"Nothing on the feed."

"No one in the lobby at all?"

"I see the doorman take a call and leave his post. I see the lobby sit empty for a while and then I see him come back."

"And no one's there? Nor did you see me get out of the elevator."

"Nope."

"Then we have an even bigger problem than I thought."

Another string of expletives echoed through the phone. "Bugger got through my security. I've got that feed programmed to alert me to any tampering."

"And nothing popped?"

"No."

Liam heard the frustration more clearly in his brother's voice on that single word than all the ranting and cursing that had come before. "I'm calling for an escort to the airport and delaying our flight until tomorrow morning. Brief Kenzi and Jack on what's going on and we'll gameplan when I get in."

"Be careful, Liam. Whoever's behind this? This guy knows way more than he should."

"Got it."

He disconnected with his brother and for the first time had to question what was really going on. He'd faced tough jobs before—they all had—but this was on a different level.

And he couldn't shake the fact that whoever was after Isabella knew the House of Steele was going to help her.

"I'm sorry about before."

She turned away from the window, her hands still fluttering in the silky material of her blouse where it hung around her waist. He wasn't sure why that constant worrying of her fingers had him intrigued, but it did. The subtle proof she was human touched him way more than it probably should.

"I take it your brother didn't find anything."

"Not yet."

"And I take it he also doesn't believe me when I say someone was in my room last night."

Liam cycled through the conversation in his mind. He'd been more than careful to keep any indication from his side of the conversation that Isabella might have been wrong yet she'd sensed it anyway. "Campbell just likes to be sure. Especially when he can't find a technological answer to the problem."

"And I take it the lobby visitor wasn't visible on your building's cameras?"

"Right again."

Her face fell at the news, whatever lingering hope that had shimmered in the depths of her green gaze fading. He could still taste her on his lips, the subtle flavor of her coffee a shocking aphrodisiac. The urge to give comfort had him crossing to her, determined to offer reassurance.

"Then I shouldn't be putting you in danger. Or taking up even more of your time with a full day of delay." Her subtle feint to the left ensured she maintained a physical distance between the two of them and he stilled, surprised by the stiff set of her shoulders.

Where was the responsive woman who'd clung to him, fully engaged and kissing him back?

And why did the sudden urge to drag her back into his arms pulse through him with the heavy throb of a line of bass drums?

Their eyes met and that bass throb amped up another level, pushing him to take some action. To reach out once more and touch her, just to see if she was as soft as he remembered. To see if her lips were as enticing…

Liam shook off the thought and took a few steps back.

Isabella Magnini was a job, nothing more. He'd take care of her and see his responsibilities through and move on. It was what he did and it was how he lived his life. He'd built a structured, orderly world around himself that he controlled.

And he'd be damned if a frightened woman who'd discovered the potential to unleash hell changed any of that.

Isabella stayed where she'd been told and watched Liam through the sliding doors of one of Heathrow Airport's many concourses. As he'd confirmed with his brother, he'd made good on his plan of hiring an armed escort to take them to the airport and was now thanking the man for his services.

The exchange was brief but it gave her the opportunity to observe him in action. The late morning rain coated the air a misty gray yet he stood out against it, as bright and vibrant as the sun.

The long, trim lines of his body captivated her, but it

was something beyond the physical—something far more ephemeral—that drew her in as she traced his form with her eyes.

Competence shone from him in the simplest of actions. His quick handshake with their guard. The flash of his hand as he snagged his rolling suitcase. Even the quick flick of his wrist as he brushed drops of rain from his hair.

All of it bespoke of a man comfortable with himself and his surroundings, secure in who he was.

Was that what made leaders? No, she quickly amended, that's what made conquerors.

The idea took root and she let it simmer as Liam walked closer, evaluating him through that new lens. Their elevator kiss the day before had certainly reinforced the notion and the events since—the quick, competent change in plans, the work with his brother back at headquarters, even the possessive order to stand inside the doors and wait for him when they'd arrived at the airport.

Here was a man used to giving orders he expected would be followed.

So why was she letting the simple fact that their elevator kiss meant nothing to him chafe at her like sandpaper on skin?

The thought had kept up a steady tattoo in her brain for the better part of the last day, even in the face of the very real—and shockingly *present*—danger she was in. Even worse, she'd spent a near-sleepless night focused on that while he looked fit and ready to conquer the day.

"Ready?"

She nodded and knew full well his question was meant to indicate their walk to security, so why did she feel something more? Something deeper at the question?

Was she ready?

She'd hidden from life for so long—had willingly buried herself in work and nothing else—that she'd missed out on so much. Her twenties, certainly, and if she kept it up her thirties would end up a blur as well. A blur of lab notes and beakers, computer analyses and charts and graphs that might calculate any number of things but couldn't assuage how lonely she was.

She was ready for something more and now that the life she hadn't put much stock in was in danger, she knew that more keenly than ever.

Liam took her suitcase in his free hand and gestured her forward with a tilt of the head. "We'll wait in the captain's lounge after we check in."

She reached for the handle but he was already out of range and she took a few quick steps to catch up, her heels clicking on the tile. "What difference does it make once we pass through security?"

"I don't want you out in the open."

She knew the lounge he spoke of—it was a premium environment for premium fliers—but she'd never been there. "Isn't that the whole point of going through security?"

He stopped and turned, the blue of his gaze penetrating as he waited for her to catch up. If she wasn't mistaken—and her ability to read social cues meant her chances were only about fifty-fifty on being right—he looked decidedly uncomfortable. "I don't like to fly. The quiet of the lounge helps me calm down before a flight."

"Oh."

He turned on his heel with the bags and continued on toward the snaking security line, his gait stiff.

A small smile she couldn't quite hold back sprang to her lips and the spiral of tension holding her stomach in a tight fist loosened ever-so-slightly. Maybe the conquering hero had an Achilles' heel or two after all.

To a mere mortal such as herself, it was an oddly comforting thought.

Whatever momentary lapse in judgment had caused her to think Liam human fled the moment they sat down in the captain's lounge to await their flight. At least eight women had given him the once-over with their eyes in the one-hundred-yard jaunt from security to the club and the elegant hostess manning the front desk—who was old enough to be his mother—had flirted like a blushing school girl.

"Would you like something?" Liam settled their bags under their table and stopped to wait for her answer.

"I'm fine, thank you." She snagged her tablet—the one she used for fun—from the depths of her purse and snapped open the cover.

"It's a long flight and the food here's better."

"Please help yourself. I'll wait for the plane."

A strange expression flitted through his gaze before he seemed to think better of responding and headed for a wall-length counter filled with every sort of food imaginable.

The moment his gaze was averted, she appraised the counter full of food and knew she'd been hasty. Fresh fruit. Cookies. Even hot sandwiches filled the wall and her stomach let up an unladylike growl in indignation of being ignored.

She nearly gave in and followed him when a tall, statuesque woman sidling up to the counter filled her line of vision. The woman's gaze was predatory and her wide mouth spread into a welcoming grin as she moved next to Liam. Isabella was too far away to hear the conversation but there was no way she was mistaken on the woman's body language.

No, sir-ee.

Every line in the woman's slender frame screamed out an invitation. And judging by the appreciative grin on Liam's face, he didn't mistake the offer.

Isabella refocused on her tablet and ignored the unfolding flirtation. She was Liam Steele's client, nothing more. She had a problem and it was his job to fix it.

End of story.

The words on the screen jumbled in front of her eyes as her vision swam with the memories of their kiss and she blinked to refocus. Slowly, the chapter heading came back into view and she threw herself into the story of a roving space pirate and the female cantina owner determined to help him put his sketchy past behind him.

She'd been enjoying the story up to now, the author a personal favorite. In her mind's eye, she'd fleshed out the big bad space pirate as a cross between Harrison Ford and Channing Tatum. How insulting, then, when he morphed in her mind to bear a striking resemblance to Liam.

Couldn't her books even be off-limits?

With a resigned sigh—and a willingness to eat a portion of crow along with a fresh sandwich from the serving bar—she glanced up into Liam's warm gaze.

"Problem?"

"Of course not. I just decided I was hungry after all. I'll just go up and get something."

"Then it's a good thing I got you a sandwich and a banana." He pulled a plate from behind his back, the promised sandwich filled to the brim with fresh-cut turkey, what appeared to be slices of pear and a wedge of soft cheese.

She took the proffered sandwich and fought the petty urge to go up and get something different. Good heavens, what was wrong with her? Her mother might have spent most of Isabella's childhood thoroughly disengaged but even she'd managed to raise a child who was well-mannered and gracious.

Not to mention thankful when someone did something nice.

After she swallowed a bite, she set down her plate and turned to face Liam. "Thank you. The sandwich is delicious."

"They know how to send a traveler off in style here."

"Yes, they do." She used his comment as an excuse to look around the lounge and away from the intense scrutiny of his gaze but his voice pulled her back to the here and now.

"We should get into JFK a little before two. My sister Kensington and her fiancé, Jack, are picking us up themselves."

"Okay." While the extra attention still felt unnecessary and overblown, Liam's caution overrode any protests she might have.

"I'd like you to stay at the family house tonight."

"I don't think that's a good idea."

"I think it is. I'd also like you to give us keys to your apartment. Jack and I can go over and check things out tomorrow. He's in security as well. Between the two of us, we know what to look for and how to suss out any threats."

"I'll go with you, of course."

"I'd prefer you stayed behind."

Whether it was lingering frustration over the long-legged Amazon and her smooth moves or the sheer insult of being left behind while someone investigated her home, she didn't know.

She was fast hitting a point where she didn't care, either.

"It's my home. I appreciate your guidance but I believe, as your client, I still have final say. I'm going with you."

"Isabella—"

"No. I'm not leaving you to walk through my apartment and look through my things while I sit and do nothing."

"Someone's proven themselves a threat to you on several occasions and, by all accounts, with increasing severity. You're better off staying where we can control the situation."

"I'm not negotiating this with you. I need to get inside my apartment and see if anyone was there. Besides, I won't be scared away from my own home."

"And I'd like you to be reasonable and let me do my job."

She pushed her plate aside and leaned over the small table, her gaze direct. "No, Liam, I won't be reasonable. Or pliable. Or pitiful. I may not be some athletic Amazon like Blondie over there," she tossed her head in the direction of the woman from the serving counter, "but I know my own mind and I know this. You're not going into my home without me."

"Blondie?"

"Excuse me for being vague. I was referring to the statuesque blonde who almost had her tongue down your ear."

"I believe her name's Stella."

"Of course it is."

"She's an old college acquaintance of my sister's who thought she recognized me and came over to say hello."

"How sweet." Isabella flung a hand, nearly knocking over her plate in the process. "Why don't you go get reacquainted?"

"Since she's leaving on a tropical vacation with her boyfriend, I'm not sure either would appreciate the intrusion."

Isabella looked over to where the blonde had sat down and had the distinct mortification of watching the woman run her hands over the rather large and imposing chest of a man she clearly had feelings for.

Damn it all to hell and back.

A few other choice expletives floated through her mind in rapid succession at, once again, being caught out of her depth. "How lovely for her."

"Quite."

She took a sip of the soft drink he'd brought her and willed the mortification to fade as quickly as possible. The cold slide of sugar coated her parched throat and while it couldn't quite beat the heat of embarrassment flushing up her neck, it did make her feel a bit better.

"I don't think you're pitiful, Isabella."

"Thank you."

"And for the record?" A small smile crinkled the corners of his eyes, those blue irises twinkling. "I sure as hell don't think you're pliable, either."

Chapter 5

So the cat does have a few claws.

Liam couldn't hold back his delight at that fact, nor could he quite shake off the sudden flash of mischief that sparked under his skin. Was Isabella jealous?

He wouldn't have thought it behind the cool exterior that had him in a permanent state of confusion, but the evidence was rather clear in her words. And over Stella, of all people. The woman was a shameless flirt and if it weren't for the fact that she was a friend of his sister's he probably would have faked ignorance when she walked over.

Of course, between two sisters who knew half the population of both Manhattan *and* London as well as grandparents who had been movers and shakers for more than half a century, his chance of going anywhere without meeting someone he knew was slim to none.

He could only be grateful his brother's lifelong behavior bordered on reclusive, ensuring they had few acquaintances in common, but even that was beginning to change. Campbell had undergone a significant change of heart since marrying Abby and the two of them now had connections as well.

It was his life and the consequence of the status his family enjoyed and he'd learned long ago to live with it. Hell, with House of Steele they'd learned to use it to their advantage. But in all that time, he'd never seen the connections in his life as more than a necessary nuisance to get him to an end goal.

Until today when Isabella unsheathed her claws.

There was something about her he couldn't define and that intrigued him. If he were honest with himself, he was used to putting women in neat boxes.

The ingenue. The model. The actress.

Each fit a specific space and while he appreciated them all and never promised what he couldn't deliver, he forgot about them quickly once they were no longer a part of his life.

Isabella, on the other hand?

He suspected she'd be a difficult woman to forget.

Maybe because she is *a woman.*

The thought rose up with such force he nearly fumbled the bag of chips in his hand.

Along with the thought came an image of his grandfather, rubbing his hands at correctly matching the two of them up, and Liam shut down whatever it was about Isabella that had him captivated.

The woman underneath the shapeless clothes and computer-like mind might be enticing, but the implications of tangling with her weren't.

"Why don't you like flying?"

The question broke into his musings—direct and pointed—just like Isabella.

"I just don't."

"You must fly often."

"At least once a week, usually more."

"Don't you think you should do something about that? Hypnosis or acupuncture or something?"

He knew it was a ridiculous fear. Hell, he'd BASE-jumped off several buildings the world over and had a surprising love of climbing. But there was something about a plane. The closed space and the very real fact that he turned his destiny over to someone else.

A small shudder gripped his shoulders.

Nope. He did not like to fly.

"I live with it."

"Yes, but you don't have to. Whether you choose modern medicine or holistic medicine or even a psychologist, there's a therapy to help you."

His toes curled in his Italian loafers as the word therapy hit its mark. He knew it was an irrational response, but he hated that word.

Hated what it suggested.

Although he'd played it off earlier with Isabella—and he did believe therapy had its place—he'd had his fill. He had given it the old college try and got out of going as fast as he could.

Talking through problems worked for others but he wasn't wired that way. And he sure as hell didn't think sitting in a chair and spilling his guts to someone else would make his parents come back or assuage the all-consuming grief that he'd never see them again.

With a casualness he didn't feel, he shot her a lopsided grin that usually had the effect of charming the woman sitting opposite and derailing whatever they were about to say next. "A few vodkas and I'm all set."

"But there are solutions. Drugs. Professionals who can help you."

He cut her off. "I'm fine. And not everything can be fixed by science. Hasn't that fact sunk in yet?"

The words hit their desired mark when her face fell into somber lines, her eyes going wide. "Excuse me then. Clearly you've given this a lot of thought."

"I have."

She took a small bite of her sandwich and he suspected he'd earned roughly the same status as a puppy kicker or hunter of unicorns.

The announcement for their flight came over the PA system and he dropped his balled-up napkin onto his plate. "You ready to go?"

"Yep."

He hated he'd made her feel bad and suspected the tight knot in his gut from lashing out at her wasn't going to go away any time soon.

But he couldn't deny the extreme relief that he was no longer under Isabella Magnini's microscope.

Edward Carrington the Third fiddled with the keys on his laptop as the hum of the coffee shop swirled around him. His trip to London had been surprisingly productive, the visit to Steele's apartment lobby producing the desired result.

The man had taken one look at him, made the threat and ushered what was no doubt a scared Isabella straight back upstairs.

Damn, but he loved when an experiment went according to the hypothesis.

The visit to Steele's apartment had been part impulse and part test. He'd already achieved the objective of his trip by messing with Isabella's hotel room. The early morning lobby visit was the icing, giving him an advance look at Steele's surroundings and how the man lived. Liam Steele's reputation preceded him and Edward had no doubt the man was prepared for most eventualities.

The lobby security hadn't been hard to crack but it wasn't a cake walk either. And the lobby guard hadn't been easy to persuade either. He'd tried various scenarios for two days to get the guards to leave their posts and it was only when he'd hit on manufacturing a problem at home for the morning guard that he'd managed to divert the man.

Everyone could be diverted for a price. For some it was money. Others security. Even others it was love. Everybody had a trigger, all you had to do was find it—his research had told him that time and time again.

And there was nothing that delighted him more than seeing his research come to life in practical application.

He finished up a quick status email to the Doc and closed the lid of his computer. Isabella had been a thorn in his side for way too long and it felt good to imagine her finally getting her comeuppance.

Magnificent, actually.

He drained the last of his cappuccino and looked around the small store. A few people sat in pairs, their quiet conversation humming around him. Several others sat like him, tapping away on keyboards, lost in their own thoughts.

It was funny, really. If any of them knew *his* thoughts they'd likely run screaming.

He'd spent his life as a refined, productive member of society, hiding how he really felt about everyone else. The weakest—yet oldest—son of a wealthy clothing merchant in New York.

How excellent then, that his life had taken such an incredible turn these last few years.

All because of Isabella. He wasn't sure if he should kiss her or kill her and that was the real rub.

He stowed his laptop in a thin neoprene case and dropped his empty cup on the way out. Neat. Orderly.

He didn't leave traces.

A skill he'd put to use once more after the cozy couple arrived back in New York.

Hot damn, he loved it when a hypothesis became a cold, hard reality.

Isabella took a small sip of her champagne and avoided looking over at Liam. He wasn't fidgeting, per se, but he certainly wasn't settled, either. His large form sprawled in the first-class seat and he'd shifted several times to get comfortable.

By the continuous shifting, she could tell he clearly wasn't at ease.

She was pleased to see the second dram of vodka still sat on his tray, unopened. Although she didn't think he had a problem to have a few drinks on a six-hour flight, it was still somewhat comforting he wasn't downing the midmorning drinks like water, either.

He has too much self-control for that.

The thought swirled through her mind, yet another reminder of how he fascinated her.

What did she care if he drank himself into oblivion to get through the flight to New York? They were being picked up on the opposite side.

His personal choices were none of her business.

With the deliberate precision that had marked her behavior her entire life, she kept her eyes glued to her tablet, turning the electronic pages with a regular cadence. The pages were all for effect—she hadn't read a word since opening the book—but it gave her something to focus on.

She refused to have any sympathy for him. Nor could she quite squelch the thought that he'd earned his discomfort fair and square.

Not everything can be fixed by science. Hasn't that fact sunk in yet?

No, she wasn't the best at reading social cues and perhaps she'd pushed a bit harder on his fear of flying than she should have.

But he had no right to speak to her like that.

The heavy press of his hand on her forearm caught her attention and she turned to look at him.

"Would you like another glass of champagne?" He reached for the small bottle of vodka and waved it. "I need more ice."

"No thank you, I've had enough."

He resettled himself after ringing the call bell and she refocused on her tablet, the awkward mantle that shrouded both of them only growing more oppressive under the silence.

"I'm sorry for what I said."

The words were quiet and she'd barely heard them, the ringing laughter of the stewardess he'd waved down for ice still echoing over her head.

"Oh?"

"Before. You were just trying to be helpful and I was an ass."

"Yes, you were."

"I am sorry for it."

She'd never been a person to hold grudges—had often wondered, in fact, why others found it all too easy—yet she couldn't quite let the matter go. "That's the second time you've insulted me and my work. It's clear you think things are my fault so why have you taken on my situation?"

"You need help."

"So do lots of people, including lots of people who likely come to your firm for services. Surely you have an evaluation process?"

"Of course."

"And do you take on every case that comes in?"

"No."

"Yet you took on mine."

The discomfort that had his large body restless in his seat took on a new dimension. Where he fidgeted before, now his large form grew still, yet she could practically see him quivering in anticipation.

"I made a business choice along with my family. Our grandfather's voice carries significant weight and he believes we should help you."

She knew her grandfather's decades-old friendship with Alexander Steele had gone a long way toward greasing the wheels, but it didn't change the fact that Alexander wasn't in the field, handling cases. She had no doubt if Liam hadn't wanted to take on her case he'd have found a way out of it.

"And what do you believe?"

"I don't make it a habit to explain my behavior."

"Well, maybe I'd like an explanation."

Liam fought the waves of discomfort that pulsed under his skin.

How had she turned the tables so neatly? And since when did he get so off his game he'd allow the tables to be turned in the first place?

"I've given you an answer, but it doesn't seem to satisfy."

"It's a simple request. I'd like to know why you've decided to help me when you're so disdainful of my work and my situation."

The penetrating stare and the softly spoken words hit with the force of a bomb exploding at his feet.

Why was he helping her?

He'd done nothing to understand her situation and had, just as she'd suggested, gone out of his way to belittle her when given the opportunity. Before he could even consider his words, they were cascading from his lips like a waterfall.

"You created something without thinking through the consequences. For a woman as smart as you are, I find it hard to believe that your actions were completely innocent."

Even if she *is* innocent.

And that was the real rub, Liam knew. He wanted to paint her as the calculating woman, in full possession of a diabolical plot to wreak havoc. Instead, he had a woman who had unleashed something she wasn't prepared to handle and had put herself in the crosshairs to boot.

When she claimed she didn't know the deeper consequences of her actions, he believed her. And when she said she was committed to keeping the science out of the wrong hands, he believed that, too.

"My actions weren't innocent. I've created a capability I now must live with for the rest of my life. Do you think I don't understand that? That I'm somehow unaware of the implications of my work?"

The truth shimmered in the depths of those green eyes, lit softly by the plane's overhead lighting. Even with the muted glow, he saw the truth there.

"No. I don't think you're unaware."

"Yet I came to you and your family for help. I went around my grandfather to one of his oldest friends in hopes I can stem the tide on those implications."

"You haven't told him?"

"No. He's already lived with the bone-deep disappointment of his son's betrayal. I can't do that to him, especially as I stand here, repeating history."

And there it was.

Her father.

Damn, but he was a raging idiot. "You're not the same as your father."

"It depends on what side of history you're on for that argument to hold any weight."

"It's not the same." Urgency lit his words and even with his earlier judgment, it was important she didn't think he equated her actions with her father's. "I don't think it's the same thing at all."

"Well, whatever you believe, rest assured I'm not ignorant of what I've done. I'm anything but."

Her words pelted him like an icy rain, abrading the skin with sharp edges. "I won't do it again."

"Then I accept your apology."

The clouds lifted from her eyes so quickly if he hadn't been looking at her so closely he'd never have believed they were there to begin with.

"That's all?"

"Yep."

That strange sense of being so far off his game as to be playing a different one rose up once more, throttling him. "You're not still angry? Or holding a grudge."

"What would be the point? You've apologized."

"Then you're the rare woman, indeed, if you're not still angry."

"All right. If you want to ignore the fact you apologized, which I think is rather significant, I'll keep going. I hate conflict and I have to spend a lot of time with you."

"And?" He let that single word hang there, his mind still whirling through her litany of reasons.

"No more ands. That sums it up." She took the last sip of her champagne, her glass punctuating her comments. "For the record, I've seen men hold a grudge, too. And while the reasons tend to be different, men are as adept at it as women."

"It's not the same."

"It's exactly the same. Do you know how many colleagues begrudge another for their work? Their accomplishments? Their grants? It's practically an industry sport."

And there it was again. For a woman who seemed somewhat immune to social cues, she'd hit the mark square on the nose.

"You've observed this behavior?"

"Repeatedly. No one's immune from petty jealousy or human foibles. We're just wired to get irritated about different things."

His thoughts from earlier refilled his mind and the impish urge to press her on her comment filled him. "Is that why you were angry about the airport lounge? Petty jealousy."

"No." Her mouth snapped shut as a light flush crept up her neck. "Of course not."

Those urges pressed him on, tempting him to push harder. He leaned toward her, his gaze direct as his voice dropped to a low hum. "You weren't the slightest bit jealous of my conversation with Stella at the bar counter."

"Why would I be jealous?"

"I don't know." He tilted his head for effect, as if he were trying to come up with the answer. "Maybe because we had that explosive kiss in the elevator and then didn't talk about it."

That delightful blush crept higher and filled her cheeks with a rosy glow. "That meant nothing. You even apologized after. It was a simple defense mechanism to ward off the threat in the lobby."

"There's no threat now."

Even as he said the words, Liam knew them to be anything but the truth. *She* was a threat. A threat to his ordered world.

A threat to his self-control.

And damn the woman, a threat to his sanity with those lush lips and large green eyes a man could drown in.

She swallowed hard and nodded her head. "No, there isn't."

"Then why do I want to kiss you so desperately?"

Chapter 6

Isabella stared into those endlessly deep blue eyes and wondered how she'd gone from crushed and defeated to the top of the world in a matter of moments.

Was that the true miracle of attraction? Highs and lows with very little in between?

The strange thought tunneled through her subconscious as her very active conscious fought to hang on and stay in the moment. "Somehow I don't get the feeling you're a man who asks for kisses all that often."

Was that her voice? Those seductive, breathy tones that sounded like they came from the deepest part of her?

"I can't remember ever wanting one more."

He hesitated for the briefest moment, those vivid blue eyes sparking with fire, before pressing his lips to hers. Where she thought the awkward angle of their airplane seats would make it difficult to enjoy his kiss, it did the opposite. The barrier actually made the kiss sweeter, a subtle reminder they needed to work for what they wanted.

Or, reach out and take it.

The thought hovered in the back of her mind as she laid her hands on Liam's shoulders. If their kiss in the elevator had been a surprise assault on the senses, this was a lush invitation.

His tongue was cool, the lingering effects of the ice in his glass an erotic counterpoint to the heat emanating from his large form. He drew her in, moment by moment, with the press of his lips and the subtle pressure of his mouth. He kept his hands at his sides and that restraint—counterbalanced by the thick muscle of his shoulders under her fingertips—played a sexy counterpoint.

Control. Barely leashed yet absolute.

What would it be like to make him lose it?

Emboldened by the thought, she matched the thrust of his tongue, wrapping her mouth around his erotic assault. Although she couldn't hear his moan over the heavy hum of the airplane's engine, she felt its light echo from the back of his throat.

He lifted his head, sexual need shining from his eyes. Without warning, the space pirate from her book came to vivid color in her mind. She'd imagined Liam in the role earlier, but she now finally understood what her subconscious had already figured out.

Here was a man who lived life on his own terms. By his own rules.

The thought was thrilling. And more than a bit scary.

The moment was broken by the arrival of their stewardess with the ice he'd requested, her bright, vivid smile amped up like the lights in a stadium. Liam thanked her, but offered nothing further.

Isabella observed the exchange and wondered at it. "She's rejected."

"Excuse me?"

"You smiled at her before the ice and now you've dismissed her. She's hurt."

A puzzled frown flittered across his face, the look of surprise so genuine she had to believe she was reading him correctly. "I thanked her. I'd hardly call that dismissing her."

"She was expecting something more."

"It was just some ice."

"I guess it was."

Isabella picked up her tablet once more and flipped to her book. She needed to put the observations on hold for a while and let her thoughts simmer. In the meantime, she'd read about her space pirate and let the lingering feel of Liam Steele's kiss on her lips bring the words to life in a way they never had before.

She now knew what it was like to be plundered.

As the late morning sun stole through her bedroom curtains, Kensington Steele stared at the diamond winking off her left hand and marveled at how her world had changed in a matter of months. She'd spent years purposefully marching through life, anxious to tackle the next big challenge and prove to herself that she could do whatever she'd set her mind toward.

And all the while she'd been missing the simple joy of sitting still with the one she loved. Of holding his hand in hers and allowing the quiet to wrap around them in a warm cocoon. Of laying her hand against his chest, the strong, steady heartbeat underneath reassuring her she had a partner on the journey.

"I can hear your mind whirling." Jack's voice was sleepy

but she didn't miss the note of humor threaded underneath his words.

"I was thinking."

"Damn, but I didn't do it right. Morning sex is supposed to be lazy and all-consuming. No thinking allowed." He tightened his arms around her. "I'd better try again."

"Oh don't worry." She ran a lazy finger over his stomach, pleased when the firm flesh of his abdomen contracted at her touch. "You did everything exactly right."

"I still think I should try to persuade you once more." He pressed a kiss to her forehead and punctuated it with a light tickle to her ribs.

She wiggled from his arms and sat up in bed. She knew herself and the voracious appetite he'd managed to unleash in the past three months. If she stayed in his arms she'd be in the exact same spot until they left for the airport to get Liam.

Which wasn't such a bad idea...

"Jack!" He tickled her again and it was the incentive she needed to put some distance and step out of bed. "I'm serious."

Those dark brown eyes—hungry with that incredible need for her that never seemed satiated—captured her own. "So am I."

On a sigh he sat up and settled his large frame against the headboard. "Then I go back to my first question. What's got your mind whirling like that?"

"I can't get over my conversation with Liam."

When he just sat there and waited for her to continue, she was once again reminded that she had a partner in all aspects of her life.

He *got* her and that was such an incredible gift all by itself.

"He's convinced the guy in his lobby yesterday morning

was a problem and Isabella had the problem at her hotel."
She slipped into her robe, supremely satisfied when a small
moue of dissatisfaction tightened Jack's lips. "Add on the
fact that Campbell can't find a scrap of video in either location's feeds and the likelihood they're both right is high."

"I never took your brother for one to imagine a threat."

"No, but we don't know Isabella. She's scared and you
know as well as I do that can make a client see the boogey-
man where he isn't."

"Or it can make them alert and heightened to the danger around them."

"True." She sat back down on the edge of the bed and
worried the silk tie of her robe in her fingers. No matter
how she spun it, she couldn't fully dissuade herself of the
unnamed danger underlying the assignment. "But why is
the threat in London *and* here in New York? She claims
her apartment's been broken into and strange things have
happened at her lab. And she wasn't even supposed to be
in London but ended up going at the last minute. And—"
she broke off at the smile covering Jack's face. "What?"

"Keep going, you're on a roll, Sherlock Holmes. Put it
together for me."

"Don't you need a new stand-in? Last time I checked
Watson and Holmes didn't sleep together."

"More's the pity for them." He ran a finger down her
arm, his touch leaving a small layer of gooseflesh in its
wake.

She nearly gave in—almost—but held back. "That
would have made for quite a different story."

"I'll say. But come on and enlighten me before I can't
constrain myself any longer and strip that silk off of you."
He tugged on the same tie in her hands. "Slowly."

Her scrambled thoughts struggled to keep up at the

image he painted and she stood once more and put some distance between them. The wolfish grin she got in return had her refocusing on the task at hand.

"Why is there a threat in both places? If this was a threat from a professional operative she'd have been taken out already. Instead it smacks of cat and mouse. Who does that? Especially if they want the research she's squirreled away."

"Someone with a grudge."

"And access to intel."

Jack's expression changed, the sexy twinkle in his eyes morphing to all business. "From the files you shared with me and the feedback from your grandparents, she doesn't have anyone to hold a grudge against her. Parents are out of the picture. No exes or messy relationships. Her life is her work. Who could be after her?"

He stood and dragged on a pair of slacks. Kensington allowed her gaze to drift over the firm planes of his body, momentarily distracted by the flex of muscles in his quick, efficient movements. Dragging herself back to the point at hand, she pressed on. "Everyone has enemies."

"No, darling. Everyone in *our* business has enemies. Most people live their life day to day, pleasantly free of that particular problem."

"You have a point."

"But so do you. Someone's after her, even if nothing obvious pops." He stretched out a hand to her. The gesture was simple. Warm. Loving. "Let's fire up your computer and see what we can find."

A hard shift in the cabin had Isabella coming awake with a start. She hadn't slept long—and the few moments she had gotten were filled with endless images of Liam's mouth pressed along every inch of her body—but another hard dip of the plane had her coming fully awake.

A quick glance over at the object of her erotic dreams had them vanishing, concern rising up in its place. "Are you all right?"

"I'm fine." His fingers were pure white where they gripped the arm rests and his jaw appeared cut out of marble.

She reached for his hand, prying his fingers loose and wrapping them tightly within her own. "It's fine. It's just some turbulence."

As if to punctuate the thought, the captain came over the intercom with an apology for the bumpy ride and a promise they were climbing to a higher, smoother elevation.

"I'm sure it is."

"It's like waves on an ocean."

The tight set of his jaw relaxed ever-so-slightly as he turned to stare at her. His pupils were wide disks inside those orbs of blue. "What?"

"Flying. We're flying on the air the same way a boat floats on the waves."

"It's hardly the same."

"Scientifically, the principle is exactly the same."

Another layer of fear peeled away and she felt the tension in his fingers relax slightly. "So we're flying in the perfect storm? Somehow that doesn't make me feel any better."

"It should. But if you really want to feel better I can bore you with the specifics of my research. That should put you right to sleep."

What she'd meant as a joke hit its mark and Liam shifted in his seat, interest sparking under the white-eyed fear. A small part of her thrilled at the fact he hadn't removed his hand, even if his voice was all business when he spoke. "I'd say now is the perfect time."

She walked him through the basics of cell structure and

the mapping of DNA, pleased when he so obviously kept up. His nod to keep going had her releasing his hand to grab the second tablet from her carry on—the one with all her notes and data—that she kept on her person at all times. Flipping it open, she tabbed to the presentation she'd been building for the *New York Times*.

"Here. Let me walk you through this."

Slide by slide, they moved through the data, Liam asking questions here and there, but each one was additive to what she'd already explained.

"You really get this."

"I get by."

His wry smile had her rephrasing the statement. "I didn't mean it that way, but usually I have to slow down when I explain my work, even to many of my fellow scientists. You seem to have a natural aptitude for this."

"It's interesting. You've defined what makes us…us."

"That was the goal."

It was a victory—albeit a small one—that he did understand on some level what she did.

"So explain to me how this can be abused."

And there it was. The proof that he also understood how her work could be misused and twisted. She flipped a few slides forward and walked him through the remaining highlights of her research.

"This point right here. The genetic material can be altered at these two points with the introduction of a new material, carried to the cells by a virus."

"I saw something about this recently. A young girl's cancer was cured by injecting her with a modified HIV virus."

"Yes, it's all part of the same underlying body of work." She also knew several recent blockbusters had played with the same basic idea and it was amazing how close to the mark those films had been with the technology.

"So how is your work different? If it's already been successfully trialed by others, what have you discovered that's caused such an uproar?"

"All of the work to date has been around modifying damaged cells. The cancer cells, for example."

He nodded and for some absurd reason, she suddenly wished her hand was wrapped up in his, fingers entwined once more.

"All my work has been with healthy cells. Healthy DNA. I've discovered how to reprogram it to make it stronger and less vulnerable to mutation or attack."

"Which could prevent disease?"

"Yes, it could."

"I'm still not fully seeing a downside. If research has already proven we can cure those who are sick, why not fix the problem before they get sick."

"When I began my work, that *was* my goal. Finding gaps in DNA that caused both mental and physical illness with the intent to cure those strands. But that's only half the equation."

"And the other half?"

"Once we know how to make our DNA stronger, it's a small step to then remove what we don't want or need."

"Designer genes."

"Exactly. Remove our faults and we remove our innate balance. Remove our faults and we become invincible."

Invincible.

That single word had haunted him for the last hour.

Although he'd had a pretty good idea why her work would be so appealing to the world's governments—the ability to create a race of super soldiers certainly perched atop the list—the ramifications went far deeper.

Superhuman intelligence. Superhuman strength. Superhuman *everything*.

And power-hungry leaders who would be all too willing to ignore the bigger risks inherent in altering nature for their own benefit.

Liam dragged their carry-ons from the overhead bins and gestured Isabella from her seat to deplane in front of him. He'd already gotten Kensington's text that she and Jack were waiting for them outside. They didn't have to collect baggage so after a brief hold up in Customs, they'd be on their way.

Quick. Easy. Efficient.

Just like he liked his life.

Which was an odd thought considering he'd spent the past five hours thinking about Isabella. She was anything but simple—as a person or in the current state of her personal life—and he wasn't sure what he thought about that fact.

Or why he couldn't stop thinking about her in the first place.

Although he'd been prepared to think the worst, her explanation of her work had shed new light on the problem. While it didn't change the fact she could have had more forethought into the implications of her work, the passion in her voice and her depth of knowledge went beyond the cursory.

She loved her work. And she had a passion to solve the puzzles of human existence to make life better.

"I always hate this part." Her words broke into his musings as Isabella settled her shoulder bag against the handles of her suitcase. Within moments she had the entire ensemble rolling smoothly behind her as they walked.

"Customs? Why?"

"It always feels like I'm under a microscope."

Their first-class accommodations meant they'd deplane first and the queue was small. He turned to her, unable to hold back the smile. "Don't you make your living with microscopes?"

"And computers."

"Then you should feel right at home."

"You know what I mean. It's not like my name's not in their databases—" she broke off a flash of red highlighting her cheeks as her mouth broke into a small frown. "Because of my father."

And there it was again. That subtle—or perhaps not-so-subtle—reality that she lived with. The betrayal of a parent that meted out emotional punishment as well as tangible, living reminders on a regular basis.

"You weren't responsible for his actions."

"It doesn't keep government officials from keeping track of the connection."

Liam knew his grandmother had given him the basics and Kenzi was more than capable of filling in the gaps, but he found himself needing to hear the words from Isabella. "What did your father do, exactly?"

The bright hues of passion that had lit up Isabella's gaze like shiny emeralds were nowhere in evidence when she finally spoke. "He's a scientist."

"You speak of him in the present."

"He's still alive."

"He is?" Liam knew he could have handled his reaction with a bit more aplomb, but the news that her father was alive and well was a surprise.

"Technically, he is. I have no contact with him, so..." She broke off, her words fading on a light shrug. Despite the apparent nonchalance, he'd have had to be blind to miss the heat that flared high in her gaze.

Her hands fumbled at her waistband in that gesture he was coming to associate with her before she seemed to decide something. Moments later, she exhaled on a rush, her words like bullets. "He built his body of work during the Cold War. Heavy nuclear research and new technologies to deliver more streamlined payloads."

"What made his work treasonous?"

"It wasn't his wartime work but the dirty bombs he built on the side."

Liam knew the bare basics on jurisdiction around treason trials, and for her father to have been convicted, the evidence must have been overwhelming. "How many?"

"Enough to put him in demand. He was caught selling several to a well-known terrorist cell nearly a decade after the Cold War ended."

He wasn't a man prone to sympathy and often reveled in the stoic demeanor he was known for, but the murmured words slipped out before Liam could stop them. "I'm sorry."

"So that's why I don't like Customs." She waved her passport in the direction of the glass booths that held the government agents. "It's intrusive. The only part that's even tolerable is the cute little dogs that come sniffing around."

"The beagles looking for illegal food?"

She nodded, her first smile since stepping off the plane lighting up her face. "I love them. Their tails are always wagging and they look so friendly."

"That's why they use them. Many people feel they're not as threatening because they're smaller. Well, that and the fact they can find food faster than pretty much any breed of dog."

Liam thought of the hounds his grandfather had kept for decades at their country property in England. He hadn't visited the place in years and his grandfather had long ago stopped keeping a line of dogs, but it was funny to think of those days now.

"You have a dog?"

He shook his head, the image of his boyhood summers growing brighter in his mind. "No. I was thinking of my grandfather's hounds. My father grew up with them and always spoke lovingly of the beagle he had as a boy. He called him James Bond."

The memory did its job and Isabella was laughing as they took the turn around the last stanchion in their Customs line. Several people had joined the queue and he could only be grateful they were at the front.

"That's a rather impressive name to live up to."

"He was a rather impressive dog, from my father's stories of him. Small but mighty. Bond could sniff out any and all food no matter what wing of the house he was in. My great-grandparents lived out their lives on the estate and I take it he tangled more than once with my great-grandmother over a stolen morsel in the kitchens."

"He sounds like quite the scoundrel. One who lived admirably up to his name." She pulled her passport from her purse and slid her declaration inside the pages. "So no dog for you, even with such good memories to light the way?"

"No. My schedule doesn't permit it."

"Mine either."

He wondered at that. Although he suspected she traveled internationally to see her grandfather and probably on occasion for her job, the role of scientist and researcher didn't seem to be one that precluded pets.

"You don't want one?"

"It's never seemed feasible to have one. I work long hours. I get absorbed and easily distracted by my work. I don't know," she said, shrugging, "it just seemed unfair to leave pets to fend for themselves."

They were called forward and he was prevented from probing further, but he couldn't shake the image of her coming home to an empty apartment.

Just like you do, Steele.

Customs passed with little incident but Isabella could have sworn the agent spent extra time reviewing her computer screen before dropping that heavy stamp into her passport.

Shake it off.

The admonition couldn't change the experience but it did go a long way toward resetting her equilibrium.

Liam did the rest.

He'd entertained her throughout the wait, painting a picture in her mind of a merry little dog who shamelessly stole food and it had made the wait better.

It had made everything better.

Instead of standing there alone, lost in her own world, she'd shared someone else's. Even the discussion of her father's transgressions couldn't quite shake the easy camaraderie and simple comfort.

A loud shout caught Liam's attention and he raised his hand, hollering back to a couple who stood side by side in front of a large black Mercedes-Benz. She couldn't know for sure but she suspected the car was outfitted with the latest in security and safety measures and once again she was reminded of how far out of her depth she was.

Although she was only a few feet behind, Isabella stopped, entranced by the warmth of the moment.

The woman ran forward first, wrapping Liam in a tight hug, and the resemblance between the two of them was hard to miss. Although Liam had her beat by almost a head, the matched coloring and the vivid blue eyes confirmed the woman had to be his sister, Kensington.

Isabella found herself pulled from her trance and into a tight hug before Kensington stepped back. "I'm so glad you're here. We'll take good care of you."

"Thank you."

Was that the right answer? Isabella supposed it would have to do. After all, she wasn't used to speaking to goddesses and that's pretty much what the slender woman opposite her made her think of.

Long, lush hair that framed her face before spilling behind her back. Those penetrating sky blue eyes that drew you in. And a handsome man on her arm that had Isabella thinking of movie stars of old.

The movie star turned all that wattage on her with a gentle smile. "I'm Jack. Let me help you with that."

Jack's outreach had her looking down and Isabella realized she'd not yet stowed her passport from the walk through Customs. "Give me just a sec and I'll put this up."

Her oversize tote bag still rested on top of her rolling suitcase and she reached for its large, zipper-front pocket that gaped open. She slid her passport into the opening, surprised when her hand hit a hard piece of paper.

Distracted by the warm smile and large man before her she almost ignored it, but old habits died hard.

She knew what she kept in her bags. And she knew she hadn't placed any paper inside the front pocket.

With fingers that suddenly trembled without warning,

she pulled the folded paper from the pocket, her breath catching in her throat at the single word scrawled on the sheet.

GOTCHA.

Before she could say anything, a loud series of pops split the air.

Chapter 7

Liam threw his body over Isabella's, dragging her against him as they fell to the hard ground. From the corner of his eye he saw Jack do the same with Kensington and he fought to make sense of the moment even as his ears rang with the overpowering noise of gunfire.

With careful movements, Liam followed Jack's lead. His future brother-in-law and his sister were closer to the back passenger doors of the Mercedes-Benz and Jack was already tossing a loudly protesting Kensington into the backseat.

Liam followed suit, his hold tight on Isabella as he maneuvered her while still shielding her with his body.

"I'm not staying here!" Kensington's loud complaint rose up again, before he cut her off.

"I need you to stay with Isabella. She can't stay here alone. Is the gun still in the front console?"

"Is the Pope Catholic?" When he didn't bother to respond to the attitude, she added, "Fine. Go."

Liam backed out and slammed the door on a wide-eyed Isabella. He'd worry about calming both of them down later. For now, he took off after Jack's retreating form, weaving through the heavy traffic and now-screaming travelers who'd witnessed the shots.

The heavy throb of sirens echoed through the air and Liam fought to keep up with Jack. The arrival of police would slow down whatever he and Jack could do assuming they got their hands on the shooter and he wanted as much time as possible with the bastard.

Jack had a head start but Liam's longer stride had him catching up before he kept on going. The retreating form they'd followed had zigzagged his way through oncoming traffic before vaulting over a half wall of plastic roadblock.

Excellent.

Liam couldn't hold back his satisfaction the man had disappeared into a closed environment and pushed himself, adding another burst of speed to keep up the hunt.

That continued whirl of sirens grew heavier and he heard shouting in the distance. A glance over his shoulder showed Jack stopping to talk to the first officer to arrive and Liam knew he was about out of time.

A shooter in public would draw the law in any jurisdiction. But in the middle of New York City's international airport?

The whole place would be in lockdown in a matter of minutes.

He vaulted the same half wall as his quarry and hoped Jack could get him the time he needed. The fact the man was in security—operating a firm of his own—would go a long way toward greasing the wheels, but there was no way they were quietly sweeping this one under the rug.

Footsteps echoed off the thick concrete of the garage and he struggled to get his bearings. The sound was distorted enough to make it difficult to know which way the guy had gone. Add on the coward had had enough of a head start that he'd cleared the visible perimeter of the parking garage and Liam knew the man had more than enough time to either hide himself behind a car or get to one on his own.

"Freeze!"

Liam stopped where he was, the arrival of the cops stopping him from going any further.

Damn, but if he'd only had a bit more time. His heart slammed in his chest, a pounding indicator of frustrated effort. He kept his hands lifted and allowed the police to sweep the area around him until they were satisfied.

But as he stood where he was, his quarry getting farther and farther away, Liam couldn't help but wonder how the hell he was going to keep Isabella safe.

Isabella glanced around the rather impressive meeting space at the House of Steele and fought the urge to scream. She was on her third hour of questioning and had already spoken to two detectives and a lieutenant from the NYPD before a pair of federal agents arrived and took over the show.

Isabella had no doubt the interrogation was designed to wear her down, but she had nothing to give them. She was as puzzled by the events as anyone else and the note she'd discovered in her bag had already been taken into evidence to be checked for fingerprints.

From her perspective, she had no idea how the note had even gotten into her bag. The front pocket had been empty of anything save her passport when she'd boarded the plane. She'd unzipped the zipper and transferred her passport to her purse for the walk through Customs and had left the zipper open.

Over and over, she retraced the time with Liam through her mind. No one had bumped into them. Or even touched them, for that matter.

So when had someone had a chance to slip a paper into her bag?

"Dr. Magnini." The first detective who'd questioned her smiled broadly. If the gesture was meant to soothe it fell short with its fake and insincere undertones. "Why were you out of the country?"

"I was in London visiting my grandfather. I do that frequently." Information she'd already shared and which, she had no doubt, they'd already culled from the manifests of her international travel over the last several years.

"Yet you were traveling back with Mr. Steele."

"His family and mine are old friends."

"You've known Mr. Steele long, then?"

Liam pushed off his position on the wall and came to stand next to her, his hand resting warm on her shoulder. "As Dr. Magnini pointed out, our families are old friends. A simple fact that's easy enough to verify. I'm curious why you keep pressing it."

"We're trying to get a picture of why she'd be in danger. With your line of work, Mr. Steele, it stands to reason a shooter could be after you as easily as they are after Dr. Magnini."

"True enough." Liam's tone grew darker and his hand remained steady against her shoulder, even as his index finger ran over her collarbone in lazy, sweeping motions. Whether to soothe or to suggest something more intimate between them, she didn't know, but the small motion had set off sparks under her skin and she was having a hard time keeping up.

"Regardless of the reason, it still doesn't explain why you've been interrogating Isabella for almost three hours.

Nor does it explain away the fact that she's answered all your questions, despite the fact you've not come up with any new ones since the first fifteen minutes of the discussion."

"We could hold this meeting downtown."

"Yet you chose to hold it here which means you know you don't have enough to keep going with this."

Words flung back and forth across the table with the ease of arrows and she took it all in, suddenly more grateful than she could ever say for the help of the Steele family.

No matter how many challenges she'd faced in her life, this was simply not something she could handle on her own.

From the touch of his hand to his ready defense and quick answers to the agents, Liam was a force to be reckoned with. Isabella shot a glance toward Kensington, where she sat at the head of the long table, the woman's presence only adding to that sense of reassurance.

"We're offering you a courtesy, Mr. Steele." The second agent piped up. "Your firm has been more than helpful over the years and we'd like to show our gratitude."

Courtesy, my ass.

If there was anything she'd learned since her father's disgrace it was that the government did nothing without careful calculation.

Benevolence was a strategy, *not* a general way of acting.

"We're taking Dr. Magnini's security very seriously. No one was injured today and it's obvious the targeting of us at the airport was deliberate and focused as opposed to an attack that was broader in scope." Kensington had said little and Isabella got the sense it was driving the woman crazy to stay in the background.

Clearly when she did speak, it was worth the wait. The woman's words were couched in a pleasant smile that fooled no one, least of all the government's representatives. Both agents nodded at the thinly veiled reference to terrorist activity and she could see the hard set of their shoulders relax slightly.

Protecting citizens from terrorism took a shocking amount of their time and no one wanted to own the results of not paying the proper attention to a bad situation. Much as she resented the interrogation, she sympathized for the reason.

Her sentiment took a decided turn south when the second agent sat up straighter, a thought clearly registering in the man's mind. "Dr. Magnini. How well-versed are you in your father's work?"

"I'm very well acquainted with his work, Agent McCray. It haunts me, as a matter of fact, as does his tarnished reputation."

"Tarnished?" The first agent raised his eyebrows, interest sparking deep in his eyes at the line of questioning his partner had opened. "That's a rather lenient description of someone who sold weapons to terrorists and was ultimately tried as a traitor."

"And the British government prosecuted him fully for his crimes." Isabella refused to drop her gaze or allow it to waver for the slightest moment. She'd lived with the pain of her father's choices her entire adult life, but never before had she felt such a deep-seated humiliation in front of others.

No matter how she tried to distance herself, she'd never be free of it. How funny, then, that in her attempts to understand where she came from through her research, she'd virtually scripted the current circumstances she found herself in.

With a weariness born of the absolute weight of her father's betrayal, she stood, effectively ending the conversation. She'd learned to live with the humiliation, but she was unwilling to expose the good people who'd offered their help. "I believe both Liam and Kensington have been more than accommodating, holding the meetings here in their home. As Mr. Steele mentioned, you have no right to keep me, asking the same question over and over. It's an imposition on my time as well as on my friends."

The agents stood in kind and Isabella relished the small victory.

"I'll see you out." Jack piped up from next to Kensington and ushered the interlopers from the house.

Kensington kept her lips pursed and offered up a subtle shake of her head, pointing toward the open doorway. It was only when they heard the heavy slam of the front door that she finally spoke.

"That was fun." Kensington let out a heavy breath before getting up and walking toward the sideboard. Although Isabella hadn't paid much attention since walking in, her full focus on answering the officials' questions, she took in the room now that the immediate threat had receded.

They appeared to be in a large dining room, converted to a meeting room. The dining room furniture was still intact, but so were several bookshelves and a low credenza that looked like a filing cabinet.

Liam's gaze swung to hers. "Are you doing okay?"

The low hum of adrenaline that had stayed constant in her bloodstream for the past three hours took a nosedive, and whatever polite veneer she'd managed to drum up vanished in the blink of an eye.

Legs heavy with pent-up anger, she slammed her chair back, catching the wooden arms just before the chair fell out of reach.

"How the hell can you ask me that? Not only am I now

being shot at in public venues by a madman but I've put the very people who are trying to help me in the cross-hairs as well."

"We can handle this."

He laid a hand on her arm but she shrugged off the comfort, backing away from the table. "How? By person-ally escorting me? Because fat lot of good that did since I ended up with a threatening note in my luggage all the while standing right beside you!"

Each word she spoke ratcheted up louder and louder until she felt the heavy prick of tears at the backs of her eyes and a matching telltale knot in her throat. "Excuse me."

And then she ran.

Liam was on her heels before his sister snagged his arm, dragging him to a halt. "Kenzi—"

"I'll go." The usual fire he saw in her gaze—the one that telegraphed how much she enjoyed tangling with him on every subject under the sun—was nowhere in evidence. Instead, all he saw was the sincere notes of sympathy. "Let me talk to her."

Where a good old-fashioned fight between siblings would have only fired him up more, the simple under-standing in her gaze was his undoing. "Fine. Go."

Jack walked back into the room, obviously keyed into the conversation. "What happened?"

"Adrenaline and a dose of female tears." Kensington kissed her fiancé on her way out the door. "I'll be back in a minute."

Liam watched his sister go and it took everything in him to avoid following her. Jack crossed to the credenza. "Drink?"

"No. I had a couple on the plane."

"Suit yourself. But, since that was several hours ago and the house is locked down, you may want to reconsider."

Liam eyed the bottle of wine Jack held up and shook his head. "I'm good."

Jack fiddled with the cork, saying nothing until he had the bottle open and a glass swirling in his hands. "They don't have a case. It's pretty clear today's incident wasn't a terrorist act, perpetrated against innocent Americans."

"No, damn it, just one innocent American." Liam flipped through the business cards the various officers and agents had left behind, disgust curdling in his stomach like bad fish. "Damn Feds. They're going to be after this one like a dog with a bone."

"She doesn't have anything for them on that front. And despite her history, she's an American citizen with an impressive record of professional work. They'll tire soon enough." Jack took a seat. "What she does have is someone who doesn't want her to share her research. But the bastard's going to have some fun with her for a while."

Jack's words only reinforced his existing fears, all while confirming a few more. "So it's not just me who feels like it's a game."

"It's personal, Liam. And the only way we're going to protect her is to figure out who it is."

He wadded up the business cards, tossing them in the trash. "She doesn't believe anyone's out to get her."

"Kensington and I did some digging earlier. Nothing's popped yet but she's looking. And you know as well as I do, no one hides from your sister for long."

Liam knew the depth of his sister's skills. Campbell might have the electronics work down cold, but Kensington was a whiz at digital forensics. Between the databases she subscribed to and the ones Campbell got her into, once she was there she knew how to tug leads and pull just the right strings to unravel a mystery.

If there was something to find on who might be after Isabella, his sister could get after it.

But even Kenzi's skills couldn't change one simple fact. "She's alone in the world, Jack. Who the hell could be after her?"

"Old boyfriend jealous of her success?"

That sour feeling in his stomach turned decidedly rancid at the idea of Isabella with a boyfriend. She was a grown woman, he well knew, but the idea of her with someone else…

He pushed the image from his mind and focused on the core of Jack's question. "It doesn't play. There's been no personal contact made. A former flame would want her to know it's him. Would want that gratification to express his love, even if it was a twisted way to do it."

"Colleague? Someone jealous of her work and the funding it received?"

"All her research has been funded off of an inheritance."

"Generous dead guys don't exactly scream connection." Jack swirled his wine once more, his gaze drawn to the dark red liquid. "But those overlooked for the inheritance do."

"I tried that angle but she can't think of anyone. Hell, I don't know. Maybe she's too close to it." Liam tapped his fingers on the desk before reaching for one of the empty wine glasses Jack had left on the middle of the table and the bottle of wine.

"And you?"

"What about me?"

"Are you too close to this?"

"Hell no."

"You sure?"

Liam set the bottle back on the table with a hard thud. "Positive."

"She trusts you."

"She needs to trust all of us. We're the only thing that stands between her and whoever wants to keep her from presenting her work."

Edward stowed the gun back under the front seat of his car and rubbed the ache in his thigh as he waited for the parking attendant to come give him a valet ticket. The luxury car had worked like a dream at the airport.

Although the police had the garage on lockdown, carefully reviewing anyone who wanted to leave, it was quick work to show them his traveling papers and his credentials from the university. Between the faked travel itinerary and the fancy car, he was on his way with barely a second glance.

It didn't hurt he'd already worked the camera feeds at the airport and in the garage while he'd waited for Isabella's flight to arrive. No one knew he'd gone in or out of the garage that afternoon and he'd already re-set the feed so no one would. He'd taken particular pride in the timed footage he'd captured on an alternate feed, re-tagged in the system to show Liam Steele entering the garage as he gave chase.

Edward took the ticket from the parking attendant and grabbed his bags from the back of the car. His thighs ached and he ignored the burn as he dragged his bags behind him. The pain served him right and acted as a not-so-subtle reminder.

The events at the airport had been a bit too close for comfort and he was still mad at himself for the near fumble on that one. There were few systems he couldn't hack but the airport's video feed was state of the art. He'd fiddled so long with it he almost missed Isabella's arrival. Which had further rushed the stunt with the note and his ability to get out of sight and get off a good shot.

Damned Steele family reunion.

He'd done his homework on them, too, and they might look all "rich, happy family playing at the security game" but they had some decent skills between them.

So he'd rushed and missed the best part. What he wouldn't give for a picture of Isabella when she'd discovered his note. Oh man, would that have been sweet, but he'd have to live with the memory of watching her from a distance.

The thought went a long way toward assuaging the pain and he couldn't hold back the smile as he turned up his block. He imagined her subtle panic and confused expression as she found the note, then read it, just before a bullet went winging her direction.

He'd already disguised his appearance and it had been easy enough to slip it into her tote when the Steeles were busy celebrating their little reunion. But it was his knowledge of Isabella and her manic desire for uniformity and order that had her pulling the note from her bag right then and there, setting everything in motion.

He *knew* her. Had observed her for years.

And because he knew her, he could use her weaknesses against her.

Edward nodded a greeting to his doorman as he walked into his building, then beelined for the elevator. He stifled the yawn that threatened once he was inside the car and focused on what came next.

He and the Doc had some momentum and surprise on their side and there was no way they'd give that up.

Even though he desperately needed to rest.

The elevator pinged and he stepped off, dragging himself toward his apartment. Maybe he would sleep a little. A late night always set him back and he couldn't afford the loss of strength right now.

Better yet, maybe he'd take a day. The Doc was busy with his own plans and besides, Isabella's meeting with the journalists was still more than a week away.

They had time.

Rest, then action.

He dragged himself under the covers and rubbed at his legs that had suddenly begun to throb in earnest. With the backward counting technique she'd taught him to work through the pain, he thought about the woman he knew.

Brilliant. Flawless in her research. And fundamentally incapable of dealing with the world around her.

She was a woman who consoled herself with work. It was the one thing she did well so she'd made it her life, to the exclusion of most anything else.

Oh yes, he *knew* Isabella.

And he'd set trigger points at every place she might visit now that she was back home.

As he fell asleep he imagined her panic when she found the little surprise he'd left waiting for her in her lab.

Chapter 8

Isabella glanced around the small library, curious in spite of herself. She'd always imagined what the inside of a real New York brownstone would look like, but until her arrival at the House of Steele headquarters a few hours ago, she'd never been inside one.

Her mind already whirled with the details of the room, cataloguing memories as she paced. The activity kept her mind busy as she worked to process the events of the day.

But no matter how elegant the room's drapes or how fascinating the rows of books on the shelves that lined the walls, she couldn't escape from the reality of what had happened.

Someone had snuck up on her at the airport and planted the note and then proceeded to shoot at all of them. Her work had put them all at risk.

She had put them all at risk.

"Mind if I come in?"

Kensington stood in the open doorway and Isabella

waved her in. "Of course not. I was just admiring your home."

"Do you know the story of it?"

"No, I'm afraid not."

"Come sit with me and I'll fill you in. After, of course, we get a bit of wine." Kensington crossed to a small, hidden bar that was barely visible where it was tucked away in a corner and pulled out a bottle. "Red okay?"

"Of course." Isabella used the conversational reprieve to catalogue the things she didn't already know about Kensington.

For instance, the woman knew how to open a bottle of wine in under twenty seconds. A feat that, if not unique, was certainly impressive.

Isabella also knew the woman had an aura of kindness about her. Kensington kept up a steady stream of chatter as she opened the wine, then filled two large bowl glasses with the rich red.

But what she realized most of all was the subtle understanding and veneer of sadness behind the woman's bright blue eyes when she finally took the seat opposite on the couch.

"I'm sorry for the interrogation by the police. If we could have stepped in sooner we would have. I was practically kicking Liam under the table to move things along."

"I'm not sure anyone could have moved them off their goals."

"Likely not." Kensington took a small sip of her wine, before gesturing to the room at large. "But since it was more than obvious to anyone who bothered to look that you were an innocent victim, the questioning got old. We've worked hard to be a solid resource to the government when they need it and I'm not happy they used my home as a place to detain you."

"How long have you lived here?"

"None of us live here any longer. We just use it as the House of Steele headquarters." Kensington smiled and settled her glass on the coffee table. "It was my mother's family home and the home Liam, Campbell, Rowan and I grew up in."

"That explains why it feels so comforting, even if the things taking place inside aren't—" Isabella broke off, the words at odds with the kindness Kensington offered.

"Even if the things taking place are sordid and ugly."

"Yes."

A warm hand covered hers and Kensington's gaze was direct when she spoke. "We're going to take care of you. All of us."

"I know."

"Your work is important. Groundbreaking. It deserves the proper care and the right audience."

The wine in her glass sloshed as Isabella's hands began to tremble. "It's dangerous work. I don't know why I didn't fully understand that."

"It's necessary work. And you're hardly the first to work in the field."

"No."

"Understanding who we are and how we're made. That's a natural human longing. You simply have the tools to dig down deep and find out the reasons why."

"The scientific reasons, yes."

Kensington's gaze grew sharp. "Are there others?"

"I never considered them before, but now? I'm not so sure. I think biology only tells us so much."

She'd always believed in science. The mathematical surety and basis in facts one could measure. It was comforting somehow, that in the natural world all one needed to do was look for order and patterns and from there, you could understand the chaos.

"Sort of like this wine?" Kensington's smile was gentle when she lifted her glass. "Grapes are grapes. Same molecular structure. Same DNA. Same familial roots. But the soil and the sunlight and even the weather that year have an impact on the wine they become."

"I suppose."

Kensington's hand was warm when it covered hers. "I know you're scared. And I know you've spent a long time searching for answers. Maybe you've been asking the wrong questions."

Liam stared into his wine glass and wondered when an evening spent with the cops was a reason to have a family celebration. Kensington had been closeted away with Isabella for the past hour and in the meantime, the rest of his siblings had descended on the house en masse.

Not that four extra people was exactly a mass of humanity, but things had certainly gotten louder in the old dining room.

"Pass me the spicy mustard, Campbell. O'Callaghan's never puts enough on their subs." Rowan's voice echoed from the opposite end of the room where she sat next to her husband, Finn.

Campbell tossed the mustard down the table along with one of his trademark taunts. "Stay away from her, Finn. After all that spicy mustard and a sub full of onions she's going to be a tasty morsel."

When Finn leaned over and gave Rowan a smacking kiss on the lips, Liam suspected his besotted brother-in-law was past caring.

Campbell's wife, Abby, swatted her husband on the head

as she reached for a stack of napkins. "Newlyweds are immune to mere human foibles like onion breath."

Campbell pulled Abby in close, tickling her ribs as he dropped a kiss on her lips. "I sure as hell hope so."

Liam couldn't quite define the sensation of seeing his younger brother and sister in relationships so he opted for subtle amusement and left it at that. He hadn't been a big part of his siblings' interpersonal dynamics since his parents died and he hardly had a right to comment on things now.

Even if every time he was with them he couldn't shake the feeling they expected him to play elder statesman. It wasn't a mantle he was comfortable with—or the responsibility that lay heavy on his chest when he thought about it—but it was there all the same.

He was the big brother and he'd spent enough years as one, as well as researching the dynamics of other families, to know birth order had an effect on everyone. Nowhere had that been more prevalent than in his own family after their parents died.

And the subtle realization that they all needed him to step up and share his feelings.

To set the tone for how they'd move forward as a family.

How the hell did a person do that? Lose the glue that kept them together and then try to figure out a way to manufacture it? To start all over and make something new out of the pieces. He'd never thought of himself as that person and when Kensington had stepped up, fully engaged in the matriarch role among the four of them, he let her have it.

So why was it now, when their family dynamics had changed once more with the addition of Abby, Finn and Jack, did he suddenly feel the loss?

Rowan glanced up from where she doctored her sandwich. "So fill us in on what happened today. Kensington texted us to come over and bring food for a family meeting. That's all we know."

He and Jack took turns filling them in on the events at the airport and he did the heavy lifting on Isabella's background, adding context to the case file Kensington had already distributed.

For all their easy banter and teasing, everyone was quiet through the telling and it was Finn who finally spoke first. "I've run into Agent McCray a few times. He's not a bad bloke but very by-the-book. If he thinks there's anything to this that threatens public security he's not going to rest until he finds something."

"This wasn't an act against the public." Liam stared down at his sandwich, the untouched food suddenly unappetizing, even though Campbell had brought his favorite—corned beef.

He'd let Isabella down. He was supposed to be protecting her, yet he'd allowed the enemy to get close enough to slip something in her bag.

Close enough to…

"Well isn't this a motley crew." Kensington's voice broke into his thoughts from where she stood at the entrance to the dining room. Isabella stood next to her, her features pale, but stronger than when she'd run from the room.

Kensington made quick introductions before gesturing Isabella into the empty chair to his right. He fought the urge to touch her and reassure himself she was okay. "Everything go okay with Kenzi?"

"Fine. We just talked. It was…" Isabella broke off before a soft smile tilted the corners of her lips. "It was nice. I don't usually have any girlfriends to talk to. It was good to get a woman's perspective."

Unsure of what else to say or how to reconcile yet another glaring signpost of just how alone Isabella had been, he fell back on the role of polite host. "Would you like anything? Rowan brought enough to feed half the neighborhood."

"I'd love a sandwich." Her lopsided smile shot straight to his heart. Add on the twist of her fingers in the hem of her blouse and he could see she was overwhelmed by his familial horde, yet she'd smiled through all the greetings. "I didn't realize how hungry I am."

"Then let's get you something to eat." Abby interjected, grabbing a plate of sandwiches on the center of the table and a wad of napkins. Isabella offered up a quiet thank-you and settled her napkin in her lap as the din of conversation restarted around them.

Liam couldn't stop looking at Isabella, his gaze drifting toward her at each shift of the conversation. A goofy joke from Campbell. An adventure story about a recent museum job that Rowan and Finn traded off telling. A fish-out-of-water moment Abby recounted from a recent business trip to Sweden.

Each moment pivoted into the next and all the while, Isabella sat there, studiously taking it in.

"We're a bit much when you get us all going." Liam leaned over and snatched a chip off the corner of her plate.

"Oh, I don't know." She lowered her voice so only he could hear. "They're much nicer than you."

"Excuse me?"

"Your family. I'm not sure where you came from but they're much nicer. And none of them scowl."

A heavy laugh he couldn't hold back welled in his throat. "Give them time. Campbell's got a puss that could scare off a line of soldiers at twenty paces."

"I heard my name." Campbell looked up from where he was fixing his second sandwich. "What's so funny?"

"I was just sharing an observation with Liam." Isabella wiped her lips with her napkin. The move was dainty and, if Liam read her correctly, was a bit overlong for effect.

"And?" Kensington pressed.

"I'm not really sure why you all keep him around."

Rowan let up a loud cheer and raised her glass. "Family. It's a tough commitment but somebody's got to do it."

As Liam gazed around the room at all those smiling faces, glasses held high, he saw the other side of that commitment.

The side that didn't weigh on him, heavy as lead.

As he looked at Rowan, Campbell and Kensington and the partners they'd chosen to share their lives with, Liam knew he had a band of allies to help keep Isabella safe.

The smell of chocolate chip cookies wafted from the kitchen and Isabella fought back a groan as Abby walked into the dining room, a platter held high. How did these women stay so thin?

She didn't consider herself fat, per se, but her genetic material had always ensured she had a bit of meat on her bones.

A sedentary lifestyle with her research didn't help, which was why she maintained a steady, three-day-a-week regimen at the university's gym. Although not on par with an Olympic athlete, the treadmill and elliptical did keep the beast at bay.

Until she started downing warm, out-of-the-oven cookies at midnight.

Liam had departed with Kensington, Jack and Campbell to somewhere upstairs to review some video footage and Rowan and Finn had left to prep for a lingering assignment they were fielding in the morning.

Which left that whole tray of cookies for her and Abby.

"Snag a few while they're hot. They're Campbell's weakness and I can promise you there won't be any left after he gets into them."

Unable to resist, Isabella snagged a cookie, supremely satisfied when a melted chocolate chip stuck to her index finger. "These look good."

"I've gotten pretty good at them, which is a surprise since I could barely boil water a year ago." Abby grabbed a cookie of her own and glanced at it. "Let me amend that. I could boil water and scramble eggs. That was about it."

"And now?"

"I learned how to make cookies because I have someone to make them for."

The thought was so simple—and so powerful—Isabella set her half-eaten cookie down on a napkin. "That's lovely."

Abby's cheeks turned a healthy pink. "And besotted and probably a whole lot of dopey. Not to mention, my husband is going to gain fifty pounds if I don't stop. But, well," the woman shrugged, her bright smile only adding to her appeal. "I'll love him anyway so I guess it doesn't matter."

Had she ever seen anything like this up close? She knew from stories that her grandparents had experienced a warm, loving marriage, but her grandmother had died before she was born, as had both her mother's parents. And *her* parents…well, that was certainly not a love story in any way you attempted to define those words, Isabella knew full well.

"Everyone's found each other in that time? Rowan and Kensington, too?"

"Yep. And don't think Alexander hasn't been rubbing his hands in glee. He's over the moon his grandchildren are settling down."

"And no one minds the dangerous jobs?"

"Jack and Finn understand it the best. I've had to come

around a bit." Abby hesitated. "My half brother had it out for me and that's when I called the House of Steele for help. Campbell was assigned to protect me. And he helped me through it. I decided that I can be scared of what he does or I can be his partner and believe in him and stand by him. It's not easy some days, but I wouldn't change it. And I wouldn't change him."

Isabella moved the crumbs neatly to the center of her napkin, processing Abby's comment. Liam had been assigned to her personal detail and she'd sensed the undercurrents at their London dinner with his grandparents that Alexander was pleased by that fact.

Did he think he'd somehow strike matchmaking gold again?

Her life was a far cry from Abby's. She'd gotten the basic details during their long flight home from Liam and as a woman who ran a major telecommunications company, Abby's life was light years away from her own.

She'd also gotten the very sad information that Campbell had been the one to kill Abby's half-brother after the man held her hostage.

"Your work is groundbreaking."

Isabella glanced up from the small pile of crumbs. "Yes. It's cutting-edge in my field."

"My work is often similar. Telecommunications is a competitive business and what we provide has global implications, not all of them good."

Abby reached for a cookie, then pushed the plate closer before continuing. "I know what it's like to have a technology that others have the power to abuse. And I know why you press on, anyway. What you've discovered? It can help people with illnesses. With cellular abnormalities. You can make their lives better. That might not be the full reason you began and it might not be what others want, but your work is valuable. And good. Don't forget that."

Unable to resist, Isabella took another cookie. "My work has the power to hurt a lot of people."

"Lots of things have the power to hurt people. It's how we take responsibility for them that makes all the difference."

Abby's comments and the small olive branch of friendship carried Isabella upstairs and into the private domain of the Steele family. Although Kensington had told her they now used the old family home as headquarters, she passed a few made-up bedrooms on her way to a large office space that housed several computers and a wall of screens.

"This looks like something out of a movie." The words spilled off her lips before she could pull them back and it was Campbell who spoke first, a large grin suffusing his face as he grabbed a handful of cookies from his wife.

"Welcome to my lair. And this may look like the *USS Enterprise,* but I can promise you, I've got mad skills way more advanced than Captain Kirk's crew ever dreamed of."

"With manners on par with Pigpen," Abby scolded him as she handed him a napkin. "Quit dropping chocolate chips on the desk."

The same observations she'd had earlier came back to life. Abby and Campbell were lovely, but it was something more. They were partners. They had each other's backs and wanted what was best for one another.

"While my brother finishes stuffing his face, come see what we found." Liam's voice was cool and cultured, at odds with his brother's playful banter. Funny how that cold exterior drew her in and made her feel unbelievably warm.

Even as it left her with more questions.

Why was he so cool and aloof? He obviously depended

on his siblings and despite their teasing exchanges, they all cared for each other.

Yet there was something missing with Liam. Something he held back while the others let loose with their emotions.

She moved toward a bank of monitors Liam gestured toward. "What am I looking at?"

"This is the parking garage I chased our attacker into today." He played with a toggle button on the desk. "This is what was recorded on the video feed."

She watched as an image of Liam came into clear view, leaping over a half wall of plastic roadblock into the parking garage. Saw him stop and look around, his attention focused as he took in his surroundings. Then she saw him run again.

"You see that." He pointed toward the corner of the screen. "That's where I saw him move."

He tapped a few keys, then toggled again. "This is the camera that captured what I was looking at."

She leaned closer to the screen, trying to understand what Liam was pointing to. Other than several rows of parked cars, she saw nothing. "And?"

"And no one's there."

Chapter 9

"How can no one be there? You chased the man into the parking garage." Isabella leaned over the desk and mimicked his movements on the computer, toggling through the various screens. "You chased him. You saw him. How can you be there and he's not?"

Campbell came up behind them and wiped his hands on his jeans before tapping on the screen. "Because someone with extraordinarily good electronic skills erased himself. Or he's working with a partner who erased him."

Liam heard the distinctly complimentary notes layered over disgust. If it could be done with a computer, his brother had figured it out and even Campbell was impressed with this guy's digital skills.

Skilled or not, the timing still seemed off. "How is that even possible? I'm there in the frame. He's not. That takes some time and effort to sync up two feeds. The police and the Feds had this footage within minutes."

"Which makes it a major slip. He'd have been better off wiping the feeds entirely. We might not have been all that useful to the Feds today, but they sure as hell aren't going to believe Liam chased himself."

"So he planned it out." Once again Liam had to give the guy grudging credit. This took time, effort and planning. It also proved their arrival at the airport hadn't been treated as an opportunistic attack.

"Wait, wait." Isabella split the screen and he was again impressed with her speed on the equipment. "Here's Liam running in and here's the corresponding feed. There's no gap. Look, the time's even match—"

She'd nearly said "matched" when they all saw it.

A hair's breadth of difference in the time stamp when it turned over to a new minute marker.

"No, it's not matched." Isabella stood to give him room and Campbell dropped into her vacated seat. By unspoken agreement, they all backed up as Campbell went to work, his hands flying over the keyboard.

Liam leaned toward her and pointed toward the wall of screens. "Your computer skills aren't so bad. You knew how to get back and forth in that program pretty easily."

"Years on a computer."

He wasn't sure if he saw pride or embarrassment and finally settled on both when a bright light filled her green eyes, matched to a light shrug of nonchalance. "Seriously. You're good."

"People think of lab work as just microscopes but it's a ton of computer work. Add on several lab partners who speak geek as their first language and it was either learn to keep up or perish."

"Hey!" Campbell hollered over his shoulder. "I speak geek as my primary language."

Abby bent and pressed a kiss to his forehead. "And it

rocks my world, darling. But I still wouldn't go bragging about it."

Campbell dragged her onto his lap and proceeded to drop a line of kisses along her neck. Liam wasn't sure if he should avert his eyes or give them some privacy for their overtly affectionate display.

Was this his brother? The one who'd spent so much of his adulthood behind a computer, or, in recent years out on ops, barely interacting with the world? The change was a welcome one, but it was still a surprise.

And it only punctuated how much he'd missed by staying away.

In all those years had he ever thought to make an outreach or attempt to get Campbell engaged in life?

No. Not once.

"Ewww. Get a room." Kensington's command rolled over all of them as she and Jack came back into the office, her laptop in hand. "Take a look at what Jack found."

"Me first." Campbell pointed to the screen while still juggling Abby on his lap. "Look right there and there."

Liam followed Campbell's index finger as he pointed out the time stamp on two split-screen images.

"He's good but he's not perfect. Right there. When you blow out the time stamp. The feeds are a few milliseconds off."

"What do you have?"

Kensington placed the laptop on the counter and did some pointing of her own. "Right there."

The screen was lit up by a series of numbers and Campbell and Kensington bent their heads over the screen as she hit a few keys to move the program up onto the wall of monitors for them all to review the figures.

Again, Liam marveled at the funny shorthand his siblings had with each other and, by extension, their partners.

Although the House of Steele had been a group endeavor from the start, he'd opted for more time in the field than here at home.

And it showed, he mused to himself.

"Those look like bank statements." Isabella's gaze locked on the screen. "Where did you get them?"

"You probably don't want to know." Jack's smile was oddly reassuring but Isabella wasn't deterred.

"No, I would like to know. I realize my current situation suggests I'm comfortable working outside the certain moral boundaries but I'm not. I also realize we're fighting an enemy, but I want to do it legally."

Kensington dragged her gaze off the screen and gave Isabella her full attention. "I have government-secured access to certain data warehouses. Access I've not only jumped through several hoops for but which we pay through the nose for and are re-licensed to on a quarterly basis."

"Oh."

Liam laid a hand on Isabella's arm. He had to give her credit, she was willing to hold her own for what she believed in. Much as he'd have enjoyed watching her go toe-to-toe with his sister, he redirected the conversation. "Your work doesn't lack moral boundaries. I don't think that and I don't think anyone else does."

A series of agreements filled the room.

"That's a rather big change of heart since the other night at your grandparents."

"So it is. I've thought a lot about what you said on the plane. How you described your research. There's value in your work. Advancements that will go a long way toward helping people live better lives."

"Thank you." Her lower lip trembled and Liam fought the urge to run his thumb over that plump flesh.

Abby was the first to speak and of anyone, Liam knew she had the best sense of what Isabella was going through. Her telecommunications company was a leader in technological advancements, one of which was used to spy on her and Campbell the previous fall. "Science is filled with examples of advancements that have been misused or abused. Hell, every technology brings with it challenges and risks for abuse. That doesn't mean we don't advance or move forward."

Campbell pressed a quick kiss to his wife's forehead before chiming in. "We've got your back, Isabella."

"All of us," Liam added. He wasn't sure when it had happened, but somewhere in the last twenty-four hours he *had* gone through a change of heart. He gestured toward the screen, refocusing them on Kensington's data. "So what does this say?"

"Jack reminded me of the oldest piece of detective work in the book and we followed the money."

"And just to add one more cliché to the mix, we found something rather odd. It seems dead men do tell tales." Jack filled in Kensington's gaps as he pointed to several dates on the screen. "Isabella's benefactor has had several transactions on his bank account."

"Daniel?" Isabella shook her head, shock coursing through her with all the force of a gunshot. "It's not possible. He passed away more than three years ago."

"Is there anyone else who could be on this account with him?"

Liam's voice was calm and she took solace in those even tones. "I suppose anything is possible but he was never married. No children and parents long since passed. I don't know who would be on the account with him. That's part of why the will was never contested by anyone when he provided the funding for my research. There was no one to contest it."

"This is his account. Jack and I traced the dates and it's had steady activity going back years. No gaps and nothing to suggest the holder stopped using it at any point in the last three years."

Isabella struggled to keep up with the facts flying at her with lightning speed. Daniel had died. She'd gone to his memorial service and had been at the reading of his will. He'd *died*.

Even if there hadn't been a body to cry over.

The thought crept in and she fought the suggestion. Daniel Stephenson was her mentor. Her friend. There was no way he was still alive without her knowing it, especially with how badly he suffered at the end.

"This simply isn't possible. Daniel was ill for many years. A disorder of the nervous system that steadily weakened his muscles. It weakened him until he'd deteriorated so badly—"

She broke off. It had been so hard to watch him those last few months, struggling in the lab to get through each day, his exhaustion so deep she wondered how he could stand it.

Ire and bone-deep anger struck like a hammer on an anvil. Who would dare to steal from him? To abuse his memory and steal his legacy? "We need to get the Feds to look into this. Here's the real criminal." She flung a hand at the screen. "Someone's been siphoning off of a dead man, sponging at money that's not theirs."

"We can't do that." Liam spoke first but she could see the anxiety painted on everyone's faces.

"We're not turning this over to the Feds. Especially not until we can dig in further and understand what we're dealing with."

"But they were here and grilling me. We can't hold back evidence. They can use this." Isabella fought back the shock thrumming down her spine at the blatant withholding of information. "They can find the guy who threatened us. Who's abusing Daniel's legacy."

Liam didn't give an inch. "Or they can throw more red tape at you and drag you down to their offices. I want you to stay here where we can watch you."

"So I can be your prisoner instead of theirs?" The words flew out, a byproduct of her confusion and utter shock at knowing how badly her mentor had been betrayed.

As if sensing the brewing storm, Campbell butted in. "They're going to figure the video out soon enough. Their electronics experts aren't slouches and they're going to do the same thing I just did. But on the bank accounts, they're likely not going to know where to look without Isabella's inputs."

"I still see no reason to hand any of it to them on a silver platter." Liam's words brooked no arguments and it registered on her once again how formidable the man could be when he demanded his way.

And then he turned those penetrating blue eyes on her and her stomach cratered at the impact. "And for the record, you're not a prisoner."

Whether it stemmed from desire or the simple need to prove to him they were equals, Isabella wasn't sure, but she couldn't have held back the challenge if she'd tried. "Then stop dismissing my concerns. I want to understand what's happening to me. What forces are at play around me."

"And I want you to trust us to work on your behalf. I won't put you at risk again."

She fought off a small mewl of frustration and moved into his space. A tight, cloying sense of claustrophobia built under her skin, like a subtle itch that grew more and more persistent. "I hired you, or have you conveniently forgotten that?"

"And I'm doing my job."

Isabella suddenly noticed the room had emptied, leaving the two of them to battle it out.

"Nice job. I haven't gotten away from my siblings in two decades."

She ignored the lame attempt at humor and pressed her point. "I want to know what you meant by that."

"By what?"

She wasn't a short woman, but his solid frame took up all the space in her vision as she stared up at him. "That you won't put me at risk. Again. You didn't put me in this situation."

"You're on my watch now and I will make sure you can safely present your work."

"As I sit in this house and twiddle my thumbs."

A cheeky grin lit up his face, the cocky move as infuriating as it was unexpected. "Don't worry, Kenzi will put you to work if that's what you want."

Anger welled from the deepest part of her, fast and thick like an oil strike. "No, damn it, that's not what I want. I want you to consider me a part of this. I'm in charge of my life. I've been doing a fine job of it for the past thirty-three years and I'll be damned if I stop now."

"Right. You've done great, Isabella." The smile fell, replaced by an ire that matched her own, blue fire snapping in his gaze. "That's why you're in this position. It's why you don't have any family. Or friends. Or a lover. It's why you're all alone, you've been doing such a damn fine job."

Something dark and raw churned under her fury, erupting from her in a wash of flame.

"You know nothing about my life. About the humiliation of what I've lived with. About the betrayal of not one parent, but two."

She dashed away the hot tears that fell freely down her face, clogging her throat in a tight fist, determined to get out the rest of it. "And you sure as hell don't know what it's like to live like a freak. Someone whose intelligence and drive and innate sense of freaking order scares the hell out of everyone around her."

"Isabella—" He reached out but she flung off his hand, stepping back from the sheer weight of the pain that threatened to drag her to her knees.

"You can't know what it's like. You have a family who loves you even though you keep them at arm's length for some puzzling reason known only to you. You have a reputation that's sterling. You even have an endless parade of women content to share their time and attention. I have nothing." He reached for her once more, but she flung him off. "Nothing!"

And then he had his hands on her and he was dragging her close and she was trying to breathe through the tears and the need and the most desperate desire to connect with someone.

No, she amended as his mouth crashed on hers with the force of a hurricane. She had the desperate desire to connect with *him*.

With Liam.

Hot, wild need sparked under her skin everywhere he touched. His hands were on her shoulders, on her lower back, roaming over her stomach before reaching up to cup her breasts.

She should have been shocked or felt some sort of embarrassment that she'd been wearing the same clothes for nearly twenty-four hours or that her stomach wasn't flat enough or that her slacks hadn't been ironed but none of it seemed to matter to the man who had her in his arms and demanded she give him everything she had and then some.

And oh boy, did she own up to the task.

Her hands matched his for fervor, the hard lines of his shoulders a sensuous feast for her fingertips. She explored his body, even as their mouths never broke contact and as he walked her backwards toward the wall. She willingly let him lead, ready to follow him anywhere.

His tongue thrust into her mouth, a carnal feast that mimicked a joining of their bodies and she sucked hard before biting his lip.

Isabella felt his fingers lock with hers and then he had her hands up on either side of her head, holding her steady as he plundered her and still, she gave it all back to him, every move countered with one of her own.

The temptress she never knew lived inside of her skin came to life under his tutelage and, if the low moans echoing from the back of his throat were any indication, was having a grand time teaching Liam Steele a thing or two about desire.

"Fifty bucks they don't come back downstairs."

Kensington threw a fresh wine cork at her brother and shot him a dirty look. "That's why we closed the door."

Campbell dodged the missile and smiled, the look of the family imp riding high on his cheekbones. "Did you see the way he looked at her?"

"Like he wants to strangle her and make love to her, all at the same time." Abby's dreamy voice floated down the table.

Kensington couldn't hold back the giggle when matched expressions of horror crossed Jack's and Campbell's faces at the image Abby painted but it was her brother who voiced their feelings. "I do not want to think about that. Ever."

Abby swatted Campbell's hand when he reached for yet another cookie from the near empty plate. "You certainly don't seem to mind when you're dragging me onto your lap like a caveman."

"That's because you're my woman."

Abby's eyebrows rose in an arch almost high enough to touch her bangs. "Want to run that by me once more, Cowboy? I believe those vows were better or for worse, not 'you may possess her like chattel.'"

Campbell took Abby's hand in his and pressed a quick kiss to her knuckles. "And I count myself the luckiest of men."

"Damn straight."

Kensington glanced down where her hand already rested in Jack's before pressing her larger point. "I realize I started this hen fest, but I do think Liam has a point. We can't let her leave here. And we need to keep an eye on him. Whether he wants to admit it or not, they've both been targeted."

"Sure, because keeping up with Liam is just that easy."

Jack squeezed her fingers before snatching a cookie with his free hand. "Campbell's right. You guys can't keep up with him on a good day. What makes you think he's going to sit still and ask for help on this one?"

"He has no choice. He might have signed up for this gig but it's going to take all of us to work this one."

Campbell snatched the last cookie off the plate. "I vote we make Rowan tell him."

Liam fought to surface from the sexual haze that had gripped him the moment Isabella began yelling at him. He'd gone from irate to turned-on in the blink of an eye.

He had to admit he preferred the latter.

"Are you still mad at me?"

They were still plastered against the wall, hands locked tight. Liam disengaged their fingers to play with a curl that rested on her shoulder.

"Are you going to keep acting like an overbearing, obtuse male?"

"Of course."

"Then I'm still mad."

"Why won't you be reasonable about this?"

Isabella slipped from his arms and straightened her blouse as she put some distance between them. "I could say the same to you but we'd be right back to the circular argument that got us here. So I'll try a different one. I understand you and your family are protecting me and I don't want to put any of you in jeopardy. But I *will* need to leave. I need time with my research and my notes to finish preparing for my interview. I also need to visit my apartment. I can't exactly live in a small suitcase of clothing for the next ten days."

If their circular argument got her back in his arms, Liam was all for it, but he knew it wasn't that easy. "We can buy you new clothes."

"It's bigger than that and you know it. I have a life and I can't live in fear. And most of all, I owe it to Daniel to figure out what's going on with his legacy."

As she stood there, her body stiff with her convictions, Liam thought about all the facets of her he'd seen in the past forty-eight hours. From the wet umbrella on his grandparents' front porch to the vibrant, amazing woman in his arms, to the determined scientist actively preparing to take responsibility for her work, he'd seen a surprising array of emotions.

He knew dangerous situations often brought out extremes in personalities, but Isabella had shown a fortitude that would fell most.

"I'll work out a game plan with Jack. Between the two of us we can figure out the best way to move you back and forth between here, your lab and your apartment. And Kensington can keep digging on the bank account front. No one tugs a financial line quite like my sister."

"That's a start."

"Am I still overbearing and obtuse?"

She narrowed her eyes but a small smile ghosted her lips. "The jury's still out."

"Can I see you to your room?"

"I should, um, probably go up myself. I know how to find it. The blue guest room on the third floor. Kensington showed me earlier."

He knew what she meant—and figured she was probably right about going alone—but it didn't escape his notice her fingers were clutched tightly in the hem of her blouse as she walked from the room.

It wasn't much, but he took some solace she was as close to the edge as he was.

Isabella lay in bed, the clock flipping over to 3:00 a.m., and berated herself for declining Liam's offer to see her up to her room. She wanted him. If they'd let things go on much longer in the office she might have had him.

And wouldn't that have been a glorious outcome.

Not to mention horribly awkward.

This strange attraction was heady, certainly, but she was smart enough to know it was a side effect of the adrenaline rush and the danger surrounding both of them. Attraction might blaze between the two of them, but it couldn't change the words he'd spoken before the spark between them flared to life.

She *was* alone.

And she hadn't had a boyfriend let alone a man in her bed in too many years to count. There had been that researcher a few summers back. Late nights in the lab and a genuine compatibility had led them to bed, but it hadn't lasted.

Nor had it rocked her world.

A few scattered relationships here and there that never seemed to ignite and catch fire went back even farther in her mental museum.

Regardless of those interludes, she was alone. And assuming she survived the next few weeks, she was going to stay that way.

Men like Liam Steele didn't settle down or change their ways. He barely kept tabs with his family so the likelihood of him doing anything more permanent with her didn't bear thinking about.

Or fantasizing about.

Even if they were damn good fantasies.

She eyed the clock once again. Three-oh-two.

On a heavy sigh her mind drifted once more to her fling with the summer researcher and she counted backward two, no three—well, damn it, four—years.

She hadn't had sex in *four* years?

Counting once more, she knew she was right. Victor had been their guest in the lab the summer before Daniel died.

Daniel.

The stark reality of her dry spell was eclipsed by the financials Kensington and Jack had discovered. Who could possibly have access to Daniel's finances?

And why were there any finances to access?

His estate should have taken care of things after his death, closing all outstanding accounts and distributing the proceeds according to his wishes. Daniel's wealth was extensive, a legacy of family money he'd always seemed a bit embarrassed by, but there still should have been plans for it. Especially since he was so ill for so long, he had to have made provisions.

Although Liam had diverted her attention, now that she'd thought about Daniel her mind opened up a whole new avenue of inquiry. Could someone who knew him be behind what was happening to her? While the will hadn't been contested, the large sum he'd bequeathed her for her research had drawn attention. Was there a jealous researcher behind the attacks?

Someone she might have overlooked?

Question after question flooded her thoughts, none with answers. Lost in thought, she nearly missed the ping of her cell phone, indicating she had a text message.

When the ring went off the second time, she rolled toward the end table and picked up her phone.

And dropped it when Daniel Stephenson's name and picture filled the screen.

Chapter 10

The scream echoed from the hallway, dragging Liam from the erotic visions that had kept him company since climbing into bed an hour ago. Without stopping for the gun he'd stowed in the end table next to his bed, he shot down the hall toward Isabella's room, his only focus getting to her.

Hall lights came on as he slammed through her door, evidence his siblings had heard the scream, but he didn't stop until he had Isabella out of bed and in his arms. She clung to him, her arms wrapped so tightly around his waist he nearly toppled over her on the bed.

Bracing his feet, he reached for her arms, struggling to control her trembling body with hands that shook of their own accord. "What is it? What happened?"

"My phone. A text." Eyes wide, she pointed to the slim phone that looked as if it had been tossed to the floor, wedged under the corner of the end table.

"What is it?" Campbell was through the door first, the

guest room he and Abby were sleeping in being on the same floor.

Liam held on to Isabella and pointed toward the phone. "Something spooked her."

Jack followed on Campbell's heels with Kensington and Abby not far behind. "What the hell happened?"

"She got a text." Campbell held up the phone and swiped a finger across the screen, a dark frown edging the corner of his lips. "From her late boss."

"Read it." Liam ordered.

Campbell's gaze darted toward Isabella. "The message is simple and threatening. It says, 'You're next.'"

"Who's doing this?" Isabella trembled once more and Liam settled her on the bed, then sat next to her, dragging the covers up around her shoulders. "Who would be this sick?"

The same sensation he'd had earlier—that someone was delighting in toying with her—struck him yet again. Just like everything else that had happened so far, this latest stunt had more psychological and emotional overtones than any real threat. Even the airport shooting seemed more theatrics than anything else. The gun shots had gone wide, with no evidence of any attempts to aim at a target.

"Liam. Can I speak to you?" Kensington caught his attention and Abby moved forward quickly to soothe Isabella.

"Now?"

"Please." Kensington stepped from the room and he followed her into the hallway.

"This can't wait?"

"Doesn't this seem strange to you?"

"Strange is the best you can come up with? The bastard's taunting her." Liam fought the urge to slam a fist into the wall. "He's using her life and the few people she cared about against her."

"Don't you find the timing odd? It's two hours after we find evidence someone's been tampering with the man's accounts. I don't like it."

"What are you suggesting?" The heartbeat that had finally begun to settle slammed once more in his chest. "That Isabella did this?"

"You can't rule it out."

"You don't believe her? Bloody hell, Kenzi." He fought to keep his voice level but it crept up several degrees in spite of himself, his grandfather's favorite curse punctuating the moment. "You can't really think she's doing this on purpose."

"You don't think it's suspicious?"

"No, I think it's freaking personal. We're protecting her and now you want to make her into a suspect."

He knew his sister—knew her to be innately fair—and he also knew questioning a family friend wasn't easy, but she pressed on. "You had your doubts at first."

"Before we were all shot at in plain sight leaving the airport."

"Liam. Look at it. First we discover her benefactor still has an active bank account. Then she gets some weird text message from him. Why is his number even in her phone if he's been dead for over three years? You can't tell me you're so besotted you can't acknowledge something's not right here."

He respected his sister—respected her mind and her ready ability to puzzle through complex details—but he wasn't going to sit still for this. "Watch it, Kenz."

"I'm not saying it to insult you."

"Don't say it at all."

Fire sparked in those eyes so like his own but she backed

off, her iron-clad control taking over. "All I'm asking you to do is think about it."

"Fine. But even you can't deny this is personal. Someone knows her and is playing with her, cat-and-mouse style."

"Yes. It is personal. That's my point."

He chose to ignore his sister's jab, instead pressing his point. "Who else could possibly benefit?"

"Isabella, Liam. She's the one who stands to benefit. Daniel Stephenson's her benefactor but his investment is the tip of the iceberg versus what she stands to make back on her work."

"She's not behind this."

"Then let's clear her and find out who the hell is."

Soothing tones and muted voices filled the room as Abby and Jack kept up a steady stream of conversation while Campbell fiddled with her phone. Every few minutes Abby would suggest her husband tap in a few new codes into the phone but nothing quite gave Campbell the satisfaction he was looking for.

"I can't find the source."

"We can run it in the lab tomorrow." Abby's voice never rose above soothing and controlled but it wasn't hard to read the underlying message she relayed to her husband.

Leave it for now.

Isabella appreciated the concern, but all she could focus on was the conversation she couldn't quite hear from the hallway. And the embarrassment at how she'd reacted. "I'm so sorry I screamed."

"There's nothing to apologize for." Abby's smile was gentle. "I don't think any of us were sleeping anyway. Too much excitement today."

"I know my work has enemies, but I don't understand

this. Daniel was the biggest champion of my work. Always. None of this makes any sense."

"We'll figure it out. And in the meantime, the house is on about eight different types of lockdown, so you're safe here."

Isabella wanted to believe her—knew Abby believed it herself—but she couldn't quite agree. And now she had to worry about the fact she'd exposed seven other people to risk.

"Has anyone called Rowan?"

"I'll go do that now." Jack tapped a hand on her foot before backing away. The move was sweet and awkward and Isabella belatedly glanced down to see the top of one thigh peeking out of the covers.

"Oh no. No wonder Jack raced out like his feet were on fire. I'm half-dressed."

"I think he'll survive."

"Hopefully with minimal scarring."

Abby stood up to help her with the covers and Isabella couldn't quite shake off how nice it felt to have others there.

"I've been there, you know. This amorphous place, between safety and the abyss. It will get better and the Steele family has the resources to help. They'll find whoever's doing this."

No matter how hard the last few weeks had been, staring into Abby's warm brown eyes Isabella knew a kindred spirit. Here was a woman who'd battled her own demons and not only come out the other side, but now thrived.

"Will it ever go away? Even after the threat is gone, will the fear go away?"

"Slowly, it does. And Campbell and I have both worked hard to seek help when we need it. I wouldn't have him if it hadn't been for the experience and I remind myself of that every day."

Isabella nodded, not trusting herself to speak.

She was happy for Abby and Campbell, but she knew her ending wouldn't be quite so neat. She had faith the House of Steele could help her, but that didn't mean her happy-ever-after waited on the other side of this mess.

As if punctuating the thought, Liam strode back into the room. Abby shot her a wink, then made a quick excuse and left, shutting the door in her wake.

He had on a pair of workout shorts and nothing else and it took her several long, dry-mouthed seconds to realize the fear in her stomach had morphed into something else entirely.

His body was exquisite. Athletic and strong, he had lean muscles that tapered down to a slim waist. A light dusting of hair covered his chest and she abstractly wondered if the hair would be soft or coarse to the touch.

"I'm so sorry I riled everyone up. I shouldn't have screamed."

"It must have been a shock." Something strangely formal hovered beneath his words and she searched his face, trying to match something in his expression with what she sensed in his tone.

The hard lines of his body tempted and enticed her to take action, but she held back. Whether it was lingering melancholy from her talk with Abby or the adrenaline rush of the text message, she supposed it didn't matter.

Both had left a gaping well of sadness she knew needed a bit of time to close.

"While I'm sorry for the shock, the bastard couldn't have picked a better method for his deeds. Between Campbell's computer skills and Abby's telecommunications expertise, we'll get to the bottom of the phone message."

The lure of attraction faded even further in the sudden anger that rose up and squeezed her chest with tight fists. "The idea someone's been using Daniel, even if he can't be hurt by it any longer, is upsetting. And seeing his name after all this time…"

The words faded as Liam sat down at the edge of the bed, replacing the spot Abby had just vacated. "It's a personal attack. Designed to strike at your emotions."

She nodded, the crazy adrenaline rush of the last ten minutes filling her eyes with helpless tears. "He was a good man. And he took me in and gave me a home in his lab. He believed in me. In my work. And now someone's using him to lash out at me."

Liam wrapped an arm around her and it was the last piece that shattered her composure entirely. A hard sob exploded from her throat along with the words. "It's like I've lost him all over again."

Large arms enveloped her and she sunk into his warmth. Where she'd felt protection before, now she felt compassion. And sympathy. And the very real evidence she didn't have to process this alone.

Without warning, an image of her mother rose up in her mind's eye, along with those endless days of her father's trial. They'd sat through every bit of testimony. The reading of the charges, the increasing evidence he'd committed horrific acts of treason against Queen and country and, finally, the clear evidence he felt no remorse for his actions.

Yet they went, his only family, resigned to supporting him through it all. Day after day, seated in the courtroom, watching their world collapse.

She'd used her mother as an example of how to behave in public. Stone-faced. Stoic. And absolutely unwilling to let anyone see the pain inside.

But she'd never have expected her mother would exhibit

the same when the two of them were alone. Her only ally in the battle for their family had deserted her, leaving her to fend for herself in an emotional wasteland of betrayal and heartache.

"Why is Daniel's number still in your phone?"

That same sense as before—that something hovered under his words—struck with swift and terrible claws as the memory faded in the face of Liam's skepticism. She unwrapped her arms from his waist and shifted on the bed, seeking some distance. "I never deleted it."

"Your phone doesn't look that old. Even with a standard upgrade you would have gotten a new phone since he passed away. Why keep his number?"

"My cell phone provider ported the data from my old phone to my new one."

"Yes, but why keep his number?"

"I forgot to delete it."

Although the truth, the words felt hollow on her lips. It was only when he remained silent, his gaze boring into hers, that she matched the question with Kensington's rush to the hallway. "You think I did this."

"No."

"Or your sister does and she's convinced you of that fact."

"That's not true." Liam hesitated, his mouth opening and closing as if he warred with himself, before he finally spoke. "She pointed out the fact that you still have Daniel's number. I have to agree with her. It is strange."

"And I explained that I had my contacts ported over." She wiggled farther away from him, slipping from the opposite side of the bed. She felt the lack of warmth from his body heat but simply wrapped her arms around her waist for protection. The old college T-shirt she wore offered little in the way of body armor, but she simply couldn't sit next to him for another moment.

"Why keep the contact information for a dead man?"

His use of the word *dead* stabbed into her but she held her ground. She'd grieved Daniel's death and the loss of a life cut too short far too young. She'd be damned if she was going to apologize for clinging to a small memory of him. A small connection that made him seem not quite so far away. "I think you should go now."

"I'd like an answer."

"And I'd like you to leave."

Edward Carrington stared at the computer program he'd written and chuckled to himself. He'd gotten the ping earlier that someone had looked into Daniel's accounts and had known it was time to flip the next switch. The sweet knowledge made up for the ringing alarm that had woken him from restless, pain-tinged sleep.

They'd planned and planned but even he couldn't believe just how well everything was coming together. Nothing like having a rock-solid strategy and seeing it through, each and every step of the way.

He sat back from his computer and rubbed at his wrists. Like Daniel, he still fought the side effects from the changes in his body but his continued DNA therapy seemed to be working. The pain still ebbed and flowed but he knew his time at the gym should keep it at bay.

Ignoring the trembling in his fingers, he reached for one of his wrist-strengthening hand grippers and began to work his aching muscles. His gaze roamed over the tendons that flexed beneath his skin and he ignored the pain as pride speared him clean through.

The weak boy his father had spent most of his life berating was frail no longer. He had the body one of New

York's proudest blue bloods could finally be proud of. Too bad his father thought him long dead and was unable to appreciate a bit of it. "Ah well," he muttered to himself, "we all make sacrifices for the cause."

Others had paid a far bigger price.

He set down the gripper and ran a few more programs, satisfied nothing else had set off his electronic traps. While his first love was the lab, he was no slouch in electronics either. It might have been a byproduct of too many years stuck inside with only a computer for company, but the resulting skills more than compensated.

As he logged off for the night, he thought about the video footage he'd rewatched of Isabella's face when she got the note at the airport. Confusion had warred with fear and he could still taste the rush of adrenaline that had flooded his system with such awesome power.

He'd spent years—endless years—watching her sympathetic eyes travel over him as he pushed himself to get around the lab, first on those damned crutches and then later increasingly dependent on the wheelchair. Watched as she held herself back from helping too much when it was painted plain as day on her face that it killed her to leave him to his own devices.

Pity.

There was nothing on earth he hated more.

Liam ran through his paces in the gym they kept in the basement, ignoring the burn in his lungs as he pushed himself into mile four on the treadmill. He was tired and his muscles ached from nearly thirty-six hours of sleep deprivation, but still, he pushed himself on.

Fool. Idiot. Chump.

The litany kept pace with the thwapping of the treadmill belt and no matter how hard he pushed himself, the words wouldn't stop.

He'd hurt Isabella and he knew that. He'd let his sister's doubts become his own and instead of being honest, had tried to use a quiet moment to dig for information.

When had he become so callous and inconsiderate?

When unwanted images surfaced in answer to the question, he resolutely tamped them down. He would not lose focus.

And he *refused* to go back to that dark day.

Besides. He still didn't think Kenzi was right and had every confidence Campbell would figure out who'd generated the text message. But he'd let the doubt in anyway.

And then he'd pushed it onto Isabella in the very moment when she needed comfort and support.

The creak of stairs caught his attention moments before Jack came into view, dressed in an old T-shirt and shorts. "Mind if I join you?"

"Be my guest."

Jack snagged a couple of waters out of a small fridge Kensington kept well-stocked in the corner and dropped one into the cup holder on Liam's treadmill before climbing onto his own. Liam kept up his furious pace, suddenly curious to see what his sister's fiancé could do on the machine.

They'd all known of Jack for years. His competing firm, Andrews Holdings, had gone up against the House of Steele on several assignments. It had only been when Jack and Kenzi had paired on a job in the Italian countryside the previous December that any of them had really gotten to know the man.

While he gladly lived with the general assumption no one was good enough for his sisters, Liam had to admit he'd reluctantly come around to Jack. The big man knew the business forward and backward and had a nose for sniffing out b.s.

"Kenz fill you in on last night?"

Liam would have elaborated but he knew Jack was well aware of what his sister thought about Isabella's late-night text message.

"Why do you think I'm down here?" Jack tossed him a rueful grin as he moved from steady warm-up strides into his own run. "The two of us went more than a few rounds last night fighting over this one. I'm still pissed off."

"So you think she's wrong."

Jack let out a heavy breath as he punched the speed higher on his machine. "Hell yes, I think she's wrong. Damn stubborn woman. She had the nerve to tell me not to fall for the damsel-in-distress routine. Like I don't know any better."

Liam slowed his strides to a brisk walk and ramped up the incline. While he didn't envy the man his lost night of sleep, he was pleased to know he had some support on this one. He also hadn't been able to shake the image of Isabella sitting straight up in bed, her eyes huge orbs in her face, wide with fear.

"There's no way she made it up."

"No, and I don't think she did. But I respect the fact Kensington needs to ask the question."

"No stone left unturned."

"Never with your sister."

They moved in companionable silence for the next several minutes, each lost in their own thought. Liam sucked down the cool water and let his thoughts drift over the events of the last few days. If he'd manage to get his head in the game and *off* images of Isabella, he might find some thread that led them to the threat.

Her research sat at the core of the problem, yet every overt threat hadn't been about the research.

Why?

Liam upped the incline once more on his machine and let that idea sink in.

The invasion in her home, lab and London hotel room. The note in her bag at the airport. Even the text message last night. All presupposed knowledge of Isabella's quirks and habits.

Had they overlooked the obvious?

As the idea took root, Liam gave it room to fill out. As a plan it seemed fraught with challenges, but maybe there was something there. With a sideways glance at Jack, Liam gave voice to his thoughts.

"How hard would it be to fake your own death?"

Chapter 11

Isabella wiped her hands on her jeans, the nervous motion her only comfort as she descended the back stairs to the kitchen. She wanted to face Kensington Steele about as badly as she wanted to present her chest to a firing squad, but simple biology would be her undoing.

She didn't skip meals. Ever.

Which was as insulting as it was humbling since she estimated the glamorous and slender Kensington Steele likely skipped meals all the time and still managed to function like an automaton.

Which made it that much more frustrating when she rounded the last portion of the landing, stepped off the last stair and saw the object of her irritation seated at the kitchen table, a large bowl and a laptop in front of her.

"Good morning." That penetrating blue gaze, so like Liam's, greeted Isabella before she gestured toward the stove. "Please help yourself to whatever you'd like. I made extra oatmeal but you're welcome to whatever we have."

"The oatmeal's fine."

She hated oatmeal, the gloopy, glue-like substance on her top five list of things she'd prefer never to eat, but Isabella refused to show that weakness to the House of Steele's resident goddess. Maybe if she dumped half a bowl of sugar over it on the sly it would be edible.

Her gaze alighted on the bowl next to the coffee pot and she offered up a small prayer of gratitude they at least had sugar in the house.

A few minutes later, her doctored coffee and oatmeal in hand, she knew she couldn't hide any longer or she'd risk her oatmeal turning to a thick, inedible paste.

Kensington was the first to extend the olive branch as Isabella took her seat. "Did you manage to get any sleep?"

"A bit." She shrugged but refused to lie. "Not much, and what I did get was filled with strange dreams, but it was something."

"You're still doing better than I did. Jack and I had a wicked fight so I haven't slept at all." Kensington's gaze never strayed from her bowl as she scooped out the last of her oatmeal and what looked like blueberries.

"I'm sorry." Was she? And why would she care if the two of them had a fight?

"He felt I was monumentally unfair for not believing you."

"I agree with him."

Kensington's eyes were wide when she glanced up from her bowl before she added a soft smile. "You like being right."

"A trait I'm sure you can understand."

"In spades."

It wasn't a truce, per se, but it was something and Isabella took the first bite of her oatmeal, satisfied they'd gotten through the hardest part of the morning. The flavor wasn't good, but it wasn't quite as pasty as she'd remembered and she didn't miss Kensington's calculating smile.

"I add cream to it otherwise I'd never get it down."

"It does make it better."

"I'm going to make bacon and eggs in a few minutes when the guys come up from the basement. You're welcome to wait."

"What are they doing in the basement?"

"Working out was the ostensible goal, but I think it gave Liam and Jack a chance to bitch about me." She hesitated, but then pushed on, obviously anxious to say whatever it was she needed to say. "It's my job, Isabella. To calculate the angles. Work the odds. I know it makes my family nuts. Heck, it makes me nuts, but it's what I do."

"And?"

"And I have to factor you in. Either because you're guilty or to rule you out, but you have to go into the equation."

Maybe it was the analogy to an equation, but she finally got it. "I understand. You run the obvious to make sure the answer isn't."

"Especially when it's equally obvious my brother is attracted to you."

Whatever she was expecting, that revelation wasn't part of the mix. A dark flush lit up her chest and spread outward, heating up her body with the unexpected scrutiny. "That's not...I mean, it's not..."

"There's something there."

"I'm not his type."

Kensington cocked her head, considered, before she pressed on. "No, you're not. Which, I'll add, is a good thing and incredibly refreshing. He doesn't bring his dates around often because Liam doesn't come around often, but the few I've met have been about as interesting as that bowl of oatmeal."

"Long-legged and beautiful, no doubt."

"Yes. Very pretty, empty packages. Empty packages who, I suspect, don't wake up with gorgeous hair." Kensington pointed at her own ponytail. "I'd kill to get mine to look like yours first thing in the morning."

Isabella avoided touching her hair as Kensington's words sunk in. The raw truth about the women Liam dated should have been hurtful, but for some reason she couldn't quite define, it wasn't. Maybe it was the casual compliment or, better, the pleasant glow that came from one given with honest sincerity.

Or maybe it was the simple joy in sharing confidences with another female.

"I'm not looking for him to change his life and I'm not changing mine."

"Famous last words."

Isabella was prevented from saying anything when the basement door opened, voices heavy from the other side. Jack filled the doorway first, followed by a sweaty Liam. If she'd thought his bare chest made an impressive picture the night before, a tired, sweaty version of him wasn't too far behind.

"Morning."

Kensington shot them both a disgusted look before she got up and pressed a kiss to Jack's cheek. "How did either of you find time to get in a workout? I can barely keep my eyes open."

Jack dragged her in close, rubbing his sweaty, beard-roughened cheek against her neck until she let out a small squeal. "Jack!"

"Serves you right." He released her.

"Watch it or you're not getting the bacon and eggs I'm about to cook up for you."

"Never dangle bacon in front of a man. It's the food equivalent of sexual manipulation."

Kensington shot him a sassy grin over her shoulder before she opened the fridge door. "All part of my diabolical plan."

As apologies went, it wasn't much, but Isabella figured it was enough.

Equilibrium had returned to the House of Steele.

Liam fought the urge to stare at Isabella and cursed the consequences of bacon for breakfast. Damn it if Jack hadn't been spot on—it *was* the food equivalent of sex— and it was the only reason he could summon up that he and Isabella were now riding uptown in the family car.

Yes, the Mercedes-Benz was reinforced with bulletproof glass, was regularly combed for bugs and was the proud owner of a nifty little computer program Campbell had designed to alert the driver to any tampering, but they were still *in* it.

Out of the house and out in the open.

He'd gone soft as she and Kensington made their play for why the two of them needed to visit Isabella's lab, along with mapping out the safest way to get there and back.

Of course, he could blame the bacon all he wanted, but it had been a poor substitute once he'd caught sight of Isabella in bare feet, curvy jeans and a loose-fitting blouse that hinted at the sexiest swath of cleavage he'd ever laid eyes on.

Damn, but he'd been an easy mark and he knew it.

The smell of bacon hadn't managed to rouse Campbell or Abby, so it had ended up being the four of them having an intimate breakfast in the kitchen. And through piece after piece of bacon, Isabella and Kensington had laid out a plan of action.

"You all keep the house well-stocked considering no one lives there."

"It's all my sister's doing. Well, and my sister-in-law's if you count the cookie dough." He slowed at a light on the West Side Highway and glanced over at Isabella. She'd added a blazer to the outfit but that wisp of cleavage was still visible and he fought to keep his eyes level with hers.

"We've converted much of it to headquarters but it still functions as a house when we need it to. And as evidenced last night, it's incredibly handy when working late nights."

Of course, he'd barely known that fact *until* last night when his sister-in-law dragged warm cookies into the conference room or when his sister led him to a made-up bed, fresh and ready to sleep in.

Yet again, the resounding gong of "Liam spends no time at home" went off like the freaking bells of Notre Dame.

Kensington and Jack. Rowan and Finn. Campbell and Abby. The six of them had formed a unit and he sat on the outside, a well-connected visitor. Had he been asked if it bothered him he'd have answered with a resounding no, louder than those church bells he now imagined.

But faced with the evidence of that family unit, it chafed to realize reality was an entirely different story.

The light turned red and he crept slowly forward, their destination only a few miles away despite the traffic that stretched in front of them.

"It bothers you."

"Yes, damn it, it does."

He slammed on the brakes just before hitting the car in front of them who'd come to an abrupt halt, the motion an odd punctuation to the roiling emotions he fought to keep at bay. There was no reason to be upset. No reason to care about his siblings' choices.

They made theirs and he made his. They'd all been doing it for years.

"Why does it upset you?"

"It's humbling to realize your younger brother and sisters have all grown up. Moved on, found lives and don't really need you."

"I don't think it's a matter of need. And surely you all see each other. You do work together."

Yes, he saw them, but how much time did he really spend? And why was that fact so glaringly obvious all of a sudden?

"Maybe until this trip I hadn't realized how much everything had changed."

"They're all married. Or almost there. That changes the dynamics, especially when the people they're marrying are all as unique as the four of you."

"Yes, that, but it's more. They're—" he broke off, the words stiff and mechanical. "They're a unit. A high-functioning unit that depends on each other. Watches out for each other."

"And so it bothers you."

Just like her observations on their plane ride from London, he realized that she saw things.

And her vision was a bit too sharp for comfort.

The denial was rising on his lips before he risked a quick glance at her, diverting his attention from the traffic. And the clear understanding and gentle support in her warm smile was his undoing. "Yes it does."

"They care about you. I'm sure they'd like you to be a part of things."

"And I care about them. It's not about caring. It's just different. *I'm* different." Again, he broke off, emotional landmines detonating under his feet. "It's always been there but it started after my parents died."

Liam wove through heavy traffic, pleased the other cars kept his gaze on the road and off the ready sympathy he knew would be in her eyes. He hated talking about his parents. It was bad enough they were gone, but then that immediate wellspring of pity and sadness that inevitably crept into the conversation...he hated it.

"Kensington mentioned how they died last night when we were in the library and she told me about the history of the house. My grandfather's mentioned them several times as well through the years. He had quite the soft spot for your mother."

The image she painted eased the tight knot of his stomach. The image he'd always carried of his mother—her wide-eyed beauty and broad smile—filled his mind's eye. "She was larger than life and had a personality that drew people to her, effortlessly."

"Each of you has that."

He thought of each of his siblings in kind. Kensington and Rowan certainly had that gift and even Campbell, when he turned on the charm. He'd always saw himself as far more aloof.

Distanced.

He kept people out and always had, well before losing his parents. Their deaths had only exacerbated the trait.

"The girls do and Campbell as well. I'm the curmudgeonly older brother who gives orders."

"You do look like you have a digestive disorder from time to time."

A hard bark of laughter escaped before he could hold it back and he turned toward her, surprised to see an impish smile dimpling her cheeks. "Careful, there. I might think you weren't still mad at me for last night."

"I'm not mad at you. I was. And then I was really mad at your sister, especially since she's gorgeous," Isabella waved a hand. "But I'm over it."

"What do her looks have to do with it?"

"She's perfect."

He avoided a snort—just barely—at the evidence Isabella spoke of his stubborn, bullheaded sister. "Perfect isn't a moniker I toss around lightly and certainly not in reference to any of my family."

"Well, take it from me, she's intimidating."

"Kenzi?"

"Yes! Who else?" She sighed, her irritation evident that he wasn't keeping up. "But she complimented my hair so I feel better about her."

Liam tried to keep pace with the odd notes of the conversation and stopped. His sisters had a special sort of conversational shorthand and it was obvious Isabella was in on the joke.

"Look. My only point is, I'm not like them. I don't know how to be effortless with others. Or smooth instead of blunt and pointed. I don't do well with others. Or with commitments."

His statement hovered there, roiling between them as the traffic opened up and he sped up the West Side Highway. And underneath the syllables, he heard the excuses.

Don't get too attached.

I can't be the man you need me to be.

I'm not the one for you.

And he knew Isabella had heard them, too.

Commitment.

That lone word—concept, really—was the story of her life. Commitment to the job. To goals. To a scientific idea. *That* she had in spades.

Commitment to others?

Not so much.

Funny, how hearing the words drip with such certainty from Liam Steele's perfectly-formed lips had made it all clear.

At some point in his life he'd chosen to run from commitment and he had no intention of turning back.

With a hard shove on the passenger door, Isabella ignored the tension that skittered up her spine and stepped from the car. She'd be damned if she'd continue to live in fear.

Summoning up a smile through sheer force of will, she met him on the sidewalk. Her lab was at the edge of university property—loosely affiliated but privately funded—and Liam had already parked in the spot reserved for her, despite the fact she took the subway everywhere.

Useless privileges.

The thought rose up quickly and sprouted seeds. She was proud of her work. Proud of her mind and the research system she'd worked in for more than a decade and a half. None of that changed some of the silly excesses that wrapped around that life.

The need to prove your work to others. To showcase what you were doing and brag to the world how far you'd come in achieving your goals.

That's what put you in this position, a quiet voice taunted her. That need to show off her achievements in a way that others would notice, too.

"What's that look for?" Liam waited while she ran a keycard over a scanner, then pulled the door wide for her once it snicked open.

"I was thinking about my parking spot."

"As in 'it gets a lot of shade during the day?' Or because others try to park there?"

"More about how useless it is." When he only kept that understanding gaze locked on her, she shrugged and pressed forward. "It's silly, I suppose, to even give it a thought. But the whole concept of the spot seems trivial. I don't own a car and never have, yet there's a spot that sits there with my name on it. A useless privilege someone decided was important."

"We humans are a funny lot. We often place importance in strange places."

"I used to think it was a practice in the scientific community, but I'm sure other professions are no different." They walked down a long corridor toward a bank of elevators. Her lab was on the third floor and she buzzed them into the elevator for the quick climb.

His grin flashed—distracting and devastating in the extreme. "Even though I may complain about them, why do you think I like working with my siblings?"

"No fights for parking spots."

"Absolutely not. We fight about more important things like who's going to get the evening's takeout order or who gets to pick the day's radio station."

She laughed in spite of herself as they stepped off the elevator. Even with the picture Liam painted she couldn't quite see a roomful of adult Steele children fighting over the radio station.

"This is quite a facility."

Her smile hovered as a surprisingly warm memory filled her mind's eye. "You should have seen where we used to be. The building next door is still connected through the basement. My lab was off that basement-level corridor. We called it the dungeon."

"Sounds warm and inviting."

"I wouldn't go straight to inviting, but it did have a certain charm."

"So why's this place so empty? For a place this big we really haven't seen anyone."

"Only about fifty people work here and it's still early."

"That's all? This is a huge facility."

She marveled at how fast his mind moved, always observing. Always cataloguing. "It's my understanding there's been a move to change that, but the facility was completed as Daniel died and I've heard it's been wrapped up in a lot of red tape. Until that's worked through, they haven't let in tenants."

"How many were on your research team?" Liam asked as she pushed open one last door.

"When Daniel was alive there were five of us who assisted him. After his death, the team disbanded over time. I have three colleagues now and about five graduate assistants that rotate based on their school load."

"Streamlined team. Why'd the others leave?"

"I think some might have been hurt I was the recipient of Daniel's generosity. Or others had new opportunities they wanted to pursue. I don't know and I'm ashamed now to say I didn't try to find the answers." She fought back the sigh at the further evidence of what others must see in her actions.

Cold disinterest.

She flipped on a bank of lights. "Nothing was the same after we lost him."

"Was his death sudden?"

"Maybe a better way to explain it was not unexpected. He was ill for a long time. I never expected the end to come as abruptly as it did, but—" She trailed off, memories of her mentor warming her.

How many months it had taken her to walk into her lab

and not expect to see him? Or to think she'd take a quick jaunt into his office after a long day and discuss her research, only to remember he wasn't there.

Daniel always had time for her. Always wanted to know what she was working on and pressed her with questions she hadn't yet thought of on her own.

"He sounds like a special person."

"He was."

"A saint, almost."

The comment was so odd—so out of place—she stopped at one of the long lab tables. "What's with all the questions about Daniel?"

"It was an observation."

"No, it wasn't." She abstractly felt the cool metal of the lab table underneath her fingertips and willed herself to calm down. She and Liam had already had one fight over a misbegotten series of questions.

She refused to make the same mistake twice.

"Daniel Stephenson was a special man. He was my mentor and my boss and I thought the world of him. But he was still a person. Moody and mercurial like anyone else. He also suffered from his illness and had many bad days where he was a challenge to be around. He wasn't a saint. No one is."

"All right."

"So why all the questions?"

"I ran an idea by Jack this morning and I can't quite shake it off."

Was that embarrassment that flitted through his gaze? When she added up the distinct shifting on the balls of his feet, the observation had more merit. "And?"

"I need you to keep an open mind."

"I'm a scientist. That's part of my job description." She

meant the comment as a joke, but his discomfort only grew more pronounced. "What's the matter?"

"What if Daniel isn't really dead?"

She searched his face, convinced she couldn't have heard him correctly. But no matter how hard she stared, those clear blue eyes remained somber and oh-so-serious.

"No way."

"Think about it."

Think about it?

Think about an idea that packed a comparable punch to going over Niagara Falls in a barrel? She was gobsmacked. And more than a little surprised an admitted cynic would even have landed on something so fantastical.

"You cannot be serious. It's absurd. Not to mention weird and impossible. We had a funeral. There was a will. And the money. All of this," she flung a hand to her surroundings. "It's all because he died."

"Money can buy a lot of things and can keep a lot of people quiet."

"But he was sick. I saw his blood work many times over. His illness was degenerative and it had attacked all of his major muscle groups." Her gaze alighted on a row of computers and an idea hit. There was no need to continue discussing this—the answer was in the data. "Come here. I'll show you."

He followed her toward a row of computers that ran along one of the countertops and waited as she keyed in her credentials, then a series of search queries. Their database was large, the reams of data the research generated requiring several servers and another round of backup at an off-site location.

"What are we looking at?"

"My work is catalogued across cellular research, tissue samples, blood work. We also have loads of data tied to the computer models that processes all of it. Every result is logged into the database with a variety of tags. Come look at this."

She tapped several keys before pulling up Daniel's information. With a few more clicks, she dug into the file she recalled so vividly. "I put the majority of his data in myself. We often used Daniel's blood work for many of the tests we ran."

"Why? He didn't have a mental disorder."

"No, but his disease is parked on a very specific piece of DNA code. It's pure, as it were, and fairly easy to find."

"Which means you can manipulate it. Like we discussed with the virus."

"Yes, we could have, but we never did that with Daniel's cells." She hesitated, the pain of losing him before they could have helped him a very real reminder of how many people could truly be helped by her work. "He didn't live long enough."

But what if they'd figured out several pieces sooner? What if his body could have held out longer? What if they'd only gotten promising results sooner?

What if, what if, what if?

A useless exercise that could make you crazy if you allowed it to.

Liam pointed to the computer screen. "What does this mean here?"

His question pulled her back from endless questions that had no answers. "Those are his various labs."

He tapped the screen. "There. That one's dated a week ago."

"It can't be. This file is specific to Daniel only. His research. His blood work. His DNA."

"Then why are there several files with date stamps going back years?"

She saw where Liam pointed and clicked on the most recent file. The serial code unique to Daniel came up first—assigned to him their first week on the project—followed by sequences of DNA code, all date and time stamped by the computer.

It was part of their standard research protocol and she couldn't have changed it if she'd tried.

With trembling fingers, she clicked the mouse once more to look more closely at the strand of DNA that had always defined his illness. The gene markers that had sequenced his disease were gone.

And in its place was a perfectly clean strand of DNA.

Chapter 12

Liam caught Isabella as she backed away from the computer, shaking her head. "It's not possible. It…No…Just *no*."

He knew the details were a shock—hell, he couldn't believe it and he'd already been toying with the idea all morning—but he needed to keep her calm and able to interpret the data that winked back from the computer screen.

"Explain it to me. Tell me what you're looking at." He dragged one of the lab seats from a nearby table to the counter and guiding her, settled her on top. "Walk me through it."

Fingers trembling, she moved the mouse once more. "I'll show you his older labs. Ones I ran before he…*died*."

Liam heard the strange emphasis she placed on the word "died" but said nothing. They'd know soon enough what they were dealing with.

For several long minutes, she walked him through the

details, pointing out several markers of Daniel's illness and explaining how the DNA coding worked. Although Liam didn't have his brother's skills for computer code, he had a head for patterns and at its core, many components of her work were an exercise in recognizing them.

"See these spots." Isabella pointed at three different points of the screen, then back to the notepad she'd dragged from a nearby drawer. "They all indicate abnormalities."

"But they're gone on the most recent tests."

"Yes."

"When did they vanish? Let's trace it back."

The work took a while, the large files taking time to load and then search through. Liam settled into the moment, curious to see the side of Isabella that emerged as she worked.

While he'd seen several aspects of her personality, from the concerned friend to the nervous houseguest to the fierce warrior, the competent professional was a new one.

And oh, how she shone.

Her proficient fingers flew over the keyboard as she navigated through the various programs, jotting down notes and identifying each stage of what appeared to be Daniel Stephenson's healing from a terminal illness.

Her long dark hair curled down her back and she continued pushing the heavy mass behind her ear as she worked her way methodically through the data. The traces of embarrassment that seemed to tinge other aspects of her life were nowhere in evidence as she trod the familiar paths of her work.

He fought the urge to run his hand through those lush strands—that fierce concentration was the only excuse he had for the fanciful thought that came next. "You love what you do."

She twisted her head at the words, her fingers stilling over the keyboard as her gaze met his. "What?"

"Your work. You love it."

"I do." A light crinkle worked its way between her bright, expressive eyes. "Why do you ask?"

"As you've more than accurately assessed, it's easy to suspect your motives. My family and I have been rather suspicious of you."

"Suspicions that—"

He interrupted her, the twin demands to explain and apologize pushing him on. "That all vanishes watching you. You love what you do and it shows."

Her dark, enigmatic gaze searched his face, as if judging the sincerity in his words. Whatever she looked for, he could only assume she found because her voice was quiet when she finally spoke. "I want to find the answers."

Liam had always believed himself immune to the emotions that came so easy to others. Love. Understanding. Compassion.

He wasn't heartless—or tried damn hard not to believe himself capable of it—but he knew he didn't view the world as giving. Or kind. Or indulgent of those filled with gentler dispositions.

But staring at Isabella Magnini, that long mane of hair wild about her face and her slender shoulders wrapped in an oversize gray sweater, he knew his world had changed.

"I want to help you find them."

Isabella stuffed the large hard drive into her bag and pulled tight on the zipper. Her eyes had nearly crossed at all the reams of data they'd reviewed but she thought she'd captured the pieces they'd need to now run everything through Campbell's databases back at the House of Steele headquarters.

What was far harder to organize were her wayward thoughts about Liam.

She knew he'd been warming up to her over the last few days, both in what he said and even more in what he didn't. But in the past few hours she'd felt a real change.

Like the sands-shifting-beneath-her-feet sort of change.

Grateful for a private moment, she watched him as he moved around the lab, righting the various drawers they'd sifted through and stowing several reference manuals she'd pulled out while running Daniel's labs. His movements were brisk—efficient—but none of it could hide the ripple of muscle across his back as he reached for an overhead cabinet or the slender taper of his waist where his shirt tucked into his slacks.

The man was devastating.

And now that he was truly her ally, that fact was only more dangerous.

When Isabella looked at him now, she saw a partner. One who was in this, not because he felt he needed to be, but because he wanted to be. And she was humbled to realize how impactful that small shift really was.

He lifted their coats and held hers out. "You ready to go?"

"I suppose we should. I've downloaded as much as I can, but there's still a boatload sitting on the server."

"You got all the reports that show the corrected abnormalities. That's what we need the most. Campbell can overlay a few programs on it to run the other gene sequences to confirm the source DNA is all the same."

"Is there anything he doesn't know how to do?"

Liam stilled in the process of reaching for her bag. "Are my siblings giving off some sort of superhero pheromone?"

Whether it was the subtle indignation that filled those gorgeous blue eyes of his or the very real disgust she heard in his tone, she didn't know, but Isabella couldn't hold back the laugh. "Superhero?"

"First my sister is perfect this morning. Now my brother is a computer genius."

"Isn't he?"

"Well—"

Her laughter faded. "You don't like being bested by them, do you?"

"Hell no. And I refuse to apologize for that."

"I'm not asking you to, but it galls you to think they've got some skills you don't."

"I'm not *that* bad."

She shot him a dark gaze, her hands falling to her hips. "Seriously?"

"It's just…I'm…"

"You're what?"

The small "O" that formed his lips snapped closed. "Nothing."

"Come on, it's something. And you know I'm curious enough not to leave this alone."

"I'm the big brother."

"Of a quartet of grown adults."

"I'm still the oldest." Her laughter faded altogether in the face of his obvious discomfort but before she could say anything, he pressed on. "I don't begrudge them their talents. Hell, I'm prouder than anyone of Campbell, Kenzi and Ro. But they're mine. I'm supposed to take care of them."

"I think they feel the same way about you."

"There's no need. I know how to take care of myself."

Wherever she'd thought their conversation would go, this raw, exposed nerve wasn't it. "Is that why you stay distant? Stay away?"

The broad shoulders she'd admired a few moments before stiffened at the verbal assault and a very real struggle played across his face. Where she'd originally thought him harsh and, at best, indifferent, in his efforts to explain himself she saw something very different.

Fear.

"I don't stay away on purpose. I have work. We all do."

"Are you sure that's the reason?"

"Of course. But—" He reined in the snappish tone. "But I worry about them. Every day. And I know they're fine. I know they can take care of themselves, but staying away's easier somehow."

"Is it so bad to let them know you love them?"

"Of course not." Liam stilled, his gaze roaming the lab.

Where the abrupt change might have been aversion in another, Isabella keyed into his rapid—and sudden—change in demeanor. "What is it?"

"Do you smell something?"

"Other than the lovely, always-present scent of formaldehyde and cleaning fluid that permeates the lab?"

"No, I meant—"

Liam's words faded to nothing as the glass door of the lab exploded inward, flames filling the hall outside the door.

Liam leaped on Isabella, tackling her to the ground. Her large bag slammed against his hip with a painful thud but he ignored it over the sudden wash of smoke that filled the air above them.

"We need another door!" He hollered the words over the all-consuming sound of the fire.

"There is no other door. The fire exit's outside in the hallway."

"There's no other way out of here?"

She coughed and shook her head, her eyes watering at the immediate threat from outside. "No."

"Get to the faucet. We need to get everything wet." He reached for the thin shirt she'd layered underneath her blazer. "Pull this up over your nose and mouth."

They belly-crawled across the floor and about halfway there Isabella calmed enough to assess what was going on. She screamed his name over the noise and confusion of the fire. "Go to the wall. We've got fire extinguishers." She pointed through the smoke and he nodded to show that he understood.

The heavy extinguishers sat propped on the wall, a list of instructions behind them. He dragged the largest one from its holder, his gaze scanning the instructions for proof this kind would work on all types of fires. At the confirmation it could handle anything, he pulled hard to dislodge the large spray nozzle from its holder.

"Keep your nose and mouth covered. I need you to take your bag and keep your coat over your head to protect you from the flames."

"What about you?"

He glanced down at his shirt and knew she had a point. No matter how clean a path he cleared with the extinguisher, the flames were too high to avoid getting burned.

"Here!" She threw his coat over his head, fluffing the material so it rested over his shoulder like a shawl.

"Isabella! Come on, we need to get going."

She nodded to indicate she understood, then followed him to the door.

Heat like he'd never felt before filled the space, swimming in front of his eyes like a mirage. He started the extinguisher, the heavy foam spraying in the air in a heavy mist of white. Liam glanced over his shoulder, pleased to see Isabella had done as he asked. Her coat was affixed above her head as she followed close on his heels.

The heat was overwhelming, the thin material of his shirt tighter than a second skin as sweat ran freely down his back.

"Grab onto my waistband!"

Step by aching step, they moved down the engulfed hallway. A heavy door at the far end indicated safety and it was his only focus as they moved closer to it, inch by careful inch. Liam maintained a steady spray of foam, crossing in a large arc—back and forth, back and forth— and forced his gaze on their forward progress instead of on the hypnotic dance of flames that surrounded them.

The posters that lined the walls had long-since turned to ash in the flames and even with his laser focus on keeping them safe he couldn't deny the horrified fascination as the fire ate up everything in its path. Curtains. Wood railings. Plants.

All of it incinerated in the blaze.

The heat increased and he wanted nothing more than to reach behind to take the steady hand at his waist, but Liam kept on, arcing the retardant from the extinguisher in a steady wash. It wasn't nearly enough to stop the blaze, but it did give them just enough room to maneuver to the end of the hall.

As they reached the door, he nearly had his hand out to take the handle when Isabella's scream echoed over the blaze. "No!"

He watched as she stepped around him, her hand wrapped in the arm of her coat pocket as she pressed down on the flat handle of the door.

Of course. The heat of the metal door would have burned clean through his palm.

The solid door was hot enough to burn his finger-

tips as he held it with his free hand and tossed the extinguisher with the other. He stumbled through the entrance
and imagined the heat and flames following them, but it
was only once the door slammed close behind them that
a blessed silence filled the space.

"Are you hurt?" The edges of her coat flapped around
her face—black from the flames and smoke—and he
dragged it away from those delicate features.

"I'm fine. Come on, we have to keep moving."

He took quick stock of their bodies, satisfied when he
saw no smoldering embers flaring to life off their clothes.
Heavy black stains ran down the arms of his white dress
shirt but that was the extent of the damage—no fire had
broken through to skin.

They ran down the three flights of stairs to the ground,
the heavy whirl of fire trucks already lighting up the air.

Building alarms rang out as they pushed through the
heavy fire door but Liam ignored the thick, bleating sound.
All he could focus on was Isabella and the fact that they
were safe.

In the swell of both siren and flame, he grabbed her
hand and ran toward the fresh air.

"Preliminary reports indicate the fire was set." Kensington placed a fresh cup of tea in front of Isabella before
sitting with her own.

After spending most of the day with the police, Isabella
and Liam were now safely ensconced back at the House
of Steele headquarters. Daylight had long since faded to
black, the city's streetlights sheening the living-room windows in a fluorescent glare. Isabella abstractly saw it—
just like she kept keying in and out on Liam's family—but
couldn't make sense of any of it.

No matter how many times she told herself she was safe,

she couldn't shake the horrible cold that had gripped her insides with sharp claws.

Someone had deliberately set fire to her lab. With her and Liam in it. Whatever she'd wanted to believe up to now, today had confirmed the harsh truth.

This was personal.

No longer could she take a strange sort of solace in a nameless, faceless threat that wanted her research. A cold, governmental entity out for its own gains or a third-world dictator who thought her work was the key to advancing his goals.

In a strange, horrifying way, this was much worse. Someone was after her. And if Liam's suspicions were correct, it was someone she knew and cared about.

"Isabella?" Abby's voice was tender as it broke into her thoughts.

"Yes?"

"Do you want to go upstairs?"

"No, I'm fine."

"Come on." Gentle hands reached for hers, pulling her up from the chair. Her gaze alighted on Liam's but that bleak blue gaze—bloodshot now from the smoke—gave nothing away.

Isabella nodded, then gripped Abby's hands as the woman pulled her toward the door. They walked up the two flights of stairs to the floor she was staying on and, like a small child, allowed Abby to lead her into the room. Abby settled her on the bed, then flipped on a small bedside light. "Come on. It's all right."

Isabella hadn't cried since they'd returned to the old brownstone—hadn't even felt the telltale signs—but Abby's gentle smile when she joined her on the bed was her undoing.

Unbidden, a hard sob broke through Isabella's chest, exhaling in a hard wash of hot tears.

"Oh oh." Abby pulled her close, her arms tight. Protective. "Shhh. You're safe now. You're safe."

Isabella clung to the woman who was practically a stranger, yet in that moment the closest thing she had to a friend. She tried to apologize through the sobs but nothing came out but heavy, tear-filled breaths.

She tried once more to apologize when a large figure filled the doorway. Abby's arms fell away, only to be replaced by the hard lines of Liam's body. "Shhh now. It's all right."

Liam's arms slid around her and he pulled her close. Abstractly, she heard the door click closed but the sound was forgotten in the gentle cadence of Liam's voice, the soothing press of his hands over her back.

He'd showered when they got back to the house but she could still smell the light stench of smoke on him. Heard it in the rough rasp of his vocal chords when he spoke.

"I'm so sorry." The words snuck out, the gravelly thickness that tinged her own voice foreign in her ears. "So sorry for what I've brought to your door."

"Stop it." Liam lifted his head and held her shoulders in a firm grip. "Stop. We're in this together. Whatever else you may think, know this."

"But it's too much. Too dangerous."

His gaze never left hers, unwavering and true. "We're in this together. And we're going to get to the bottom of things. And you're going to be fine."

"But—"

His eyes searched her face as if looking for something. She saw the question—knew what he asked before he said a word—before she saw something else.

Acquiescence.

On a hard sigh, he dragged her against his chest, his arms wrapping tight around her. Where the feeling should have been oppressive, especially after escaping from a building with too-little air, it was heavenly. Safe.

Demanding.

His mouth came down on hers and he slid his tongue through her lips.

And as hers slid out to mate with Liam's, Isabella surrendered.

Chapter 13

Liam cursed himself a fool and a lecher—knew in this moment Isabella needed comfort, not sex—but he couldn't seem to stop himself from kissing her. From this manic desire to have his hands on her as he branded her with his body.

She'd nearly died today.

They both had, yet all he could think was the same litany over and over.

Isabella had nearly died today.

The storm swirled in his blood, a demanding force that kept him in the moment, swamping him with wave after wave of need. Isabella was vulnerable and she needed him.

She *didn't* need his raging hormones taking advantage of her moment of weakness.

Besides, his family was right downstairs and if neither he nor Isabella returned in a decent amount of time, they'd know what was going on.

"Liam?"

"Hmmm?" He skimmed his lips along her jaw, unwilling to relinquish contact while he debated with the devil on his shoulder.

"You were here and then you left."

"What?" He lifted his head and gazed down at her. A stab pierced his heart at the red, glassy sheen that filled her eyes, a lingering aftereffect of the smoke.

Was he honestly thinking of a way to have sex with her? Now?

He shifted on the bed, putting some distance between them. "I'm right here."

"No, I mean you left. In your mind. One moment you were here and then you vanished."

"I can promise you, I'm right here."

She reached for his hand—clutched it like a lifeline—and pressed her point. "No, you're not. I'd like an explanation."

The moment was direct and real and entirely Isabella and he couldn't hold back a small smile. "I was letting my head get in the way."

"Isn't this the one time you're not supposed to think? Isn't sex supposed to be freeing?"

"Easier said than done." Her gaze dropped at his muttered words and he knew immediately that he'd misstepped. "Not because of you."

"Why then?"

"I haven't tried to sneak sex under the same roof where my sister was since I was eighteen."

"You don't want to make love to me because your sister's here?"

"And my brother and my sister-in-law. All eyes are on us, as it were."

"I doubt they care."

"I care."

"I understand." She shifted, putting some more distance between them on the bed. "Wrong place. Wrong time. Wrong girl."

He saw her withdrawal—would have to be blind to miss it—and tried to make her understand. With tender moves, he reached out and twisted a long lock of her hair around his finger, the silky strands feather-light against his skin. "I'd say you're absolutely the right girl. None of it changes the fact you deserve something better than a house full of people aware of our quiet moments together."

"Which only proves my point from earlier."

He faltered for a moment, those silky strands falling through his fingers. "What point?"

"Your family. They matter to you."

"Of course they do."

"You're used to hiding your choices from them. Hiding your life."

"I don't do that." Before the words had even left his lips, his conscience was rising up, taunting him, branding him as a liar.

"Yes, you do." She stood, her arms crossing over her chest. He didn't need the body language to know she had effectively ended their quiet moments together, but it certainly accentuated her point. "You should go."

"You're upset."

"I'll be fine. As you said, I'm safe here."

Physically, she was safe.

Emotionally, the thought of leaving her in the room by herself stabbed at him with hard, choppy thrusts. "You don't need to be alone."

"Don't worry, Liam. It's something I'm well-used to."

When she opened her door, he struggled with something to say—something that sounded less like an excuse and more of a reason why he wanted to be with her—but something kept him from exposing that raw, painful nerve.

No matter how real this was in the moment, they'd both go back their lives in a matter of days. He knew it and so did Isabella. And from what he'd pieced together about her life, he'd likely do lasting damage if he pressed for something physical.

She'd been alone for so long, starting something and then leaving would be cruel.

That self-righteous victory carried him from her bedroom and through the door. It was only as he stood in the hallway, the door clicking closed at his back, that he acknowledged the truth to himself.

What if he let her see his true self—the one he kept hidden from everyone—and she still asked him to leave?

The echo of raised voices had Isabella stopping on the back stairs above the kitchen. She'd barely slept and the blurry-eyed need for coffee had carried her down a flight and a half. But it was the shouting match that had stopped her midflight.

"You know it's a sound plan."

"Oh hell no it's not."

"Liam, be reasonable."

"Rowan does have a point, Liam."

Isabella fought to keep up, all while trying to digest the gaggle of feminine voices obviously intent on getting Liam to acquiesce.

"You can come down the stairs, Isabella. You might as well add your opinion to this."

She fought the horrified mortification at Liam's words—and briefly toyed with cutting and running back up the stairs—but knew she needed to see it through. With shaky legs, she descended the last five stairs, only to find the Steele women surrounding Liam in various poses.

Kensington stood with a dish towel in her hands, a griddle at her back on the counter. Rowan sat on the counter, her legs dangling and an oversize coffee mug in her hand. And Abby sat at the table, her arm on Liam's forearm.

"I'm sorry to interrupt."

Rowan waved her free hand. "Eavesdropping is a world-class sport in this family. But you have to watch for the creak of the stairs."

"I'll remember that."

Rowan nodded before turning back to her brother. "It's the perfect plan and you know it. We can't sit around and do nothing."

Liam's gaze flashed toward her before turning back to his sister. In the deep blue of his eyes she saw the same evidence of lack of sleep and took a strange sort of satisfaction from that.

Even if she had been the one to send him away.

"We're hardly sitting around as we assess the situation and how to get to the bottom of it. Besides, we've been out in the open for the past two days and neither has ended well." His long fingers flexed on his own oversize mug before he glanced down in disgust at what appeared to be an empty cup.

Wishing for something to do that didn't leave her standing in the middle of the Steele kitchen like a gaping fish, she walked to the coffeepot. Several empty mugs sat next to the coffeemaker and she poured herself a cup, then walked the pot around the kitchen, refilling everyone's waning supply.

It was silly, but she felt useful and that went a long way toward stemming the sea of embarrassment at getting caught on the stairs.

Even if Rowan seemed to think it was a common enough occurrence to provide tips for success.

She ignored that vague sense of being tossed down the rabbit hole when in the presence of a large number of Liam's family members and methodically settled the pot back on its burner.

They were so boisterous and loud; so determined to make their points. If she weren't vaguely intimated by it, Isabella knew, she'd sit back and enjoy observing the melee.

And the odd communication that seemed to work well for all involved.

Isabella took a seat next to Abby, touched when the woman reached over and laid a hand on her arm. "How are you feeling this morning?"

"Other than the fact I sound like I swallowed a frog, I'm none the worse for wear."

"You sleep okay? Any nightmares?"

"No." Isabella shook her head, intending to brush off the concern when something stopped her. "But I didn't sleep all that well."

"We can get you something for that."

"No, I'm good. I took tranquilizers once." *Never again.* "I didn't care for how they made me feel."

Isabella fought the shudder. She had taken them once— after her father's conviction—thinking how nice it would be to put the reality of her family's situation out of her mind.

Instead, she'd spent restless dreams filled with the monsters that lurked in shadows filling her mind's eye. Even now, years later, she could still remember the strange fog that had numbed her mind but couldn't numb the reality of her situation.

She refused to be that vulnerable again.

To run away from her mind's capability to engage in rational thought.

"Maybe a hot bath then?"

Abby's soft smile and kind eyes had anxiety ratcheting down a notch, even as Liam, Rowan and Kensington's pitched battle raged on around them. "Now that's an idea I can get behind."

Polite conversation addressed, she keyed back in on the discussion. "What are they arguing about?"

"The Steele family patronizes several charities and we've got a large event this evening."

The image of Liam Steele in a tuxedo hit her with the force of an explosion and Isabella quickly settled her mug on the kitchen table to avoid the sudden trembling of her hands. "I take it Liam doesn't want to go."

"It's the perfect plan." Rowan leaped on their conversation, tossing her inputs in from across the kitchen. "We'll all be there to protect you. It gets you out for a night of fun. And the odds of someone actually attempting to hurt you in public are slim to none."

"Like the chances of getting shot at when leaving the airport," Liam said, his voice dry as the Sahara.

"It's actually safer." Kensington volleyed her way back into the conversation. "The event is invitation-only. The entrances all require security clearance and passage through metal detectors. And the governor is expected so where everyone would be on their game, they'll be doubly so."

As the image of the group of them going out for an evening shimmered to life in her mind, Isabella couldn't hold back her interest. "I'd love a night out. Something to be excited about."

"See." Rowan hopped off the counter and moved into Liam's space. "You're outvoted."

"It's not worth it."

"Oh, but it will be, big brother. We all need a bit of fun and this is just what the doctor ordered."

Edward swirled the brandy in his glass as he gazed around Daniel's study and allowed his thoughts to drift. He'd spent his life suffering from a damned disease—managing pills and medicine, watching his food and drink intake—so it was a rare pleasure to taste the brandy and not worry about its potential aftereffects.

He was a scientist and he knew how the liquor worked, down to a cellular level. Absorption into the bloodstream. A heady buzz. Then evacuation through the liver. Step by careful step, a healthy body could process the alcohol just like that. Up until a short while ago, *he'd* been the exception.

But no longer. Now he worked, his body functioning like everyone else's.

He'd missed so much in his life. And if Isabella's attempts to defend her work to the public went forward, he'd not have the easy access to continued treatment.

Continued maintenance to ensure they stayed healed.

He and Daniel had stayed off the radar because no one knew the full results of her work and he intended to keep it that way. Oh, Daniel had tried to reason with him. Had suggested several times that their contribution to science would override their choice to fall off the grid, but Edward knew better.

The things they'd done on their quest to be whole would make them targets.

And all their efforts would be for nothing if they spent their lives in a cage. No one would manage their therapy then. No one would ensure they had adequate access to medicine and lab work.

And no one would appreciate all they had gone through to get to this point.

Governments would find a way to get their hands on her work, gleefully building their fleets of super soldiers, but he and Daniel would be punished. National security might be a good enough reason to break the law, but a life free of pain and the degrading pity of others wasn't.

It was why he continued to press his point. Why he had to keep Daniel focused. They had access to the man's boundless supply of money. And between the two of them, they'd finish their work, experimenting even further on how far they could push their bodies, now that they'd healed themselves.

Or mostly healed themselves.

He couldn't ignore the sneaky fatigue that still managed to surprise him several times a day. They'd changed dosages and mixtures in the compound, but neither of them had been able to fully remove some of the side effects.

It was why he had a backup plan. There was no way he was giving up his new life.

No. Freaking. Way.

As if proving his point, Daniel hobbled into the study, his cane firmly in hand. "Getting an early start?"

Edward swirled his brandy for effect, the subtle censure unwelcome. "A single glass is hardly an early start."

"It's barely noon." Daniel's gaze was flat, the normal good humor to be found there nowhere in evidence.

"Yesterday was a big day. I was celebrating."

"Ah yes. Blowing up one's laboratory is always cause for celebration."

Edward fought the light shudder at the utter lack of expression on his mentor's face and focused on keeping Daniel in the moment, his agile mind on their plans. "It is when it's the necessary step to keep Isabella from moving forward with the reporters."

Daniel snorted but said nothing as he shuffled toward the remaining empty couch in the room, his attention drawn more to the seat than continuing their argument.

Edward observed his former teacher, the man's stooped shoulders and hesitant gait signaling a subtle alarm he hadn't felt in a long while.

Had they missed something?

He'd meticulously managed their research notes and the formulas but lately it seemed they needed more and more to simply maintain.

Even as the sly doubts trickled in, he reminded himself of their blood work. The disease was gone. Out of their bloodstream and no longer populating their DNA.

It was gone, damn it.

So why the hell wasn't he feeling better?

"The lab was too impulsive."

"She triggered the notes, Daniel. You and I knew this was a risk. We agreed this was the best course of action."

"We should have approached the problem differently."

A sharp retort hovered on his tongue but Edward pulled it back. Just as he'd learned to manage his father by tamping down on his more impulsive responses, he'd learned the same with Daniel and it had paid dividends.

His teacher had taken him under his wing. Mentored him. Healed him, with the miraculous advances Dr. Isabella Magnini's work had wrought.

It wouldn't do to ruin it now by allowing his impulsive reactions to rule him.

"Hindsight, Daniel. That's all you're feeling."

"We nearly killed her."

"We have to kill her. You know that. She can't share her work."

"There has to be another way. I've been thinking through a few theories. Gaming the outcomes to identify how we might keep her alive."

The subtle panic that tickled his nerve endings flared up a few notches to full-on alarm. "Keep her alive?"

"Her mind is too valuable. You and I both know the advances we've made on our own took twice as long as any of her research. She's the heart of this project."

And a piece of your heart, too.

That was the root of the problem, Edward well knew. He'd worried from the start their work would come to this. That Daniel would look at his protégé and when the crucial moment arrived, not be able to pull the trigger.

Fortunately, he didn't have the same issues.

When it came time to execute Dr. Isabella Magnini, he had the chops to get the job done.

Isabella vacillated between exhilarated and scared spitless as the heavy pop of a cork echoed around the room. Rowan blew on the top of their second bottle of champagne for the afternoon before asking the question of the hour.

"Who wants some?"

If the House of Steele headquarters had seemed intimidating before—when Isabella had only thought of the Upper East Side brownstone as a secure location to hide out—it was now off the charts.

In a mere three hours, Kensington, Rowan and Abby had transformed it into a boutique worthy of Fifth Avenue.

"Let's look at the indigo silk again." Kensington drilled out the order from the foot of a bed in what Isabella assumed was the home's original master bedroom.

"I want her in the purple." Rowan frowned as she refilled her sister's champagne flute.

"No." Kensington shook her head before she reached out a hand to the rich blue silk. "This is the one."

Isabella didn't miss the subtle battle of wills brewing and pushed her way into the conversation. "I'm not wearing either of them. I like the first black one I tried on."

"This isn't a funeral."

Rowan's quick retort had Abby giving her a subtle elbow before she took over the conversation. "The black is elegant but you need some color. The blue will look beautiful against your darker complexion."

The blue would look beautiful—had, in fact, looked stunning when she'd tried it on—but there was no way she was putting that much cleavage on display.

"Um. I can't."

"Why not?" Three pairs of eyes—two in that vivid blue shade unique to the Steele clan—focused on her.

"I won't be naked in public."

"It's a dress, Iz, not a bikini."

Isabella's mouth clamped closed as she digested Rowan's words.

Iz?

The name was funny—short and to the point—just like Rowan. What struck her even more forcefully was the use of a nickname at all.

"What's the matter?" The slender lines of Rowan's face fell, her blue eyes clouding with concern before she crossed the room, the champagne bottle still in hand. "I overstepped, didn't I? I'm sorry. Bull in a china shop is my usual speed."

"No. It's not that." Isabella fought the strange sensation clawing at her throat.

"What is it? You don't like the blue or the purple? The black looked good. Really good. And you've got great legs." Rowan's voice got higher with each word.

"It's silly. I'm being silly." Isabella waved a hand and willed the weird reaction to subside as she swallowed against the strange, frog-like thickening of her vocal chords. "It's just that no one's ever given me a nickname before."

"Anyone?" Rowan's eyes widened, the concern fading to skepticism in a heartbeat. "Not even in college? Or from your family?"

"No. No one."

"If you don't like it I can call you Isabella."

"Not at all. I like it. Very much." She took the champagne bottle from Rowan and refilled her glass. After all, someone like "Iz" would be a take-charge sort of gal.

Someone named Iz would also wear the blue silk.

"Why don't I try the indigo silk on once more."

She didn't need to see Kensington's broad smile to know she'd made the right choice.

Liam fought the urge to punch something as he stomped around the room, a thick towel slung around his waist. His tuxedo hung from a hanger outside his closet and every time he looked at the long, black lines he imagined any number of horrors for the evening.

And an inability to protect Isabella when they inevitably ensued.

What were his sisters thinking? He respected their abilities and rarely questioned their judgment on anything. So why was he so convinced something horrible would befall them all tonight?

Rowan kept pressing the point that the event was secure and there was no risk other than all of them having too grand a time, but he wasn't so sure.

The events from the day before in Isabella's lab were still fresh in his mind. A threat lurked. A personal one.

He shucked the towel and made quick work of the tuxedo. Despite his best efforts, he'd been outvoted for the evening. Even Isabella had disregarded any possible threat in exchange for a night out of the house.

It was stifling, he admitted to himself as he fastened his father's platinum cufflinks at his wrists.

The endless hours anticipating what might happen. The even more endless hours remembering what *had* happened.

Just like the time after losing his parents.

Those long moments of utter shock and disbelief, followed by the very real knowledge they'd never come back. Would never walk through the door or smile or laugh or even yell in frustration at their brood of teenagers.

Words of anger had been the last he'd spoken with his father and they taunted him even now. Silly, useless battles about keys to the car while his parents were on their anniversary trip.

A few heated words didn't eclipse—or would ever erase—what they shared. He'd known then and sixteen years had only cemented that knowledge.

But none of it changed the fact their last words weren't the sort a man wanted to remember.

Refusing to dwell on it, he settled his phone in his pocket and his wallet in another, then headed for the stairs. He had already spent the afternoon going over security with Jack, Finn and Campbell, along with Cam's right hand man, T-Bone. They'd even conducted a conference call with the event's lead security agent, satisfied the night would go off without a hitch.

So why was he so uncertain?

So off-balance?

Campbell was already in the foyer watching for the car when Liam came down the steps. Jack offered up a small nod before he went back to barking instructions to several security additions he'd made from his own ready stash of job mercenaries.

The vigilant action should have made him feel better, but all it managed to do was lift the hair at the nape of his neck like a whispered warning.

You can't protect her.

The taunt rumbled through his mind on a loop before the sounds of light laughter floated down the grand staircase at his back. He heard his sisters first, then Abby's quiet but firm tones. But it was the last that caught his attention. That dark, smoky voice that clenched his gut in a tight grip.

A strange prescience overtook him in the mere moments it took to turn in place.

And then he forgot to breathe.

Every reason they should stay home fled at the sight of Isabella, clad in a long, flowing sheath of blue. The deep color—as rich as sapphires—outlined her full breasts before cascading over her slender hips and endlessly long legs.

She was a vision.

A goddess.

And then he caught sight of how her hands fluttered at her waist, as if searching for a place to twist a non-existent hem. His heart clenched—hard—at the small quirk and he moved toward the stairs.

The action was so simple, so easy to miss yet so real. And in that moment he vowed to make her his own.

Chapter 14

Isabella clutched the staircase railing with one hand and reached for the train of her dress in the other. She'd nearly slapped a hand over her stomach at the swarm of bats that had taken wing before she remembered the train.

Slipping and falling down half a staircase was *so* not in the plans for the night. Or she hoped like hell it wasn't. The hard trembling of her legs had her unsure she would make it past the last step.

And then she was at the bottom and Liam was standing next to her, the long lines of his body framed to perfection in a form-fitting tuxedo.

Her fingers drifted once more to the cinched waist of her dress, but came up empty with nothing to clench and worry between her fingers. Before she could give it another thought, he had those same fingers in his hands, drawing them to his lips. "You look beautiful."

"So do you."

His eyes flashed but he kept her hand in his. "This old thing?"

"I'm not sure how your sisters pulled it off, but four hours ago I didn't even have a pair of heels with me. Now I'm clad head to toe in couture and wearing several pieces of jewelry Kensington assured me are well-insured."

The words tripped off her tongue, light as rose petals, and Isabella marveled they actually came from her.

Was this what male attention did for you? Gave you that added push to flirt and preen ever so slightly under an appreciative gaze.

Or was it something more?

As she catalogued the moments in her mind, she knew it was more.

Something uniquely Liam.

"You can smile and flirt with me, but for the record, I still think this is a bad idea."

A soft, husky laugh fell from her lips and she almost clamped her mouth shut she was so surprised at the sound. Recovering, she nodded. "I don't disagree but I'm too excited to care."

Their attention was diverted across the foyer when Kensington stepped out of Jack's embrace, issuing orders while showing off her gown in a light-footed twirl. "Tonight will be fine. We've covered all bases, prepped until we were all blue in the face and we've added several mercenary thugs who come highly recommended by my beloved. We've prepped and planned. We're good."

"We're good." Isabella felt the reassuring squeeze of Liam's fingers. She'd put her trust in these people—it was time she began to trust herself. "I know we're good so let's go. We've got a party to get to."

The men helped each of the women with their wraps and within moments their group was headed out the door.

Jack's promised mercenaries had positioned themselves at the front door, halfway to the street and at the long limo that awaited them all at the curb.

Isabella already knew the routine. The car would be manned by two of the hired guards at all times, in addition to the driver. The car itself had already been swept for bombs and would be again before they left the event.

Someone might want her dead, but they were going to have a damn hard time seeing that goal to fruition tonight.

For now, it was time to enjoy the evening.

Liam settled himself in the limo beside Isabella, their legs brushing against the tight bench seat. Although the limo had room for all of them, they were stuffed so tightly together Liam had memories of his prom night and the herd of teenagers they'd managed to stuff inside their rental.

"Is that amusement I see in your eyes, big brother?" Rowan's question was loud enough to be heard above the din.

"I believe it is." When his sister only stared at him, he added. "I was thinking about my prom and the limo ride."

"Oh, do you remember his date?" Kensington chimed in on the action. "Cressida Bogart. And no, I'm not making up that name."

"Biggest breasts in our entire school," Campbell added proudly before Abby elbowed him. He had the grace to ratchet down his smile but no one missed the enthusiasm that still lit his blue eyes. "We all adored her but Suave and Sure of Himself over there got the girl."

At the mention of his teenage prowess, Liam risked a glance at Isabella. When all he saw was a broad smile in return, he figured he was on safe ground. "She was a lovely girl."

"Who put out."

"Rowan!" Abby pretended shock while Finn just shook his head next to his wife.

"My memory's not what it used to be but I don't recall any post-prom sex. Or pre-prom for that matter." He wasn't sure why he felt the need to defend himself. He hadn't exactly made a secret of his endless string of relationships throughout his life, but for some reason it seemed necessary to set the record straight. "Cressie confessed to me that she had the hots for someone else."

"Her stepbrother." Kensington interjected before rolling her eyes. "Actually got him, too, for a few years after their parents moved on to new spouses."

"I have a renewed appreciation for your situation."

Isabella shifted next to him and Liam fought another wave of heat that ran up his side at the brush of her thigh before he focused on her comment. "What about my situation?"

"Three siblings with long memories."

Campbell's broad grin flashed in the ambient light of the streetlamps outside the limo. "We're a bit much all piled into one place, aren't we?"

"I was thinking more of how you all remember everything. Almost like your own private network of information. What one forgets the other fills in."

"Ensuring no one has any secrets." Jack said.

"It's more than that." Isabella leaned forward and he saw that light—the same one that filled her face when they were in her lab. She loved ideas and learning and it showed. "You each have different ways of complementing each other."

Liam saw how interest sparked across three pairs of blue eyes, all matched to his own. It was Finn, though, who spoke first. "Gangs work similarly. Each member hones a strength. Slick fingers. Wheel man. Con artist who initiates the mark. Everyone plays on a different skill to come together to get the job done."

"It's efficient." Isabella said. "And highly effective."

"And nosy." Liam added, with a pointed look at Rowan.

She stuck out her tongue before she patted Finn's arm. "Is that why you worked alone, baby?"

"Partly." Finn smiled and Liam didn't miss the glint of memory that flashed briefly across his face. "Or maybe I never found anyone who was as good as me."

The limo came to a stop and the tone changed immediately. The joking and easy camaraderie fled as each person in the car put their game face on.

Since he and Isabella had been the first into their seats, they were the last out and she laid a hand on his arm before he could slide toward the door. "It's nice, you know."

"What is?"

"This. Your family." She gestured to the now empty car. "Rowan's the instigator. Kensington's the mother. Campbell's the beleaguered joker who shines a light. You all play a role."

"And what's mine?"

"You're the foil."

"For what?"

"All their admiration, love and respect. You're their big brother, Liam, and no one ever forgets it."

Isabella's words were still rattling around his mind an hour later as waiters laid the main course down on their tables. He'd watched each of his siblings throughout the dinner and knew the truth of Isabella's assessment. How quickly she'd sized everyone up and figured out the roles they played.

As if to punctuate the point, Rowan's ready laugh echoed once more as she finished telling Abby and Campbell a joke. How funny, then, that Isabella had seen what none of them had ever put into words.

They functioned as a team and they always had. Long before the House of Steele, they were a unit.

A family.

Maybe that was why the loss of his parents had hit so hard. It wasn't simply the grief—although that was significant in its own right—but they'd all had to recreate new roles.

New lives.

And new ways of interacting with each other.

His gaze caught on Isabella's delicate fingers as she reached for her wine glass and he turned to her, stilling her hand. "You're pretty amazing, you know that."

"Oh. Um." Confusion and delight filled those dark eyes in equal measure, nearly turning them black. "Thank you."

"You see things."

"So do you."

"No." He shook his head. "No, I don't. I watch them. You actually see what's happening around you. It's a special and rare gift."

"It's a lifetime spent on the fringes. Add in my scientific bent toward observation and you have a recipe for constant analysis."

"Don't underestimate yourself." He slid his fingers down her arm until they entwined with hers. "You have a gift."

"For pointing out the obvious?" The corner of her lips trembled around a small smile. "Or saying inappropriate things?"

"Neither." He lifted her hand to his lips, pressing his mouth to the soft skin. "You have a gift for pointing out what is all too easy to overlook. Thank you for making me look."

"You're welcome."

They sat there in quiet silence for a few moments, each lost in their own thoughts as the sounds of dinner continued on unabated.

Despite the dinner activity and conversation all around them, Liam didn't miss the soft, subtle glances of each of his siblings.

Bradley Armstrong scrolled through email on his tablet, discarding some, reading others and earmarking several more for later. A small glass of whiskey sat on the table next to him and he glanced at it with fondness.

His wife allowed him one per day, two on the weekends. Said it kept him sharp to have some indulgence but not enough to dull his mind. Funny how as a young man it had seemed like nagging yet now as he was older—as they were older together—he understood it for what it really was.

Wisdom beyond her years.

He had a good life. A happy one. He and Rachel had built that. Day by day, year by year, they'd built a life together. Just like he'd built the *Journal of Cellular Science*.

The journal was one of the most respected in the world, unequaled in its category.

And he'd done that.

Built it on a sure knowledge the scientific world was changing. The community needed peer-reviewed work, but it also needed a line of sight to the world at large and he'd created that. Built a magazine first, later a website and now—with the miracle of science in full force—the majority of their readership consumed the content on a tablet or a phone.

He'd seen it all and he still loved his job. Loved the thrill of knowing human beings could still learn something about themselves or the world around them each and every day.

He reached for his glass, satisfied to finish off the day's indulgence when his gaze caught on an email he'd missed—one of the few that got past the company spam filters with a title that read "Urgent, Open Now."

Curious, Bradley did as the note asked and nearly fumbled his whiskey glass at the contents.

I have Isabella Magnini's notes. There's something you need to see.

He might have a scientific mind, but he had a reporter's instincts first. A note like this—one that obviously did know how to beat the spam filters—had value. And when his gaze skimmed down the note and he saw the name Daniel Stephenson, he knew he'd hit pay dirt.

Excitement warred with confusion as he reread the note. Stephenson had died years ago. Hell, he'd gone to his memorial service.

Those reporter's instincts heightened once more as he played through various scenarios. Bradley knew Isabella had taken a significant risk by talking to him. Her off-the-record comments and guarded sharing of preliminary notes had indicated as much. Despite the secrecy, from the notes he read, her work was solid. And well worth the attention it would garner.

Had Stephenson faked his own death to help her? Or was someone using his name?

Either way, the story underneath had definite meat on its bones. Maybe it was even bigger than the joint article he'd share with the *New York Times* once she shared the final pieces of her research with him.

With a hard thud, he set his glass on the end table and tapped out a reply.

Of course. He'd be delighted to meet with Daniel. Whatever time worked best for the man.

As he hit Send, Bradley knew the truth of the matter. He'd go to the ends of the earth for this story.

But as luck would have it, he wouldn't have to go much farther than downtown.

Isabella knew the laws of aerodynamics. She knew it was physically impossible for a person to float but as she moved over the dance floor in Liam's arms, she was convinced she'd defied each and every one of those laws.

Were her feet even touching the ground?

"You're a great dancer."

Liam's husky voice, whispered against her ear, sent a shiver racing down her spine. "It was the one physical requirement my mother enforced on me. I had dancing lessons from an early age, followed by couples lessons as soon as I turned thirteen."

"Did your mother go to school with my mother?"

The light tone and flash of teeth had her marveling at the difference she saw in Liam this evening. She suspected even he wasn't fully aware of the change but it was there all the same.

Danger had skirted the edges—or dive-bombed in their midst—since she met him, so it was a treat to see him relaxed and enjoying himself.

"I don't think they knew each other."

"But our grandparents do." He stared down at her, his gaze speculative. "How is it we've never met before now?"

"Maybe it's because you've been busy with all those big-busted debutantes you've been squiring for the last two decades."

"Damn Campbell and Rowan," he muttered before swinging her into a fast turn to the music's rising tempo. "They've got big mouths."

"For which I'm grateful. Getting anything out of you is harder than splitting atoms. Which, for the record, isn't nearly as easy as everyone now wants to believe it is."

"Energy is energy."

"Precisely. And immovable objects are hard to get moving."

His mouth dropped in a mock "O" of surprise. "Are you suggesting I'm the immovable object?"

"I thought I rather eloquently stated the facts. Even used some physics to back up my argument."

"A sexy scientist, out to prove her point." Heat filled his gaze as his hand tightened on her lower back and Isabella felt an answering response in the achy need of her own body.

Who am I?

The question caught her off guard and she nearly tripped at the thought, so wrapped up in Liam and the moment. Catching herself, she maintained her footing and stayed in the music.

While she knew she was harder on herself than she needed to be, she also knew her circumstances had some root in her own making.

Yes, she was a scientist and prone to introspection and the occasional lecture or two when making a point but she was a kind person. She knew how to make conversation and enjoy the company of others when she did choose to socialize.

So when had things changed? When had she given up on her youth and the dreams that had fueled her as a girl?

The music kicked up another notch, preventing any further conversation as they moved around the floor. His muscles flexed under her fingers and the heat of his body kept her in that permanent state of arousal, pressed so closely against her.

Isabella knew she was in danger of losing her heart, but in that moment, with the music swelling around them, all she could focus on was Liam.

All she saw was Liam.

All she wanted was Liam.

Chapter 15

"Are you going to sleep with my brother or not?" Rowan's question—and the heavy slur that punctuated every other word—wasn't nearly as shocking as it should have been.

Isabella abstractly wondered if it was the champagne she'd drunk or the heavy throb of sexual desire that beat in her veins that had her barely fazed at Rowan's deliberate question.

Either way, sitting in the library of the brownstone with Rowan and Abby wasn't getting Isabella any closer to her goal of crawling into bed with Liam Steele.

"Mind you, I'm all for it," Rowan added with a cheerful smile.

"You're always for sex." Kensington shot back at her sister as she crossed her ankles on the coffee table. "You practically pushed me at Jack a few months ago."

"You were looking at Jack's fine as...assets long before I started nagging you." Rowan waved her champagne flute. "You certainly didn't need my encouragement to take the leap."

"You can't ask questions like that, Rowan. Sex is a private matter." Abby waved her own flute of recently refilled champagne, the bubbling liquid sloshing dangerously close to the rim of the glass. "And you especially can't ask it of someone we haven't known that long."

"Of course she can." Isabella decided to float the family theory she tested out on Liam earlier. "As youngest, Rowan can play the vocal instigator and everyone will forgive her for it while enjoying the results she procures. It's her role in the family."

"What's mine?" Kensington leaned forward, her feet dropping to the ground.

"Matriarch." Abby and Rowan's voices matched Isabella's in timing.

"That makes me sound eighty. Besides, isn't that Grandmother's role?"

Isabella almost laughed at the small moue that lit up Kensington's face but kept her best lecture voice in place. "It is, but in her absence you handle the responsibilities. You're also preparing the family for the eventual day you become matriarch, even though we all hope it's still many years away."

"Amen to that." Kensington sighed, the forlorn sound echoing in the thoughtful silence. "I sound like a calendar."

"You *are* a calendar," Rowan pointed out. "A very beautiful one who keeps us all in line. And we love you for it."

Isabella let them continue talking—the new subject of dissecting each other diverting their thoughts off her decision to sleep with Liam—and gave herself a moment to think.

She knew herself. And she knew that she already had

feelings for Liam. Sleeping with him was only going to cement those feelings further. Would make it that much harder when things ended between them.

No matter how much time they'd spent together in the last few days, this situation was going to end. They'd go back to their lives—assuming she had a life to go back to—and keep on being the people they were before she published her damn research findings.

Why did that simple set of facts leave her so cold?

She was a scientist and she was used to dealing in data. And even now, the results weren't on her side.

Liam wanted her, of that she had no doubt. But he didn't want long-term.

Of that, she equally had no doubt.

What she couldn't quite reconcile was how she was sitting down here with the girls, talking about any number of things, instead of upstairs in Liam's bedroom.

With him.

They'd all tumbled out of the limo like puppies, Jack's mercenaries on guard for the short walk from the limo to the house. Where she'd expected Liam to take her hand in his and drag her up the front staircase, he'd disappeared the moment they'd arrived back. Oh, he'd muttered something about having to check a set of computer feeds with Campbell, but Isabella knew the move for what it really was.

Evasion.

Did she take that as solid proof he wasn't interested? Or did she go with her gut and go find him? Her time with Liam Steele was going to end in a matter of days or weeks. Did she really want to leave this experience wishing she'd made different choices?

"I'm going to turn in."

A chorus of good-nights echoed around her and even Rowan refrained from saying anything else.

Did they know her decision?

Did she even care?

When the answer to that was a resounding no, Isabella knew she'd made the right choice. She'd spent her life accepting the hand she'd been dealt and she was sick of it. She wanted an adventure and the best place to start was a night spent in Liam's arms.

His large, powerful, *capable* arms, if her memory of dancing encircled in them was any indication.

It was time to take *exactly* what she wanted.

Liam stood over his brother's shoulder in the brownstone's "command center," the scent of cherry licorice and Scotch wafting toward him. For a grown man, his brother had the strangest eating habits—only exacerbated when he worked—and Liam was amused to find himself reaching for another red twist.

"Why am I eating this?"

"Because it's sugar and it's brain food and it's good."

"It's midnight and I've already eaten. Filet mignon, as a matter of fact."

"Consider this slumming and come here and look at this." Campbell waved at the computer screen.

Liam stared at a screen of images, not exactly sure what Campbell wanted him to see. "So?"

"These are all the video feeds around Isabella's lab before the explosion."

"Right."

"I've run them back a week prior to the events and nothing's popped. Nothing suspicious beyond what appears to be a few corner drug deals. No one coming or going with anything beyond a briefcase in their hands. Which means no one carried any large incendiary devices into the building."

"We were inside a science lab. It's not like it's hard to find any number of flammable items."

Campbell dragged another piece of candy from the bag. "Which is also why I've run every feed inside or outside the actual lab building for a week as well. No one was in there when the fire started beyond you and Isabella."

"So how the hell did a fire start if no one set it?"

"It was triggered."

"How? You need a spark. Someone to light the fuse."

"You and Isabella lit the fuse."

Liam struggled to process his brother's theories. "We dug through computer files. How could someone have started a fire the size of what we experienced remotely? How would they even know it was us?"

"It's the personal again. Which is why I've been running those files you gave me from the lab."

"And?"

"And someone's planned this for a long time. They were waiting for those files to be triggered. Who knows how long ago the sequence of events to start the fire was set into motion."

"So what did you find in the files?"

"The science is beyond my rather expansive skills so I asked an old college friend a few questions about genetic sequencing. He gave me a few programming ideas and I set this baby to run before we left." Campbell flipped screens and a wall of ones and zeroes lit the face of his machine. "There's no doubt about it. The guy she used to work for. The one who's supposed to be dead. He's not."

Liam knew there were things in this world he didn't understand. He'd always known it but in the time since they'd established the firm he'd experienced more than he ever could have imagined. The depths of human curiosity and achievement were as deeply trenched as human depravity and immorality.

Humans figured stuff out. Fixed things. Learned things.

But if Isabella's work had really healed her old mentor, they were talking about an entirely different level of science.

Why would anyone want to hold that back? The test subjects alone should be screaming from the rooftops what her work had done for them. And if Stephenson had the sort of money that could build scientific labs, he should be the first to sing his mentee's praises.

So why was he hiding?

"I need you to run everything you can find on Daniel Stephenson."

"The not-so-dead guy."

"Yep."

"Kenzi ran him once," Campbell said. "Found his bank accounts, school records, that sort of thing."

"Let's run him again. He's got every reason to be on top of the world yet he's hidden away, not even letting Isabella know he's alive. Something's not right."

A light knock at the door caught their attention and Liam looked up to see Isabella standing in the door. Awareness skipped down his spine, tightening his skin with that sharp flick of desire.

"I'll get started on the data in a few minutes." Campbell cleared his throat. "After I go check on my very tipsy wife who I assume, after an hour downstairs with Isabella and our sisters, is now even more tipsy."

His brother had long legs and speed on his side but Liam had never seen Campbell clear a room quite that fast.

"Where's the fire?" Isabella's smile was lopsided as the echo of Campbell's footsteps faded down the hall. "Which is probably a poor choice of words considering what we experienced yesterday."

"Was that really only yesterday?"

She nodded, the smile fading. "Hard to believe, but yes."

"Campbell was walking me through what he's found so far on the data we downloaded for him and the information he's managed to glean from hacking the lab's backup server."

"Which means he's conclusively proven Daniel's risen from the dead?"

"Pretty much."

"Did he find anything else out?"

Liam snuck a glance at another one of Campbell's licorice ropes in a vain attempt to keep his gaze off Isabella's mouth. "Nothing conclusive yet. We'll all look at it in the morning with fresh eyes."

"Why are you avoiding me?"

"What?"

"You're up here. Hiding. I'd like to know why."

Liam knew he'd never met anyone like Isabella. She was as genuine as she was direct and he found himself unable to resist her.

Why *was* he hiding?

Even as he asked himself the question, he refused to let her see his confusion. "I'm not hiding."

"At midnight? After several drinks and a fun night out. After pulling me close against your body when we danced? Sorry if I call b.s. on your answer."

"You're still in danger."

"I know. Which is also why I know I want to make love to you. Tonight. Tomorrow. For as long as you'll have me or until I end up dead from this nameless, faceless threat determined to ruin my life."

He winced at the frank, direct language, before he heard the slight quaver underneath the bold words.

Was that fear? Or was he projecting his own feelings onto hers? "I'm not that guy, Isabella."

"What guy?" Lines furrowed her brow and all he could think was that the puzzled lines were endearing. Human. And sexy as hell.

Why did he keep fighting their attraction? Especially if he thought frown lines were the height of sexy.

"The guy who can make love to you and stay afterward."

"Oh." She nodded, the lines fading away. "I can see how that would be difficult for you."

"You do?"

"Of course. You're a good man. And honorable. And you only sleep with women who don't expect more."

He'd slept with several women who had expected more—especially if more came from his bank account—but he opted to keep that to himself. "You have a right to those expectations."

"I know."

"So you understand what I'm saying?"

"Yes."

"So we'll leave things status quo."

"No."

What?

"Isabella—" He broke off as she moved up into his arms. Her lips pressed to the open throat of his shirt where his tie lay open, along with his top button.

"What?" Her breath was hot against his throat and in that moment he knew he'd never felt anything more erotic.

Or more devastating to his efforts to stay strong and deny her.

"We can't do this."

"Then I'll go back to my room and do it all by myself, Liam Steele. I want you and whether it's in my head or physically with you, I'm making love to you tonight."

The images that sprang to life underneath her words were nearly his undoing. "You do that? I…I mean…" He snapped his lips shut at the evidence he was stammering.

"Yes, I do do that. But I'd prefer not to this evening." She took a step back, her cheeks a delightful pink while mischief rode her green eyes into dark, glittering emeralds. "So what's it going to be, Liam?"

Isabella fought the personal shock rattling around the back of her mind at her actions.

And at her words!

She *never* discussed things like that. So what had prompted her now? And why did it feel as natural as breathing?

If it were possible, she could practically hear the thoughts jamming through his mind right now. Desire and want fighting some misguided sense of honor and nobility. It would have been sweet if she didn't want him so badly.

His big hands covered hers and he shifted his head so that he was looking down at her, out of the range of her seeking lips. "I don't want to hurt you."

"Then just be with me. Love me tonight. That's all I ask." She waited—barely a heartbeat—before she added, "I promise."

And then she saw the change. Saw the exact moment his need won out over his self-control. Knew the moment when he finally saw her as a woman.

The hands holding hers tightened before he pulled her close, his lips dropping to hers in a rush. With swift, urgent demands, he used his lips and tongue to consume her.

Overjoyed, Isabella went with the moment, wrapping herself around his body like a second skin.

Long, heated moments passed, the only sounds in the room their heavy breaths as they fought a battle toward pleasure and mutual gratification and ecstasy.

His hands closed over her breasts and she pressed herself into his touch. The thin material of her dress couldn't hide her tight, pointed nipples and his thumbs found them with unerring precision, teasing the hard points until she ached with wanting. Pleasure spread, deep and low in her belly, and she shifted on restless legs as her hands fisted the material at his waist.

One of his shirt studs hit the floor, stilling both of them.

"We can't do this here."

Still wrapped up in the moment of finally having his hands on her body it took Isabella a moment to catch up. "What?"

"Here." Irritation narrowed his eyes while a dull pink crept into his cheeks. "You deserve a bed. And something more romantic than getting pawed at in my brother's office."

"I liked being pawed at." The words spilled out and she couldn't hide the grin that went with them.

"It's not very romantic."

"On the contrary." She stood on tiptoes and pressed a kiss to his lips. "Every woman dreams of being ravished."

One eyebrow quirked above that devastating blue and she saw an answering smile. "Ravished?"

"Absolutely."

"I still think you deserve better than my brother's geek kingdom. Come on." He snagged her hand and they crept through the door like they were going thieving for the good silver.

She nearly ran into his back when he stopped short. "What is it?"

While she had come to like his family quite a bit over the last few days, the last thing she wanted was to be discovered. Or grilled, in the event Rowan found them.

"I want to avoid my family."

"That makes two of us."

He turned around, the humor fading from his eyes. "Did something happen?"

"Hardly. I just don't want to get waylaid having to make small talk. Your family's sort of big. And they talk a lot."

Loud peals of laughter echoed from the first floor and Isabella figured they needed to make a run for it. "There's your chance. It's loud and no one's paying attention. Move!"

"Aye aye."

He kept his hand firmly wrapped around hers and dragged her toward the staircase.

She raced behind him, joy settling in her chest in carefree abandon.

Liam Steele had her in hand. And in a matter of minutes, she was going to be making love with him.

A heavy, throbbing mix of heat and humor flooded his veins as Liam took the stairs toward the third floor, Isabella's slender fingers trapped with his in a tight grip.

Had he ever raced through the house with a woman before?

If he were honest, the fact it hadn't happened hadn't been for lack of trying. He'd have happily snuck Genevieve Kincaid up to his room their senior year of high school when they were chemistry lab partners, studying for finals in the family kitchen.

But other than a few misguided attempts that May afternoon, he hadn't actually ever succeeded in sneaking a woman up to his room in his own home.

Why did that only add to the experience?

And had he ever felt so carefree with a woman before? The night he met Isabella in his grandparents' study—rain-soaked and scared—he'd have never pictured the mousy scientist as a woman who made love with equal parts laughter and mind-numbing sensuality.

Yet here they were and he couldn't wipe the damn grin off his face.

He pulled her close as they cleared the landing, then rushed her in front of him down the hall toward his room. They ran in and he closed the door, pulling her against his body the moment the door clicked closed.

Ravenous, he devoured her mouth once more, the thirty-second run upstairs like a lifetime away from her. Isabella met him in the moment, her hands roaming over his shoulders and back as she pulled him close. Restless, her hands shifted toward his chest and he felt the heat of her palms through his shirt like a brand.

"You're wearing too much." The words came out on a growl and in that moment he knew just how far gone he was. Their light, carefree moments had shifted into something darker and more serious, the demands of both their bodies ratcheting up the urgency of the moment.

His hands drifted toward the zipper he'd noticed at the back of her gown earlier and he slid the material open until it hung loose over her shoulders. He dragged on the silk, mesmerized as it slid down her slender arms, over her full breasts and then caught on her hips before it pooled at her feet.

The ripe fullness he'd only felt in his palms was on display as she stood before him in nothing but her bra and panties. His breath caught as his gaze traveled over her skin and it was with renewed reverence that he ran a finger down the full slope, before caressing the underside of her full flesh.

Her head fell back, exposing the long column of her throat and Liam took the opportunity to press his tongue there, the heavy throb of her pulse beating a heavy tempo under his lips.

It was desire, raw and wonderful, delightful and wicked.

In that heavy throb he felt it. And in the soft moan that rose up from her lips he heard it. And in the light flush of her skin he saw it.

And knew that he wanted this woman in a way he'd never wanted another.

Isabella finished the work she'd started in the office, dragging the studs from his shirt until it hung loose over his chest. With tantalizing efficiency, her fingers drifted lower, unfastening his slacks and slipped inside the opening. He sucked in a hard breath as her hand brushed against his rigid flesh, then nearly lost his mind as she slipped inside his briefs.

"Isabella." Her name fell from his lips in a heavy moan as her clever fingers worked his flesh from base to tip and back again.

"You were saying?"

He fought to keep his eyes open—fought to keep any semblance of control over the moment—but couldn't stop himself from pushing into her palm as she worked his erection.

Possession.

The thought flitted through his mind along with a thousand other fragments as she pushed his body to its breaking point.

She'd possessed him. Bewitched him. Damn, but the

woman owned him. She played his body like an instrument and he couldn't grasp on to anything coherent.

It was only when he felt his control begin to slip that reality came flooding back. He gripped her hand, stilling her movement.

"Not yet." He gritted his teeth. "Together. We do this together."

The delight that shone up at him in her dark green gaze was all the encouragement he needed and he dragged her toward the bed. He stopped to rid himself of his clothes, the slamming of his heart and his painfully tight body leaving his movements awkward and needy as he fumbled to remove every last stitch of clothing. He nearly forgot the condom in his wallet but remembered it at the last minute before his pants fell to the floor.

Dropping the small foil packet on the end table, he rejoined her on the bed. Her arms wrapped around him as he came down beside her, the silk of her bra and panties a tantalizing barrier between them. "I think you're still wearing too much."

Before she could answer, he flicked open the front clasp of her bra, her breasts spilling from the material. He slid the straps off her arms, then kept moving toward the thin lace at her core.

If the moments before had filled him with a desperate need, the moment his hands slid that scrap of material down her thighs gave him the blinding urge to brand her as his own.

"You're beautiful."

"Then love me. Please."

He didn't wait another moment, but kissed his way up her body, over her belly, over the full beauty of her breasts, along the slim line of her collarbone before pressing his lips once more to hers. With swift movements, he snagged the condom from the end table and sheathed himself in moments.

Isabella's hair spread out around her on the pillow and despite the urgent demands of both their bodies, he gave himself a moment to look his fill.

Her gaze was direct as always, even with a thick haze of passion clouding her irises.

And then there were no words. No more questions. No more moments of waiting.

He slid between her thighs and she guided him deeper, the moment bright and alive as he began to move. He set a hard, heavy rhythm she met thrust for thrust and, just as before, he fought to hold on.

Fought to prolong the pleasure for them both.

It was only when a hard cry left her lips, in counterpoint to the heavy clench of her inner muscles around him that he pushed forward, driving them both toward their moment of fulfillment.

"Liam!" His name echoed in his ear, the sweetest sound as it fell from her lips.

And as he followed her into the abyss he knew the night would change him forever.

Chapter 16

Liam lay in the dark in the bedroom of his childhood, Isabella wrapped in his arms, and wondered how he'd ended up back where he'd started. Of course, his teenage self hadn't ever had such an enticing and enchanting bed partner, but putting that one difference aside, it was fascinating how he'd truly come full circle.

Isabella's observations over the last few days hadn't been off the mark, either. He *had* distanced himself from his family. The transformation had been slow, but if he were honest with himself, it was deliberate. A calculated effort to keep his loved ones at arm's length. To keep the memories at bay.

And avoid the pain of making new ones.

No one knew him like his family. And no one but his siblings knew of the private moments they'd shared with their parents. Family movie nights. Vacations. And an endless string of days filled with the love and support of two people who embraced the uniqueness of each of their children, celebrating the individual each was destined to become.

He knew full well he'd come a bit close to romanticizing them over the years, but he also knew the Steele family had shared something special until that lone day a car speeding too fast had collided with his parents'. In moments their anniversary celebration had turned deadly and nothing had been the same since.

Isabella shifted in his arms, her fingers clenching around his hand where they still lay linked in the dark.

Had he done the right thing, making love to her? Even as he knew it would have taken a supreme act of willpower to walk away from a willing woman. He knew he should feel something other than bone-deep satisfaction at making love to Isabella but he couldn't conjure the effort. Hell, he could barely conjure the energy to keep breathing.

But he still would have expected to feel something along the lines of regret. Maybe a bit of remorse at taking advantage of her vulnerability despite her protests to the contrary. Or acknowledging there wasn't a future for them together. Or maybe even the slightest family embarrassment he was carrying on with the granddaughter of a dear family friend.

But no, all he could summon up was a deep-seated satisfaction like nothing he'd ever known. Which, if he were being honest, should be a bit scary.

Only it wasn't.

Isabella was a study in contrasts. Although reserved on the outside, she was passion and fire and warmth on the inside. Something he'd already seen in her work and in her willingness to defend her ideas.

And now he knew that same wellspring of passion existed in her personal life as well.

So why weren't any of the usual alarm bells sounding when a woman clung too tight wrapping around his neck like a noose?

Maybe because you're the one clinging.

That insistent voice rose up, loud and clear, breaking through his smug thoughts.

A dull panic layered over the smug, forcing him to acknowledge the truth.

He was in this position because he wanted to be. And when she began to move her backside against his increasingly interested front, his body once again dragged him toward the generous warmth and passion that was Isabella.

"You're voracious." Her words floated toward him, husky with sleep, as she wiggled her backside against his fully *awake* body.

He nuzzled the warm skin of her neck and abstractly wondered why those urgent thoughts about getting away and leaving her to her much-needed rest began to fade as if they'd never been. He pushed aside the heavy mass of hair that floated over her neck and shoulders before pressing a line of kisses down her neck, whispering along the way. "Vixen."

"Thank you."

Liam didn't miss the self-satisfied undertones in her comment but was fast coming not to care as the moment—and the innately responsive woman in his arms—demanded his full attention.

She turned onto her back, the bounty of her body displayed for optimal view and he ran a lazy finger down her throat, over her chest before tracing slow circles over her breast. Her nipple puckered under his ministrations and he bent his head, taking it between his lips as she arched into his mouth.

With aching slowness he shifted, pressing his lips to

her other nipple, satisfied as it grew harder on his tongue. Even more satisfied when he heard her soft moans. Opportunistic and greedy, he kept up his ministrations as his hand slipped between her thighs, his fingers sliding through the warm wetness he found there.

She was such a responsive partner, as in the moment as he was, and he found it only increased the pleasure they shared. As the night cocooned them both, he made love to her once again.

And fought the suddenly real fear he might not ever want to let her go.

Daniel Stephenson limped into his office and closed the door, flipping the lock behind him. His rambling brownstone on the far north end of Riverside Drive had been in his family for several generations and he took some small comfort in the quiet of the late hour and the scent of leather and old books that surrounded him.

It hadn't been easy to keep his home, but it was surprising what money and some well-placed bribes with less-than-savory practitioners of the law could buy.

Ignoring all he'd done to get here, he focused once more on his office.

The comfort was minimal, but it was *something*. Something to get his mind off what he'd allowed to happen. At the reminder of his crimes, his heart slammed in his chest and he couldn't get the image of his old lab exploding into flames out of his mind.

Hell, it had been nearly two days and he still couldn't calm down. Isabella could have died. Had their plan worked, she would have died.

And it would have been at his hands.

Edward may have rigged the explosives, but Daniel had

fully endorsed the action and no amount of excuse could change that.

What had he done?

When Edward had first suggested they needed to deal with Isabella and keep her from going public with her findings he had agreed. Her research had far-reaching implications and letting it get into the hands of government officials meant it would be far too difficult to keep the more experimental aspects a secret. He and Edward might live off the grid, but they still interacted with others for their supplies. He'd wrapped their identities in secrecy and funded them with offshore accounts, but they couldn't become fully invisible.

Nor could any amount of money fully erase the lives they'd expended to get here.

He had sinned. Had believed in Edward's promise of a pain-free life and had accepted the temptation. He might have regained his life, but at what price to his soul?

He flipped through a series of photos he kept on his tablet. Images through the years of his lab team, captured agelessly in pixels.

Just like Isabella's research.

Her work was done, and nothing could put the genie back in the bottle. Even if he found a way to destroy every last lab note, the knowledge now existed.

And if Isabella had figured out how to reverse biology, it was only a matter of time until someone else did, too.

Someone who might not have her compassion. Or smarts. Or innate warmth.

For all his bravado, that was what Edward fundamentally didn't understand.

Isabella's research might have saved their lives, but several experimental branches of the world's governments, not to mention a handful of well-funded, enterprising terrorist organizations—were playing a much bigger game.

Edward might think him weak, but he preferred to think of himself as cautious. And he had a very real sense of what he stood to lose.

It was his own fault he'd taken so long to realize it.

Isabella Magnini had been like a daughter to him. She'd been the gift he'd never biologically have on his own and he'd let his own selfish desires get in the way of that.

His hand shook as he removed the notes he kept locked away in his top drawer. His meeting with Bradley was in less than twelve hours and he wanted to check once more that he'd covered all his bases. That he'd ensured the calculations were as precise as he knew them to be.

At the core of his notes was a copy of Isabella's work, then his own calculations layered over top. She'd unlocked the genome, but he'd further modified it as part of his treatment. Like a skyscraper rising to the sky, she'd built the frame but he'd ensured it far exceeded expectations, dazzling the senses in the sheer magnitude of the accomplishment.

His last, great gift.

"What did Campbell find last night?"

"Find where?" Liam mumbled the words around a mouthful of toothpaste from the bathroom attached to his room.

"I overheard him saying he'd run the lab files. What did he find?" Isabella let the sheet fall away as she stood up from Liam's bed and delighted in the sweet ache of her muscles.

The night before had been exquisite. She'd spent the past ten minutes turning other adjectives over in her mind—

magnificent, exhilarating, phenomenal—and while good, none had quite the ring of exquisite.

Had she ever felt this *good* before?

Despite the aches—or maybe because of them—she was a mix of supremely satisfied and shockingly gratified. She'd gone after what she wanted and the results had been…well, phenomenally exquisite.

Liam's voice pulled her from her self-induced stupor as she recounted several moments from the previous evening. "He tried to explain it to me but whenever my brother starts speaking geek I have a hard time keeping—"

Liam's words faded as he stepped through the doorway, his gaze roaming over her nakedness with lazy appreciation.

"Hi." The word came out on a breathy whisper, a sudden case of nerves filling her stomach.

It was one thing to do the things they'd done. It was an entirely different thing to now stand naked before him while he was fully dressed—natty in a button-down shirt rolled at the sleeves, black slacks and a pair of Italian loafers—while she stood exposed in her birthday suit.

"You were saying?"

"I can't remember."

"Campbell. Speaking gee—" The words were muffled by his speed and the sudden sensation of being swept off her feet and wrestled backward to the bed.

All while wrapped in those strong arms.

The lingering taste of toothpaste hovered on her tongue as he shifted focus, his mouth tracing a path down her throat and toward her breasts. The mint on his tongue added a new dimension to the sensation and she felt the cool slide of his mouth over her breast.

"Liam." His name came out on a cross between a giggle

and a moan as he focused on his task. When he didn't stop she tried again, this time more forceful. "Liam!"

"What?" He looked up, a thoroughly wicked gleam in his eyes.

"We have to get downstairs."

"It can wait."

"It's after eight. I already heard the house up and about while you were in the shower."

"No way. Everyone in this house is hung over." He resumed his ministrations and made it awfully hard for her to focus.

She tried pressing on the solid heft of his shoulders, even though she'd prefer nothing more than to stay this way all day. "Then they're rumbling around with headaches."

He sighed and lifted his head once more. "I'm not doing a very good job of convincing you to stay here."

"We have to look at what Campbell found." She scrambled out from underneath him and decided to go for broke. The sloe-eyed look in his eyes had to work in her favor. "And I have to get into my apartment and get a few things."

"No way."

So much for calculating the enticements of her naked form. "I need to. All my things are there. I'm still set to sit down with the reporters in little less than a week. I need to prepare."

"Then I'll go over with the guys and get what you need."

"You can't get what I need. You won't find any of it."

"I'll call you from there."

"I need to get into my things. You can go with me. I'm fine if you bring everyone in the house as well as a few of Jack's mercenaries. But I need to get my things." She sighed and worried a section of bedsheet between her fingers. "I need to see my home."

"It's too dangerous." The mouth that had been artfully

kissing her mere moments before was now set in a hard, immovable line.

"I don't want to argue with you about this but I need to get to my things."

"Liam! Open up." Kensington's voice echoed from the other side, her orders punctuated by several rapt knocks on the door.

"Later, Kenz!"

"It's important. I already know Isabella's in there. There's a robe on the back of the bathroom door. Put it on and then let me in."

Isabella fought the momentary mortification at Liam's heavy head shake and his glance toward the ceiling as if praying for divine intervention. Also recognizing his sister meant business, Isabella scrambled for the bathroom and found the robe in the exact place Kensington had described.

"What do you want?" Liam's terse words were met with the clip of efficient heels on hardwood.

"We've got a problem."

"We have several at the moment."

Isabella fought the urge to stick her tongue out at Liam and his dry observation as she walked back into the room. "What's going on?"

"Campbell and I have been keeping tabs on anything and anyone we can possibly associate with you."

Hard, choppy waves filled her stomach and Isabella laid a hand on the wall for extra support. "Who else was hurt?"

"Bradley Armstrong."

"The editor?"

"Yes. He and his wife were found murdered in their home this morning."

A terrifying sense of cold began to spread from the center of her body out, almost as if the roiling waves in her stomach had sprouted ice caps. "No."

"I'm sorry, really I am." Kensington kept talking but Isabella felt as if she were listening to the words from a great distance as the room rushed around her, spinning faster and faster.

Bradley was dead? Along with his wife?

She'd only met him a handful of times, but he'd always impressed her with his good-natured attitude and ready excitement for science.

And his clothes.

"He wore a bow tie." At Liam and Kensington's matched confusion, Isabella added. "Every day to work. Someone always remarked on it when his name was mentioned."

"Come on. Let's sit down." She didn't want to be handled—didn't want to show weakness at the news someone had died because of her—but Liam's strong hand clasped around hers was too big an enticement.

"How did it happen?"

Kensington pulled a slender cane chair from a small writing desk in the corner of the room and sat down opposite them. "Jack's been running down everyone he knows in the NYPD to see if he can get some answers. So far it appears routine on the surface to the cops but…"

"But we know it's about me."

Kensington nodded. "That's what we believe."

Everything they'd learned in the last week cycled through her mind, thoughts flashing in a morass of images. The lab. The files. Daniel.

Daniel.

Everything they'd learned pointed toward Daniel at the center of it all, but she *knew* him. Had worked with him.

Was it possible she'd spent over a decade of her life

with a man capable of murdering a husband and wife in cold blood?

When the situation had centered on some sort of misguided revenge against her it was hard to believe, but to think him capable of a cold-blooded murder of two people?

It didn't add up.

"Let me get dressed and then I'd like to see what Campbell's discovered on the program files he's been running."

"I'll have him fire everything up." Kensington stood, her gaze shooting toward Liam as if she weighed her words before she spoke. "We're committed to your safety but I think we need to bring the police in. This job has gone beyond protection detail or basic investigation."

"Hell no." Liam stood and went toe to toe with his sister. "We promised her we'd protect her and that's what we're going to do."

"I'm not suggesting otherwise, but it's time we involved the police."

"Like you and Jack involved the damn police while you traipsed through the Italian countryside?"

"This is different."

"That's a load of crap and you know it."

"We all discussed it and it's for Isabella's safety. The police need to know what they're up against and we'll get a lot further if we help them figure out how to solve the murder of the Armstrongs."

Isabella stood, unwilling to sit on the sidelines and watch the emotional Ping-Pong match play out before her. She was done with sitting on the side. Done being a casual observer or allowing others to take care of her.

She needed to see this through.

"Of course I'll talk to the police. They deserve to know as much as I can tell them."

"We can keep you safe." Liam turned from his sister,

his ire and focus now fully tuned toward Isabella. "That's what you hired us to do and damn it, I'm seeing this job through."

"Then work with me. Take me to my apartment so I can get my things. My notes. All the pieces that will help the police catch whoever is doing this."

Kensington slipped out, leaving the two of them to their argument and Isabella was grateful for the privacy.

The blazing ire that stamped itself all over his face wasn't going to be assuaged by simple platitudes or her pleading that she needed to step in and handle this. But she'd make Liam see reason.

It was the only way she could live with herself.

"Why are you so against bringing the police in?"

Isabella's question was simple but Liam knew there were no simple answers. Just like he knew he was being irrational to want to keep the police at bay. "They're outsiders and they'll make you vulnerable. You don't know who's behind this. Who's on their payroll. Here we control the situation."

Isabella laughed, low and hollow. "Right. Because we've been so in control up to now."

"We'll crack this. Campbell's been working the technology end and we'll get this figured out."

"And how many more people have to get hurt? We were lucky the other day the lab was so empty or innocents could have been killed. And now Bradley and his wife? He was a good man. A good journalist and someone who believed in science and he was killed for it. Over *my* work." The anger that blazed across her face, heating her cheeks a vivid pink, vanished as she dropped onto the edge of the bed. "And all because of my vanity."

"This isn't about vanity or anything else you might

want to blame on yourself. This is about someone with a grudge and an appetite for destruction."

"But I sit at the center. My work and what I was so insistent on proving. It's my father all over again."

"Enough! You are not your father!" Anger shot the words from his lips like bullets. He saw Isabella's eyes widen in shock but he pressed on. "You didn't go into your work with ill intentions. Or to sell your knowledge to the highest bidder. You've worked to figure out how to make life better for people."

He slowed, the anger morphing into the very real acknowledgment that she was special. Different. And her gifts made the world a better place. "I know I didn't see any of that at first. I was harder on you than anyone and I was prepared to act as judge and jury before hearing your side."

Silent tears slid down her cheeks, the only acknowledgment of his tirade. He sat and pulled her into his arms, her slender shoulders shuddering with the pressure of her grief.

"You can say it's not the same. Can say I'm not to blame like he was, but my father's work killed innocents. He has that blood on his hands as he rots in some military prison."

He held her hands in both of his, willing her to understand. "Your hands are clean. And through your work, people will be healed. You can't even begin to think it's the same thing." He leaned down and pressed his lips to each of her palms. "It will never be the same."

Chapter 17

Liam resolutely ignored the itch at the back of his neck as he and Jack flanked Isabella up the front stoop of her apartment building. Jack had already dispatched one of his men who'd sent back the all-clear, and a second stood out front standing guard with Finn.

"We get in and get out."

Isabella's sigh was loud and long and he took it as an irritatingly good sign. "You've said that about eight hundred times since we started this trek a half hour ago."

"Then let me say it eight hundred and one. In and out."

When all he got for his troubles was an eye roll, Liam had to tamp down on the heavy bark of laughter that welled in his throat. Where was the mousy woman who'd stood on his grandparents' front porch in the pouring rain?

Had she ever really existed? Or was it simply another facet of a personality he was endlessly intrigued by?

The mercenary who'd gone into the apartment first

stood by the open door and Isabella practically ran down the hall toward the entryway.

Jack's low laughter had Liam turning around after watching her disappear through the door. "What?"

"I think this family incapable of spending time with mild-mannered individuals. You know, maybe you could have brought home a woman who would prefer to spend her day quietly knitting sweaters."

"I didn't bring her home."

Jack's cocky grin never faded. "Could have fooled me."

Liam ignored the not-so-subtle poke and attempted to deflect. "My grandmother knits a mean sweater."

Jack's grin flashed over to good-natured. "So noted."

He thought about the real question that lurked underneath Jack's ribbing. The Steele family did nothing easy. Did it make for a more exciting life? Living along the edge of danger and making decisions on the fly.

He'd always thought so, but observing his siblings over the last few days, coupled with the time with Isabella, and he'd been forced to acknowledge the truth. His seemingly full life had quite a few empty spaces.

And if he wasn't careful, those spaces were likely to swallow him up.

This job was the perfect example. Here was a change from his normal assignments and it wasn't until faced with a helping hand and friendly camaraderie from his future brother-in-law that Liam had even realized it. He lived life on the fringes, assessing motives and threats on a daily basis. It jaded a man, no matter how hard one fought it and somewhere deep inside he knew that.

Had known it for a long time, allowing a small piece of his soul to wither away as he shut out any sense of entanglement. With women, certainly, but with his family as well.

"She's rather amazing. A lot more goes on in that brilliant head of hers than I think even she realizes." Liam keyed back into Jack's words, the man's dark gaze expectant.

"She's terrifyingly brilliant."

"She's handled this situation like a champ. Scared, but pushing forward no matter the cost."

"Do you think we can stop this?" For the first time, Liam gave voice to the small kernel of unease that had dogged him from the start of the job.

Maybe it was Jack's long-term position in the world of the security trade or his increasing status as a trusted family member, but Liam knew he didn't really care. All he did care about was someone who could back up the raw screaming itch in his gut that kept warning him something was just out of reach.

Lurking.

"We can stop it. But it's not easy. Whoever is behind this has some skills. The fire at the lab, triggered remotely?" Jack let out a heavy exhale as they approached Isabella's open door. "The person behind this has the chops. And they've got an ax to grind at the same time."

"Her mentor?" The thought had been rolling for a while and no matter how many times he tried it on for size, Liam felt like something didn't fit.

"He's the most likely."

"It doesn't play for me. I get that the facts add up, but it just doesn't play."

"For what it's worth," Jack slapped him on the back before stepping through the door, "it doesn't play for me either. So we'll keep digging until something starts to whistle a tune."

It was funny, Liam though as he crossed the threshold. He'd never gone looking for a partner before, always preferring to work jobs on his own. Quite without realizing it, he'd managed to acquire seven.

Pushing his musings from his mind, he crossed the threshold of Isabella's apartment, immediately struck by the warmth inside the small space. Colorful throw pillows. A bright red couch that dominated the living room. Vivid slashes of primary tones on strategically placed paintings dotting the walls.

For a woman who chose quiet tones in her wardrobe, her home was the embodiment of the opposite.

The subject of his thoughts barreled out of her bedroom, a lock box in hand.

"You keep your notes in there?"

"Here, there and everywhere. I've got several drives in here I've culled together over time." She worked the lock, flipping open the lid to reveal several neatly stacked portable hard drives.

"This is all your work?" Jack's voice was incredulous as he pointed toward the box, lifting one of the small drives roughly the size of a deck of cards. "It all fits in here?"

"This is part of my work." A small smile flitted around her lips and Liam thought it was yet another testament to her spirit that she found a way to still smile and make jokes. "The majority of the calculations took place on a super computer and I wouldn't keep the core of my research in a lockbox I bought at the drug store."

"Are the final calculations in here?" Liam took the hard drive from Jack, and turned it over to look at it before placing it back in the box.

"Nope." She patted her chest, then slipped a small thumb drive from her bra. "I've got it right here."

Edward walked through the still-smoldering ruins of the lab, his building security badge clipped to his jeans.

No one had stopped him, but he had prepared his story all the same.

He was an administrator who had a responsibility to explain the damages to their benefactors. If that didn't work he figured he'd start boring whoever asked him to leave with stories of academic fundraising and then hightail it out of there.

But no one had stopped him. No one even seemed to care.

It was that last piece that had angered him more than he'd expected. The lab was the source of a major scientific discovery and the slobs who walked up and down the surrounding streets were clueless.

Freaking clueless.

He picked his way clear of the debris and entered the building that stood opposite. The two buildings were linked by an underground tunnel and if he'd managed the fire correctly, the passageway would be untouched.

Which made it perfect for what he had in mind.

True to her word, Isabella had packed quickly but refused to head back to the living room just yet. By her guesstimate, she had about fifteen minutes before Liam got so antsy it overtook him and he ushered her from the building.

In the meantime, she had to make as much use of the time as she could. She *knew* someone had been here— knew it to the very depths of her being—and she needed a bit of time to figure out who it was.

Daniel had only visited her apartment a couple of times, his lack of mobility and increasing dependence on a wheelchair making it hard for him to get around much. But even without a detailed layout of her place it wouldn't be hard for him to know where to look. They'd talked over the years how to keep their files secure, especially from possible natural disaster. It was Daniel who had suggested she keep her electronics in a lock box. And the fact hers had lain untouched at the back of her closet indicated he wasn't the one rooting through her home.

Or so she hoped.

It was her working hypothesis, but she knew there was still a sizeable margin of error as well. Her apartment had been invaded, but was done with a neat precision not many could pull off.

"Hey."

She whirled around to see Liam standing in her doorway. "I need a few more minutes."

"I'm not rushing you out."

The busy morning had pushed their night together to the back of her mind but the time with Liam was hardly forgotten. Instead, she knew those memories would be like a chocolate she'd take out and unwrap later when she could savor it.

A rather effective attempt at compartmentalizing—or so she thought—until she caught sight of him, standing about a foot from her bed, all tall and rangy and gorgeous.

He'd traded the morning's slacks for a sturdy pair of faded jeans and the casual look was even more attractive than the pressed black wool.

Everything about the man was attractive. Mind-numbingly so.

"Did you find anything?"

"No, but I know someone's been in here."

"Just like your hotel in London?" Where the average person might have made a joke or offered up a smirk at her precise behavior, his question held no censure or judgment.

Just fact.

It was so simple, really. Elegant. And in that moment she knew the utter simplicity and the raw power of love.

"You believe in me."

"Of course I do."

"I mean, all of me. Even the goofy parts."

His jaw hardened and his eyebrows narrowed over those incredible blue eyes. "There's nothing goofy about you."

"There's plenty goofy about me." Without waiting or second-guessing herself or wondering if she should or shouldn't, she moved up against him and placed her hands on his cheeks, pulling him down for a kiss. "And I love you for accepting me anyway."

If he was surprised at her declaration, he didn't show it as he wrapped her firmly in his arms, deepening what she began. The thick, heavy beats of his heart thudded under the palm she moved to rest against his chest. She knew her own pulse beat as rapidly and knew it was for him.

All for Liam.

"My wife's ordering pizza. Isabella, what do you want on yours?" Finn's voice echoed from the backseat as they headed uptown toward the Steele brownstone. Liam knew he'd breathe easier once they were back at the house but he was also relieved the morning had gone smoothly.

Jack's mercenaries were in the car in front of them, keeping watch and clearing the way while he, Isabella, Jack and Finn rode in the Mercedes-Benz. They also carried Isabella's research in the trunk, along with a new bag of clean clothes.

Although he'd been apprehensive about the trip, one glance at her and he knew she was happier. She seemed lighter, somehow. And more at ease since she'd stood in her own home and confirmed for herself it still looked basically as she'd left it.

Oh. And she loved him.

Liam was still digesting that news, oddly surprised to find her declaration didn't scare him as badly as he imagined it would.

What he was having a harder time defining was how he felt in return. He was intrigued by Isabella, far more then he should be. He'd known making love to her would change things—for both of them—and he'd moved ahead anyway.

But intrigue and respect and a deeper attraction that he couldn't quite get a handle on didn't change the fact the two of them led different lives. Other than the first few months when they'd started House of Steele, he barely even saw his siblings, let alone anyone else.

His life wasn't in one place. Instead, it was full of packed suitcases that were ready to go at a moment's notice and adventures all over the world. That was his choice and nothing was going to make him different.

He simply wasn't *that guy.*

The one who'd settle down in one place, have a family and be content to sit still.

"Mushrooms and olives." Isabella's voice—and the loud honking from a weaving taxi beside him—pulled Liam from his musings.

"Don't I get asked what I want on my pizza?"

"Rowan knows you want a pepperoni and sausage with extra cheese," Finn said, switching his phone to speaker mode.

Liam turned onto their street, a few avenue blocks away from the house. "Ro, make sure you order two. Campbell will have half of it gone before we get the other pizza boxes open."

"I already did. And we're going to be lucky to see Campbell. He's been swearing at his computer all morning."

"There's no amount of ones and zeroes on earth that will keep that man from piz—"

Liam forgot what he was saying as the world exploded in a wash of vivid color and black smoke before his eyes. The car in front of them carrying Jack's men blew up and he slammed on his brakes to narrowly avoid missing them and the fiery debris that winged its way toward the windshield.

Isabella's screams filled his ears and he fought to keep his focus through the utter chaos that gripped them. Jack and Finn both hollered from the backseat but he couldn't hear anything over the din and the noise and the shock.

He managed to put the car in Park, then reached for Isabella's seat belt, brushing aside her hands where she struggled with the lock. He felt the hard snap as her belt came loose, then undid his own.

Jack and Finn hollered instructions from the backseat as they each escaped out their respective doors and within moments they both had the front doors open. Liam felt Finn's hands on him, dragging him from the car. He yelled, unable to hear his own voice, and fought to stay put and make sure Jack pulled Isabella to safety.

His siblings poured from the front of the house, along with the additional guards they'd hired, all moving into action. He wanted to help them—knew he should help—but all he could think if was getting to Isabella. Staggering, he stumbled up the sidewalk toward the house, dragging her from Jack's arms into his own.

"Are you okay?" He searched her face, frantic to hear her voice and reassure himself she was alive. Breathing. Whole. A thick line of blood ran from her temple and he pulled her close, pressing his lips to her ear. "What happened?"

"I…I hit my head." She trembled in his arms, her shoulders quaking in the aftermath of the adrenaline rush. "On the dashboard."

Frantic hands grabbed at his shoulders. Rowan tugged once, then harder. "Inside! Come on. Let's get inside."

Kensington had the door open, dragging them into the foyer and he pressed Isabella toward her. "Take her and keep her close. I need to go help Jack."

"Liam. Stay here. They. I mean—"

He cut his sister off, knowing what she couldn't put to words. Jack's men had been killed upon impact. "I need to go help them deal with things."

Kensington nodded, then pulled Isabella close while Rowan flanked her other side. Liam watched them walk down the hall, Isabella moving slowly between his sisters, before he turned and walked straight back into hell.

"I need to go back out there. Those men. Jack's men." The words fell from her lips in incoherent bursts as thoughts and images assailed her. "Oh Kensington, I'm so sorry."

"Shhh." Kensington had resettled them back in the study and had her in a tight embrace on the couch. "Don't think about that."

"I have to think about it. It's because of me. It's my fault." Grief clawed at her, full of fierce recrimination as the truth of what had happened sunk in. "Jack's men. They were killed."

Rowan turned from the window, her normally animated face set in stoic lines. "They died doing their job."

"Protecting me from a madman." She shook her head, more of those random thoughts spilling from her lips. "We were talking about pizza. Rowan and Liam were talking about how Campbell eats all the pizza and to order two. And then—"

She broke off, knowing there were no words. Nothing that could make those men come back.

Nothing that could change the fact she'd argued and pushed and prodded to get into her home today.

And innocent men had died because of it.

Daniel shuffled back into the house, his planned lunch meeting ending up being a meeting for one. Bradley Armstrong had never shown up, so he'd ordered a quick lunch, then grabbed a cab home.

Curious.

Armstrong was known as much for his colorful bow-ties as his punctuality.

It was just as well, Daniel knew, as he moved on painful legs toward the kitchen. He wasn't up to sitting still for hours on end anyway. He had no idea why his drug therapies hadn't been working quite as well lately although he suspected the stress of what he and Edward had planned was taking a toll.

Yet another reason in the column for why he needed to come clean and tell Edward they were changing their plans. This madness had to stop.

The front door opened and Daniel swallowed the last of the pills before going to meet Edward. He'd committed so many sins. So many errors in judgment.

It was refreshing to know he'd finally put that all behind him.

"Edward. What happened to you?" The younger man was disheveled, his hair standing on end and a layer of dark soot covering his jacket.

"Everything."

"Was there an accident?"

"You could say that."

The human urge to rush forward to help pulled at him

yet something pulled harder inside and he stood still, puzzling at the half answers. "Are you hurt?"

"Hardly."

"Then why do you look like you've been through a war zone?" Even as the concern hovered, refusing to fade, something else buzzed under his skin. Edward's behavior was beyond odd and Daniel couldn't shake the strange sense of menace that gripped him.

"Did you hear about Bradley Armstrong?"

That sense of menace rose another notch and Daniel chose his words carefully, ensuring his voice stayed casual. "Bradley Armstrong from that science journal? No. Why?"

"Yes. The Bradley Armstrong you were supposed to meet for lunch today."

Menace turned to full-blown panic as he evaluated his ability to beat Edward to the door. The man was younger and although Daniel might have had a fair shot a few years ago when both of them were weak and frail, he knew Edward had the advantage of age on him now. "I've been as undercover as you have, hiding from anyone who could recognize me. Why would I schedule a meeting with a reporter?"

"You tell me."

"Is something bothering you, Edward?"

"Just a few things."

Daniel processed the words faster than Edward's actions. It was only when he felt the press of a needle to his thigh that he understood just how poor a calculation that was.

Chapter 18

Isabella lay on the bed in her room, the late afternoon sun flooding the space in a rich patina of gold. She loved this time of day, especially in spring when the days grew progressively longer.

And because of her, two men were unable to enjoy the same moment.

Wayne and Aidan were their names.

She'd asked Jack after he had come back into the house, saddened she didn't already know. She'd simply accepted their presence on her protection detail and hadn't even taken the time to know their names.

Now those names echoed through her mind, unceasing in the repetition.

The police were still downstairs—would likely be there for days—but Liam had convinced them to let her come up to her room to rest. Instead, she'd lain here for the past hour, repeating the names of two dead men.

Enough.

She did them no honor by lying here like a sniveling, lazy sloth. And she'd only been this vulnerable once before in her life—after her father's sentence was handed down. Inaction had gripped her that day and for so many days after and it was only when she got back to her college work and studies that she'd found purpose once more. She'd be damned if she was going to go to that dark place again.

Or ever.

Firing up her laptop, she pulled up a search engine and did a run on Daniel Stephenson. Although she knew Kensington's search programs could dig far deeper, Isabella was hunting for a history of Daniel's work. Some clue to what drove him or where he might have made advancements that laddered up to other achievements.

The pages she found walked her through much of what she already knew, from his early days at MIT to his studies abroad as a young student. She also dug more deeply into his physical condition, opening up a new search window to download the symptoms and elements of the debilitating disease that ate away at muscle and tissue, weakening bone as it destroyed.

Again, all things she knew, but she tried to reconcile the data with what she knew *now*.

If Daniel had faked his death he had to have a backup plan. The man was genuinely sick—she'd seen that with her own eyes—in the months leading up to his supposed death so something had to have changed.

But what?

She ran a few more search queries, racking her mind to come up with any sense of connection or clue to where he was and what had happened. Other than the very real assumption he'd found a way to modify her research to heal himself, she couldn't find any other connections.

The soft knock at the door pulled her from another fruit-less avenue and she called out a quick "Come in!"

And promptly lost her breath when Liam walked in, the signs of the explosion still evident in the smudges on his shirt and the grease stains on his jeans.

"You haven't changed yet."

"I was just coming upstairs to do that. I wanted to check on you first." He closed the door, but stayed where he was in front of the door. "What are you working on?"

"Right now? About two hundred empty searches on-line."

"What are you looking for?"

"That's my problem. I don't know." Willing the frustra-tion out of her voice, she shoved her hair behind her ears and gestured him over. "But a fresh pair of eyes might be just what I need. I'm trying to find any links or connec-tions. Something had to have manifested itself in Daniel's life. Before."

"Like what?"

"That's what I don't know."

He pulled a decorative chair from where it sat near the door and sat down next to hear. "So take me through what you have so far."

And just like this morning, she had a partner who read-ily accepted her thoughts and ideas. Brushing it aside—and the very real fact that Liam hadn't returned her sentiments of love—she focused on answering his questions.

"I've got his research history. The elements of his dis-ease. And the record of his family money and basic lin-eage."

"Any patterns?"

"That's the problem." She slammed a hand on the desk, jarring her slim laptop. "That's been the problem from the beginning. No matter how we look at things, there doesn't seem to be any coherent reason why this is happening. Or what possible motive he'd have for harming me."

"Jealousy?"

"Of what? My mind?" She laughed, a memory of their many games of chess played late into the night while waiting for research results to run. "The man ran circles around me."

"I've seen the laps you do and they're pretty impressive." A wry smile quirked his lips and the impact hit her square in the stomach, setting wing to a flock of sudden nerves.

"That's very sweet of you but he's brilliant. Crazy brilliant."

Liam's eyes narrowed at her choice of words. "Is he crazy?"

"No." She stopped, cycled through what she knew of Daniel Stephenson. "I truly believe he's not, but he did live with a shocking degree of pain. Monumental pain that could fell the strongest-willed individual."

"Pull up the information on his illness again." She did as he asked, then used the moment to observe him as he read the text.

Here was the man she loved. The man she'd made love to the entire night before and well into the morning. Even as warm memories flooded her thoughts, she marveled at the strange sense of wonder that filled her at how easy it was to be together.

They fit, with this strange, wonderful, breathtaking connection that didn't make sense, as if it was the most natural thing in the world.

"This disease is pretty nasty. Like the worse parts of Lou Gehrig's Disease and MS combined." He broke off as he caught sight of her. "What?"

She took a moment to clear her throat. "You're right on Daniel's disease. It's devastating."

His gaze remained locked on hers for a few more moments before he continued on. "Yet he lived with it. Found a way to persist in his work and his research despite what had to be horrible pain."

The wonder and happiness at being with Liam fled as she allowed memories of her mentor to take center stage in her thoughts. "He was so generous and so gifted with his mind. He wanted to make the world better. His focus and his life's work was to help find cures. Or ways to slow diseases. He worked so hard toward healing those who were affected by the horrible effects of illness, just as he was."

She broke off as a hard sob caught in her throat. "Don't you see? That's why I can't convince myself he's behind this. He was such a caring man. He wanted to find the answers. And he understood that drive inside of me as well."

"To find answers." He ran his index finger down her cheek, tracing away the tears that had slipped past before she could blink them away. And then he wrapped his arms around her, pulling her close against his chest. "We're going to figure this out. I promise you that, we're going to understand it."

"It can't be him." The words fell from her lips on another hard cry, as if her heart were truly breaking. The moment was surreal, the deep grief juxtaposed against the comfort from a loved one. "He wouldn't have killed those men. Wayne and Aidan. He couldn't have done that."

"Shhh."

She lifted her head from his chest, giving up the warmth and comfort to press her point. "I mean it. He worked to find *cures,* Liam, not encourage death."

"I believe you. I do. But if not Daniel, who? You've seen the lab work yourself and Campbell's been running files and simulations since yesterday. What other answer is there?"

Maybe you're asking the wrong questions.

Kensington's comment from the other day tumbled around in her brain, taking purchase like a seed taking root.

They'd looked at Daniel every which way they could, questioning his role in the attacks, yet they all kept coming up empty-handed.

So what if they weren't looking at things correctly?

"I don't know, but—"

"But what?"

"Kensington said something interesting to me the other day. It's rattled around in my mind and I think it might finally make sense. She asked me if I was asking the right questions."

Isabella fought a giggle as a look of sheer disgust painted itself over Liam's face. "What the hell kind of advice is that?"

"Good advice, I thought."

"It's hokey. 'Ask the right questions.'" He kicked his voice up a few notches in clear imitation of his sister. "'Ask different questions.' That's a bunch of psychobabble b.s."

"I thought it was insightful."

"Whatever."

Her smile fell at the dismissive tone in his voice. She'd heard anger, frustration and sibling irritation, but she'd never heard quite that combination of notes all at once. "What are you so upset about?"

"That's just like my sister. Like my whole damn family, you know." He kicked back the chair he was sitting on, knocking it to the floor as he got to his feet.

The outburst was so sudden, Isabella wasn't sure if she

should sit back and let him vent or reach out so she went with instinct and stood up to meet him. "What has you so upset?"

"You've just nailed my family in a freaking nutshell. Ask questions. Ask different questions. Push and push and push. It's all right. It'll be okay. We love you anyway."

"Liam?" She whispered his name but he was too far gone to hear.

"They refuse to acknowledge what we are. What's made us. What makes us willing to do what we do. Two men died out front of our house a few hours ago and we're all downstairs, running scenarios and simulations and my brother is fidgeting away on that damn wall of computers and none of it changes the fact that two men are sitting in the morgue right now."

Another wave of helpless tears filled her eyes at the image he painted, but she knew the root of the tears went even deeper.

Here was pain. Raw and real and *present*.

Swallowing hard, unwilling to deflect the moment with a crying jag, she pressed him. "I thought you liked your life and what you did. The work you and your family do is important. You help people."

"We also stand by while a hell of a lot of people lose their lives, too."

His shoulders stiffened and he turned, pacing a small path beside her bed, his gaze on the floor.

And in that moment she knew.

Knew something terrible had jaded him, bottled up so deeply inside he'd forgotten who he was. "What happened?"

"Nothing."

"When did this nothing happen?"

He stopped midpace to look up at her, his face drawn in a mask of bleak angles, awash in misery. "A few years ago."

Don't tell her. Don't tell her. Don't tell her.

The instructions echoed over and over in his mind, warning him of the very real truth that if he told Isabella what had happened—if he soiled her with the darkness—she'd never be clean again.

Would never be free of the knowledge, just as he'd never be free.

"Please tell me."

Liam was surprised to feel the hot wash of tears fill his eyes, the hard sting of a knot in his throat as he fought to swallow around them. "I can't spoil you."

Her movements were so fast he blinked at the speed with which she crossed the room. She pressed her hands to his face, the pure green of her eyes boring into him with passionate fire, still innocent. Still free of the truth. "There's nothing you can't say to me. Nothing. Don't you understand that?"

"No. *You* don't understand."

"Then everything. The last week figuring out who's after me. Last night together. Everything we've shared. It's all for nothing if you won't tell me."

"I can't."

"You won't." She stepped back, her hands dropping to her sides. "I meant it when I told you I loved you. I would like to hear it in return, but I don't expect it. When a man tells me he loves me, I want it to be freely given. But understand me well. I love you. Nothing you say will change that. Nothing."

That fire snapped in her eyes, arcing pure heat and

wild, all-encompassing acceptance toward him in a wash of sparks.

As the embers settled over him, he knew he was loved. And he knew love in return.

"Please sit down." He gestured her toward the bed, then took the seat next to her. He kept his hands fisted at his sides, preparing himself to tell her. She reached out and took both of them in hers, a gentle promise of understanding.

"Now tell me."

With succinct bullet points for words, he tried to tell her all about the failed mission in Prague. His responsibilities managing security detail for a diplomat scheduled to testify in a war crimes trial for a small country in the former Soviet Union. The increasing sense that something was off despite the fact that every member of the man's staff was fully vetted and cleared.

"But you still sensed something was wrong?"

Her fingers tightened around his and Liam nodded at the simple understanding. "I knew there was. But I couldn't find the hole. Who knows—" He exhaled on a hard, bitter bark of anger. "Maybe I didn't ask the right questions."

"So what happened?" Her voice was gentle but he knew the deflection for what it was and knew he was being a bastard about his sister.

"The man's brother-in-law. He was working undercover for the group being testified against. They'd turned him with enough money and promises of power, even though he was nothing more than a pawn to them."

"How'd you find out?"

"When I watched him slaughter his sister, her husband the diplomat and their two children. Mikhail and Irina."

Her fingers tightened once again as the blood drained from her face. He sensed she wanted to say something, but he pushed on, unwilling to hear her put words to the sympathy he saw in her eyes.

"It happened so fast. I didn't even get my gun out until he'd mowed down all but the baby." He stopped, the words sticking in his throat as he tried to get them out as fast as possible. "I was already firing at him when he shot her in the head."

She wrapped her arms around him and pressed her cheek to his. "You did what you could. You tried to stop him."

"Did I?" The truth ate at him, boring holes of regret into his soul like cigarette burns. "I had drinks with the man the night before. The family had thrown a party, celebrating that the trial was coming to an end. I had vodka with all of them, at their insistence. Clinked my glass in toast with a traitor."

"But you didn't know."

"I should have known. It was my job to know!" He leaped off the bed, unwilling to sit still any longer, no matter how good it felt to sit pressed against her, wrapped up in each other. No matter that it meant all the difference to finally tell someone the story of what really happened. To tell someone about the toast.

To a long and fruitful life.

He shook his head, the events as clear as if they'd happened the day before. "All my intel. All my prep. None of it mattered as the man took out his entire family twelve hours later."

"A risk of the job. And proof that you're not infallible. Intel's not infallible."

"I knew something was wrong."

"And you righted it as best you could."

No matter what he said, she had an answer.

"You avenged that family, Liam, by keeping the monster

who lied to them and manipulated them from ever doing it again. You honored them."

"There's no honor in a mistake that cost four innocents their life."

"It's a hell of a lot more honorable than someone who hides in the shadows, biding their time. Like the brother-in-law. Like the person after me. There's no honor in a life lived in the shadows, waiting to strike like a snake in the grass."

She moved toward him, her arms outstretched, and welcomed him as he wrapped himself around her. The images of that dark day still swam around him, swamping him with their power, but as her lips met his, he felt the light shine through the shadows.

Darkness surrounded him and Daniel fought to get his bearings as pain radiated down his legs in spiky bursts.

"Edward?" His voice came out on a croak, quiet and lonely.

What had happened?

Daniel struggled to make sense of his surroundings from the pool of darkness that weighed him down. He couldn't see anything but even without his sight, the darkness felt familiar. The scents around him—like a dank basement that had been disinfected with the harshest soaps—filled his nostrils.

Why did it *feel* familiar?

A quiet panic gripped him. He knew he should be upset about his lack of sight, but he couldn't quite summon up the energy.

Odd.

He shifted on the bed—cot?—he lay on, the movement bringing the metal frame in contact with a wall. Again, his senses took stock of what he knew.

The ring of metal echoed through the room, low and hollow.

The only smell he could parse out was that dank, industrial mildew, but if he tried, he could also get the barest hint of stale coffee.

The air felt heavy with moisture and his palms were damp.

He was a man who'd spent his life contextualizing his surroundings as he attempted to navigate them and, for the first time, he realized how much he understood at a sense-based level.

Slowly, consciousness, the pain in his legs and sheer curiosity pulled at him, dragging him out of the abyss. He reached for his eyes, abstractly cataloguing that his hands weren't tied.

And when he finally pulled off the blindfold shielding his vision—his hand trembling at the effort of his still-sluggish limbs—his confusion vanished.

He knew this place. Had spent years of his life here.

The harshest bark of laughter filled his throat, the irony of what he'd wrought filling him with shame. He was in his old office.

Where all his folly had begun.

Isabella pressed her lips to Liam's temple, then his cheek, then over his jaw, whispering nonsense words as she trailed a path of kisses. His body still trembled with the aftereffects of adrenaline and the emotional exposure of his experience in Prague, but she sensed a calming in the deep breaths that blew against her neck.

She'd never been a big believer in love at first sight or instant attraction, the scientific part of her mind too steeped in numbers and research and facts to accept something so fanciful. Yet here she was, so emotionally invested in this man she'd known less than a week.

Their circumstances might have heightened their emotions, keeping everything close to the surface, but these feelings for Liam were so much more.

As if sensing the direction of her thoughts, his arms tightened around her waist and he pulled her even closer, shifting them so they were stretched lengthwise on the bed. He pressed his lips to hers, his tongue seeking entrance to her mouth. She opened for him, the move natural as breathing, and welcomed him within.

Liam gently pushed her onto her back, then propped up beside her on one bent arm. He ran his hands over her breasts, down her stomach then over her hip as if sculpting her body. Heat rose up wherever he touched, a sensual brand that had her lifting into his touch.

And then her breath suspended, trapped in her lungs.

His long, sensitive artist's fingers fluttered at the waistband of her slacks before slipping beneath the material. With long, luscious strokes, he swept lazy fingers over her already-sensitized body. Sparks shot before her eyes and a helpless mewl echoed from the back of her throat when his index finger slipped beneath the waistband of her panties.

How was it possible to feel so vulnerable yet so alive?

"Liam!" His name fell from her lips as she fought the sweeping arc of passion that had the world fading around her.

"Give this to me." The gentle lover morphed almost instantaneously, a delicious taskmaster determined to take her over the edge. His touch consumed her, controlled her and forced her beyond the edge of madness.

But it was his last word—half demand, half plea—that had her world exploding into a million bright, shiny pieces.

"Please."

Chapter 19

"No fair! I'm ticklish." Liam swallowed a handful of water that splashed in his face as Isabella pushed his head under the shower spray.

"I'll show you fair."

Her giggles faded as his lips took hers, his hands ruthless as they traveled over the wet woman in his arms. He felt his body come to life against hers and wondered how it was possible she could make him feel so good.

Or how he'd lived so long without her.

Which pulled him up short, right there in the middle of the shower in the bathroom adjoined to the room he'd grown up in.

"What's wrong?" Isabella's eyes were wide, her lashes a spiky rim over that vibrant green.

"Nothing. I just—" he stopped, well aware he looked like a gaping fish. "Nothing."

Before she could question him further, he pulled her

against him, determined to return to their carefree exploration of each other.

His hands stroked her wet skin, cupping the fullness of her breasts as his thumbs played over the distended flesh of her nipples. He followed the movements with his mouth, even as the vixen in his arms turned the tables.

Isabella's hands moved on an exploratory of their own and he pressed into her palm as she cupped him boldly, her strokes over his rigid flesh drawing him closer and closer to his own release.

The daunting thoughts of commitment and forever faded from his mind as the demands of their bodies pushed each other on. The sharp green of her eyes had gone a smoky moss and he forced his gaze to stay locked on hers as the moment took them both.

But even as he felt her go over in his arms, his own release nearly upon him, he knew it was a fool's errand.

Isabella had come to mean far more than he'd ever imagined. And as he drove his body into hers, felt her ride the thrust as if they'd been made for each other, Liam knew he was lost.

Isabella lay on the bed, an oversize towel wrapped around her flushed and well-satisfied body. Liam had gone down to raid the fridge for some late-night leftovers and she allowed her thoughts to drift as she waited for him.

The past hours with him had been a revelation.

When she'd come up to her room, she'd felt bereft of any hope, convinced the death and destruction she'd brought on the Steele family was inevitable.

And now…

She knew there was still work to be done, but Liam's reassuring presence and sheer strength of will had restored her hope. Making love to him had renewed her. She hadn't known it was possible, that a physical connection could make such a difference, but it had.

In his arms she'd found acceptance and support. And the belief that they would get past the demons that haunted her.

A quick memory intruded on her musings—that moment in the shower when he'd gone from attentive lover to distant acquaintance—and despite her wish to ignore it, her analytical mind processed through those moments as well.

They'd been laughing, enjoying the moment and each other, when something stopped him. The old Isabella would have believed it was her fault and that she was doing something wrong, but she knew that wasn't the case. The same analytical mind that catalogued everything in her life had also captured the pleasure in his reactions during sex and she knew the problem went far deeper.

Fear?

The haunted glaze that had colored the normally vivid blue a dull misty gray suggested as much, but fear of what? The power of what was between them? Or something even deeper tied to letting another into his life.

His comments earlier about his family weren't simple anger, quick to spark the flame over, or even normal family frustration. The depth of his hurt had its roots in so much more. The Steele siblings might love each other and have one another's backs, but the loss of their parents had cut them all so deeply, their wounds still bled.

The buzzing of her phone caught her attention and she grabbed it from the end table, glancing at the readout. The immediate recognition had her breath catching hard in her throat.

Daniel.

She scrambled to sit up, her wet hair slapping against

her back as she answered, lifting the phone to her ear. "Hello?"

"Hello, Isabella."

The voice that filled her ear was tinny, yet oddly familiar. "Daniel?" She asked the question, even as she knew it couldn't be.

"Try again. How about Edward."

Edward? Her mind cycled through the name, grasping at who she might have known before she lit on the answer. "Edward Carrington?"

"Right again."

"It's been you?" Images of the frail scientist filled her mind's eye. His condition was similar to Daniel's, though not nearly as advanced, and she'd known the two men were close. "All along it's been you?"

"Daniel's helped."

"He's alive?" The breath she wasn't even aware of holding blew out in a rush. "Where is he? How's he doing?"

"Come see us. We're in the old lab space."

"The dungeon?"

"The very same. I thought it was oddly fitting we meet again where it all started. I may be a scientist but I like to think of myself as a man with a poet's heart."

"But how?" She broke off, the truth of what they'd believed springing to life. "The research. The lab results. They're yours and Daniel's."

"Very good."

"Why are you hiding this news from the world? It's incredible. And where's Daniel?"

"Daniel's resting now but you know how his best hours were early in the morning. They still are. Come see us and then we'll talk."

"I'm not meeting you alone."

"Then I'll come to you. The Steele brownstone is quite

a place. Looks like a fortress but a building that old has to have its weak spots."

"You wouldn't." The words stuck in her throat and she struggled around the fear that crushed her rib cage like a boa constrictor.

"Six a.m., Isabella. And if that debonair gent who's been escorting you since London comes along, he won't make it back home to that swanky apartment of his."

"No one's been escorting me."

A hard laugh chewed through the phone lines. "Lies are so unbecoming, don't you think? But let me jog your memory. Cushy lobby. Frightfully inattentive doorman. I think you know the one."

The phone went dead and she knew the choice that lay in front of her. There was only one option and no matter how badly she'd prefer to walk that path with someone, it remained hers alone.

Daniel struggled to a sitting position as the lock jangled from outside the door. Edward hadn't been in the room yet but he'd known it was only a matter of time.

He'd spent every moment since waking trying to detail a sound, cogent argument for his old student but kept coming up short. What could he say?

He'd been in full agreement with Edward until the reality of what they'd embarked upon had become a living, breathing plan. The drugs he'd taken while in the throes of his pain had made him an easy mark, but none of it excused his actions.

Or his role in helping Edward plot how to destroy Isabella.

It was all so clear now, when pain wasn't the master over his body, how misguided he'd been. The treatment that had healed him was a result of Isabella's work. Her time and effort and talent.

And Edward had convinced him she hadn't worked fast enough. That she'd taken the gift of his money and frivolously frittered it away on re-outfitting her lab and embarking on fruitless avenues of research.

When he'd begun to heal—engineered at Edward's hands—his student had become the master, telling him how much of the work was truly his own.

And he'd listened.

The door swung inward and Edward walked through the door. His gait was stiff, evidence the younger man was still pushing himself too hard. "So you're up."

"No thanks to you."

"What's the point of all this?"

Daniel's gaze shifted toward the door and Edward patted a gun in his lap. "You're not fast enough to make the door, nor strong enough to take this from me. So I suggest you sit still and listen."

"Fine. I'm listening."

"Your little protégée will be here in a few hours. When she gets here, we're going to game-plan a statement that will be issued to discredit her work published to date."

"What's the point?"

"We've discussed this. Publicizing her work any further than she already has is a mistake. Those in authority won't take kindly to the experiments we performed while perfecting the technology, nor will they be all that understanding of your faked death."

The experiments.

That had been the ultimate reason he'd faked his death. Isabella would never have agreed and he and Edward had needed reasonable results before testing on themselves.

"You're right. Of course you're right."

"So glad you're returning to the program."

"There's leftover pizza on the bottom shelf."

Liam jumped and nearly hit his head on the fridge door as Rowan snuck up behind him in the kitchen. "Geez, Ro."

"Take it easy." She grabbed the pizza box from his hand and set it on the counter.

"What are you doing down here?"

"Same as you. I'm hungry and I couldn't sleep." She hesitated a moment, very un-Rowan-like. "And I heard you slip down here."

"Oh?"

"I've been thinking." She hesitated again, then gestured him to the kitchen table. "I need to talk to you."

His little sister had two speeds, on and off. So it was a surprise to see her so hesitant as she gestured him toward a chair.

"I've been thinking a lot about our discussion a few months ago. When we were both in London and I was all up in my head about Finn."

Liam remembered the conversation—had replayed it several times over in his own mind. "The night we met and had that spicy Indian food that singed my stomach lining."

"That's the one." When the memory of the delicious vindaloo failed to even elicit a smile, he sat back, deeply curious to where she was going. "Look. I said some things that night that were at best misguided and at worst—"

On a deep breath, she rushed on, "At worst selfish and unkind."

The urge to brush it off and act like it wasn't important or hadn't affected him was strong, but he respected his sister's honesty and knew she deserved it in return. "I miss Mom and Dad, too."

"I know you do. And to imply that somehow losing them was harder on me because I was younger was insensitive. Horribly insensitive." Her gaze met his, clear and direct. "You're my big brother. It's easy to forget you're a person with feelings when I'm in the midst of my usual hero worship."

His outburst with Isabella earlier came back to haunt him, his words echoing in his own ears. *They refuse to acknowledge what we are. What's made us. What makes us willing to do what we do.*

"Thanks for telling me."

"We love you and we miss you. I felt it before but I didn't understand it. Not really. But now that Finn's in my life. Well, it just makes me realize how important my family is to me." She grabbed his hand, her fingers tight around his. "Sometimes I think we all use the business as an excuse to hide how we feel. It's like if we stay busy we don't have to think about how the people we loved were taken away from us."

Her fingers tightened once more and he squeezed back. The honesty in her statement—and the raw truth of her words—had the heavy weight of responsibility that usually lay on his chest cracking down the middle. "I think we used to do that, but I've seen a change in all of you. Since Abby, Finn and Jack came into your lives, you've all changed."

"So have you."

He hadn't changed and he knew it. Not like his siblings. They saw the world through new eyes—a fresh take on an old, miserable place—and he missed the same filter. "Come on, now. I thought I was the stoic hero, unwilling to compromise."

"Before Isabella you were. She's changed you. Made a difference."

The same panic that had turned his stomach over in the shower gripped him once more. "It's not the same."

"I think it is. But since I've already spent the last several months upset that I overstepped I won't press my point."

Rowan reached for the box and snagged a slice of pizza before pushing the cardboard back toward him. "Better get this up to her. The poor girl's probably famished."

She stood and pressed a kiss to his cheek, then left the room on the same quiet feet she'd entered with. It was only as he climbed the stairs several minutes later, pizza in hand, he had to admit his baby sister was crafty.

How the hell did she know the pizza was for Isabella?

Isabella lay in the dark and savored these last quiet minutes in Liam's arms. She knew the decision to go alone to meet Edward was akin to a suicide run, but she refused to put Liam and his family in danger.

Edward's actions had proven he wasn't thinking rationally and she needed to go to him, on his own terms. With a few tricks up her sleeve, of course. She might be dumb enough to go alone, but she wasn't going in completely blind.

She knew her enemy and she knew his weaknesses.

How funny then, that the imagined danger of her work—and the governments who could use and abuse what she'd discovered—were the least of her worries. Instead, the true threat had been nearby all along, coiled and waiting to strike.

Edward's threats against the Steeles were real—of that she had no doubt. She'd brought danger to their door and to the people they'd hired to help keep her safe and she couldn't put anyone else at risk.

Refused to put anyone else at risk.

So this is love.

The thought struck on swift wings and she marveled at the very concept. She loved. She'd known it for several days, but it was only when faced with the choice to keep him safe that she understood what it meant on a different level. Because of that love, the desire to protect was as natural as breathing.

Liam had given that to her. After a lifetime spent wondering why her parents—the very people who should have loved her without reservation, but didn't—had been so incapable, she now knew the beauty and the bone-deep satisfaction of caring for another.

What she couldn't believe was how naive she'd been.

Edward Carrington.

He'd always been one of Daniel's pets and she'd been more than willing to let him have the role. She knew the strength of her mind and her skills and she had confidence in her mentor-mentee relationship with Daniel. She'd never found the need to flaunt that to anyone.

But Edward had been a different matter. A man with a brilliant scientific mind, trapped within a rigid, brutal anger over his disabilities.

Not that she'd ever blamed him. The man lived with a set of trials far worse than anything she could have imagined and she'd never begrudged him his place to shine.

But now...

Now he was the only one to blame.

Liam's arms tightened around her in the dark and she fought the deep desire to stay there and never leave. He was safe. Secure. And she knew she was better for having him in her life.

Even if she did come back, that didn't mean they were guaranteed a future. But she'd be damned if she was going to give him up without a fight.

For now, facing Edward needed to be her sole focus. If only to return to the safe, warm cocoon of Liam Steele's arms as fast as she could.

Chapter 20

The cool spring morning lay heavy about Isabella's shoulders as she stepped out of the cab a few blocks from her old lab. Police crime scene tape wrapped around the burnt remains of the newer building, leaving a clear view of the older facility. Edward and Daniel were in there.

Every instinct she possessed kept screaming she was making a mistake, but none of it could quite bury the excitement of seeing Daniel once more.

Nor could it dampen her excitement about seeing the very real proof of her work, come to life.

Although her work had been tied to emotional triggers in the human body, the very idea it was applicable toward healing physical disease was awe-inspiring.

It was that single thread that gave her hope she might be able to convince Edward to change his mind. Whatever he might have planned, he was still a scientist at heart. A man who loved learning and puzzles and putting his stamp on the world. That had to count for something.

Didn't it?

She moved swiftly through the standard maze of sidewalks that led up to the building, taking stock of her surroundings and the preparation she'd made before leaving the Steeles'. While she didn't want them in danger, she had made sure they'd know where she was.

Leaving was the challenging part. She'd managed to slip from Liam's bedroom without waking him but the house security system had given her some trouble. Thankfully she'd watched Campbell disarm it the night before and her natural aptitude for numbers had ensured she got the code right on the second try.

If all went to plan, no one would find her note until she'd dealt with this situation.

She patted her large purse, pleased to feel the solid weight of her tablet. She had one card left to play.

Now all she had to do was pray that it would be enough.

Liam reached for Isabella, coming fast awake when his hand roamed over the mattress instead of soft, warm curves. He sat up, his eyes adjusting to the early dawn light flooding the room. "Isabella."

When she didn't answer, he came fully awake, a distinct sense of unease gripping him. Before he could act, his door flew open, Campbell in the doorway. "The alarm's off."

"What the hell?" He jumped out of bed, dragging on pants as he went. The dull throb of panic echoed in his veins as absolute certainty filled his mind. "Isabella's not here, is she?"

"I don't think so." His brother waved a piece of paper. "But I think I know where she went."

"Why would she do this?" The question spilled from his lips but he knew damn well the answer didn't matter. She'd gone and she'd done it under the cover of silence.

"She's at her old lab, but she gave me a specific set of instructions."

"The lab's gone." Liam slung his T-shirt over his head, puzzling through the riddle of her note.

"It says dungeon next to the words, 'old lab'."

Liam grabbed the note and scanned it quickly. She'd described the dungeon's location when they'd gone to her lab; had joked how cozy she'd found the dank old place. As he replayed the conversation in his mind, he began working through a plan of attack.

He reread the note through to the end. There was a set of instructions at the bottom about files and such. "Tell me what this means."

Campbell nodded toward the hallway. "Up to the computer room. I'll explain it along the way. She's left me a set of code to execute upon her signal."

"No time. I'm going to her."

His brother stopped on the stairs, blocking his descent. "Not without proper planning."

"Get out of my way. I know where she is. I don't care what the hell she thinks she's about, I'm going after her." The words burst from him like gunfire and whatever veneer of calm he tried to project shattered. In its place, Liam knew a deep-rooted sense of panic.

A panic he'd only ever felt once before, the night his grandparents awakened him to tell him of his parents' deaths.

"I know where she is, too. And you're not going in there blind. I've already rigged the feeds around her lab when I did the video surveillance work yesterday. Let me get you outfitted properly before you go and you'll have eyes inside. Bastard thinks *he* rigged the video but I've got a work-around."

Liam stared down at his brother, the image of a young

boy he'd always carried fading as a man stared back up at him. He knew his brother was an adult—had known it for some time—but in that moment, he saw the man Campbell had become and it humbled him. "Thank you."

His brother's light-hearted countenance and mischievous smile had been replaced with the serious visage of a warrior. "You're welcome."

"I can't believe she went alone."

"You can kick her ass about it later. After you tell her you love her and aren't ever letting her out of your sight again."

"Cheeky bastard." Liam muttered as Campbell snuck past him up the stairs.

That smile he knew so well reappeared on his brother's face. "Lucky for you I'm a freaking whiz at my job, too. Come on."

Isabella slipped down the hallway, the familiar surroundings of the dungeon filling her mind with an endless series of memories. She'd spent nearly a decade here before they'd transferred into the new facility. Although she didn't miss the drafty winters that had necessitated a space heater on the coldest of days, she did miss the simpler times when she'd worked here.

She'd had such excitement and enthusiasm. Such passion for her work. And she'd believed that she was making advancements that would make a difference.

And now?

Now she had to focus on staying alive. Questions about her future could come later.

As if he'd heard her thoughts, a door at the far end of the hallway—the entrance to Daniel's old office—swung open. "On time and punctual, as always."

Isabella had worked through a dozen scenarios in her

mind of how she'd play this meeting, but they all fell away as she stared at Edward. "You're standing. You're—" she hesitated, the word sticking in her throat before she continued. "Well."

"Cured." The absence of warmth and the complete lack of emotion behind his hazel eyes brought her up short.

The urge to correct his statement struck her but she held back. *No use playing your hand yet.* "I want to see Daniel."

"You don't make demands."

"It was your idea I come down here." She knew damn well his invitation had been a threat, but she was determined to keep up the ruse for as long as possible. She didn't miss the gun he held at his side, or the distinct menace that surrounded him.

Whoever she'd believed Edward Carrington to be when she knew him was now just a memory and she'd do well to remember that. "I'd like to see Daniel. Please."

"He's in his office." Edward laughed at his joke. "I'm sure he'll be delighted to see you."

She tried to keep her gaze off the gun and straight ahead of her but there was no way she had that much willpower. The handgun was like a magnet, drawing her eyes no matter how hard she tried to avoid it.

And then she was through the door and she forgot about the gun as she ran forward. "Daniel!"

Liam drove their large family SUV at top speed, weaving and swerving through the early morning streets. Jack sat next to him, giving suggestions about which streets would be best to get him uptown while Kenzi talked to Campbell and Abby back at home. Rowan and Finn had already mobilized the police, ensuring SWAT was prepped for the layout of the dungeon.

As he barreled on past Columbus Circle, Liam fought

the noose of fear that threatened to strangle him, fading his world to black.

They had to get there. They had to be in time.

He'd continued the prayer all through preparations and couldn't think of anything but getting to Isabella. Despite Kenzi's repeated relay of Campbell's data—that Isabella was fine and in her old lab with her mentor and a former colleague.

He cursed himself a hundred times over they'd not thoroughly checked out the damn colleague.

"Tell me what we know about Carrington." Liam barked the order as he sped past the 72nd Street subway station, narrowly missing an early morning bus.

Jack spoke first, his fingers flying over his phone screen. "One of Isabella's partners on Daniel's team for years. Son of a wealthy New York family, with money that goes back a few generations. Born with both a silver spoon and a condition. Nearly died four times before the age of three."

"High IQ but suffers from delusions." Kenzi added the last, incorporating her own intel. She'd left Abby behind running queries through her search programs and Liam couldn't help wishing his sister and her fiancé had stayed behind altogether.

He didn't need to be worrying about them while he went in after Isabella.

Of course, he'd been tartly informed of the same in reverse from Kensington and he had no interest in wasting precious minutes arguing with her. The only good thing was that Jack was as invested in her safety as Liam was so he had backup.

"Where are they now?" He hollered it and heard Campbell's voice as Kenzi switched to speaker.

"Still in the office. Carrington is armed but so far he's kept it at his side."

"What else do I need to know?"

"He's rigged the doors with pressure sensors so he'll know if anyone arrives. I've got a work-around but I need you to wait for my signal before you open the doors."

"You can't disarm them now?" Liam swerved around another bus and ran a yellow turning red, ignoring the honk of several taxis that lit up the morning air.

"We can't risk tipping him off." Campbell let out a low curse. "And we've got another problem."

"What?" Liam slammed on his brakes as he ran the SUV halfway up the curb, then threw the car into Park. "I don't want to hear about problems. Fix it."

He left the car running and turned toward Jack. "You've got the feed."

Jack nodded and handed him a second small tablet, displaying a full visual feed of all the cameras Carrington thought he'd overridden in the facility.

"Would you wait a damn minute!" Abstractly, he heard Campbell's voice hollering in the background but Liam ignored him and grabbed the device from Jack.

He kept his gaze on the screen as he wove his way through the large lawn that fronted the research facility. He could see Isabella in black-and-white. It wasn't much, but it was something.

His touchstone.

He *had* to get to her.

"What happened to you?" She had tried repeatedly to get information from Daniel but he kept shushing her, his attention focused on Edward. "You're alive. And you're all right. It's a miracle."

Isabella knew that wasn't the whole truth—if her research findings were any indication, he *wasn't* completely fine—but she wasn't going to tip her hand just yet. She needed to lull them both as she tried to figure out what Daniel's role had been in the attacks of the last few weeks.

"Sweet reunion."

"It's amazing." She focused on Edward, pleased to see the gun still hung by his side. It didn't calm her, per se, but it did give her hope all wasn't completely lost. "What I can't understand is why you're hiding. This is miraculous news. What we've all worked so long for."

"Which you've ruined by going public." Edward said.

And now we're getting somewhere. "How did I ruin anything?"

"You took the research public. Gave it away. Put us in jeopardy. People get suspicious when men start rising from the dead."

Isabella knew there was something underneath Edward's mania and panic, but she couldn't place it. Why hide? "But you're alive and well. And you didn't rise from the dead, not really. You survived. Thrived with gene therapy. That's what scientific research is about. What my work is all about."

"Not when it's experimental! When it's going to get people interested in knowing more. When it draws attention." Anger exploded from Edward like a canon blast and her heart pounded in a fast clip against her rib cage.

She'd overstepped. The gentle questions and scientific curiosity hadn't paid quite the dividends she'd hoped but she continued to push. "But you're living proof of the work. You're both doing so well."

"Cured, damn it. We're cured." Edward's hand shook, the gun waving at his side, his eyes darting between her and Daniel.

She felt Daniel's grip over her forearm, as if to still her

in place. "We've been suffering some side effects. Things we never discovered in our test subjects."

"What test subjects?" Despite the threat of Edward's shaking trigger finger, she needed to know what Daniel was talking about. "Who do you mean?"

"The others." Daniel shook his head, regret shimmering around him like heat rising off asphalt.

"What others?" When neither man answered, the adrenaline that had carried through the door morphed, spiking into a nauseous cocktail in her stomach. "What others, Daniel?"

Edward's eyes continued their race between her and Daniel, his smile knowing as his gaze came to rest on Daniel. "That's always bothered you, you sorry bastard. Hasn't it?"

"It was wrong."

"It was research! They died for something extraordinary."

Daniel's voice quavered, every one of his long and pain-filled years carved into the lines of his face. "They had no idea. They were drafted without making the choice themselves."

"Cracked eggs to make our omelet. Nothing more."

The callous statement had her mouth dropping in shock. Isabella had pieced enough together to know they'd used human test subjects, but to be so cold-hearted about it? Like something out of Dr. Frankenstein's lab, they'd both showed blatant disregard for human life.

Life they were sworn to uphold as scientists.

Daniel's voice was a quiet whisper, his hands shaking as he stared down at the old linoleum floor. "I'm so sorry. So sorry."

Before she could ask Daniel what he meant, Edward's eyes lit up and he reached for his phone. "He's here."

* * *

Campbell kept up a steady string of curses in the small earpiece Liam wore as he moved on toward the research building Isabella had pointed out on their last visit.

"I told you there was more. You tripped one of Edward's cameras."

"What? Where."

"Damn bugger." Campbell added a few more choice expletives before he barked a few more orders. "Bastard rigged all the cameras, not just the ones in the building. You triggered an alarm as soon as you crossed into the research campus."

"So shut it down."

"It's too late. He knows."

Liam didn't wait for his brother to say anything further. He took off at a dead run.

Edward's hands trembled, the gun waving madly off the end of his fingers. Isabella knew she didn't have much time to convince him to calm down or change his mind on his obviously clear intent to kill her and Daniel so she played her last remaining card.

"How are you feeling, Edward?"

"I told you. I'm cured." The gun shook harder but she saw a small spark of awareness flit through his gaze.

"No you're not." Daniel's voice was quiet, guilt and grief layered in every word. "You know you're not and neither am I."

"We're *fine*."

"The pain?" She pressed on, hoping like hell she could hold him off and keep him distracted. "It's bad, isn't it? I know why. I can show you where the problem is."

"Tell me."

"It's in the nerve receptors. They're deteriorating. I

brought my notes with me. I…" She added a quaver to her voice for good measure. "I can show you."

"Give them to me."

"Sit down with me and I'll show you. It won't make any sense if I don't walk you through it."

Edward hesitated as he shifted from foot to foot, his gaze darting toward the door, then back at her. "No way."

"Then promise me you won't hurt Liam. You said yourself he's coming. He's innocent. He's not a part of this."

"Give me your notes."

"Promise me you won't hurt him."

"You have no say!" Edward had the gun up, his shaking hand steadying as he took aim. "Give. Me. Your. Notes."

She opened her bag, the moment to bargain with him vanishing like quicksilver. "You won't understand my notes."

"Try me. I deciphered your mess of notes from before, I can do it again. All it took was a bit of testing on some poor unfortunates who weren't going to get better anyway."

She shuddered at the proof of what he'd done. Daniel's hand tightened on her forearm once more and his words were a soft plea when he spoke. "I'm so sorry. For all of it."

The proof of her mentor's guilt struck like a spear to the heart but the pain was nothing compared to the sight of Liam charging through the door, his gun drawn.

Or Edward's rising arms as he took aim.

Isabella screamed a warning but he didn't need it. The "eyes" Campbell had provided had Liam aiming at her captor as he came through the door. Her gaze was focused on a small man, his gun in hand, but Liam had already taken aim, his motions all raw instinct and years of training.

What he couldn't stop was the reaction of the man sitting next to Isabella on an old cot.

Daniel leaped toward the gunman. Bodies merged and collided as two gunshots fired in the small space. Liam had no way of holding back, the bullet already in motion. And he saw as it made contact with the small man's head, slamming him back against the wall as the second man fell on top of him.

"Daniel!" Isabella started for the bodies but Liam intercepted her, grabbing her close and pulling her back toward the door.

"I need to see them."

"Isabella." He kept dragging her, despite her protests and struggling form. "Wait. Please wait."

Jack and Kenzi ran toward them down the hall and Liam barked orders as he held a struggling Isabella. "Two men down. I don't have confirmation on either of them."

His future brother-in-law moved into action, his gun in hand as he went through the door. Within moments Jack hollered an all-clear from the room.

"You're okay." He dropped his gun to the ground and pulled Isabella close. "I didn't think I'd get to you."

"I need to go in there."

"Give me a minute. Please. I need you right here. For just a minute, I need you here." He ran his hands up and down her back, pleased when she finally stopped struggling. "Just right here. With me."

"You killed him. Edward." She whispered against his chest, her shoulders quivering from the adrenaline and the hard sobs that racked her body. "He's gone."

"He's gone."

"And so is Daniel."

Liam glanced toward where his sister and future brother-in-law stood inside the door, Jack's nod a silent acknowledgment of Isabella's suspicions.

"Yes." He ran his hands over her face, savoring the soft skin of her cheek. "Why'd you do this without me?"

Large tears spilled from her lashes but her voice was firm and strong when she spoke. "I love you. I couldn't put you in danger. I couldn't stand it if something happened to you."

"So it was okay you did it to me? What if something had happened to you? I love you and I spent the last hour terrified I wouldn't get here in time."

"It's not the same. Not after Wayne and Aidan last night. Not after I knew what Edward wanted. I—" Realization dawned bright and vivid in her eyes. "You love me."

"Yeah."

"I thought you were afraid and scared and not ready and a loner."

"When did I say that?"

"You didn't." She shook her head as more tears fell down her cheeks. "But I inferred from the data that's what you meant."

He knew they'd nearly lost each other. Knew the events of the morning would live with both of them forever, but in that moment he couldn't resist the sheer joy of teasing her. "What data?"

"The data I collected from your behavior. The way you looked at me in the shower. That was fear in your eyes."

"It was." The smile fell from his face and he knew he had to be honest.

Had to face his fears once and for all.

"I swore to myself I'd never love someone who could leave me. I'm stuck with my family but that was it. I was damned if I'd add anyone new."

"And?"

"And I *was* damned. That's just it. I've been living half

my life. I keep everyone at arm's length, thinking that will make me happy. Will keep the darkness at bay."

"And does it?"

"No. All it means is that I sit in the dark." He pulled her close once more, pressing his lips to her temple. Her wet cheek. Then on to her lips. "I love you. I want a life with you and I want to stand by you."

"I love you, Liam. With everything I am, I love you."

"Then can we make a promise to each other. Right here, right now?"

"Anything."

His arms tightened around her as the reality of almost losing her washed through him once more in a hard wave. "Don't ever run off without me again. There's no problem that's too big we can't face it together."

"But—"

"Ever. We're partners. And we're going to spend our lives together."

He saw that stubborn spark he loved so much light in the depths of her eyes. "I acted on the evidence I had. I needed to do this."

"Then your hypothesis was faulty."

"Now you're a scientist?"

"No. I'm a man in love. And I'm never letting you go." He pressed his lips to hers and let the world fade away around them.

She might have scientific fact on her side, but since there was no empirical evidence that could beat the power of love, Liam figured he had a fighting chance.

Epilogue

Alexander Steele's bright blue gaze had morphed from tearful joy to calculating craftiness throughout the evening and Liam wasn't sure which expression he enjoyed more.

Wily old bastard.

He'd even told Grandfather as much when the man had arrived for dinner, his hand locked firmly with Grandmother's. Alexander had only chuckled, then whispered loudly to Liam's grandmother, "See, Penelope. I told you everything would work out."

And so things *had* worked out.

He wouldn't have believed it, thinking back to that rain-soaked night at his grandparents' townhome when he opened the door to let Isabella in. Couldn't have known the shy woman on the other side of the door was the other half of his heart.

Yet here they were, a month past her thorough briefing to the *New York Times* on her research, the inherent risks and how to keep the knowledge safe.

And now they looked toward a future together.

The box in his pocket felt like a boulder and he fought the urge to keep touching it so as not to tip anyone off to his plans. Although he'd worked hard over the last weeks to share more with his loved ones, there were some things a man wanted to keep to himself until the moment was right.

Alexander stood at the head of the table, his gaze tearful once more, as he stared down the table at all of them. "My grandchildren."

Liam sat at the opposite head, Isabella on his right and she reached for his hand, entwining their fingers.

"Your grandmother and I were there on the day each of you were born. We've watched you grow. And we've watched you all live through adversity. Nothing makes me happier than knowing you all have partners to travel through life with. To lighten the load. To create a family. To share all the richness that makes up the tapestry of our lives."

Liam's fingers tightened on Isabella's before he got to his feet. "A perfect segue, Grandfather."

"Is it?"

"Your gift for proclamations is something I can always depend on."

He shot his grandfather a wink, pleased when the older man nodded, pride puffing out his chest. "By all means, then."

Liam turned toward Isabella, the box growing even heavier in his pocket. "It's taken me a long time to truly realize the rare and wonderful gift I have in the people assembled around this table. You've given that to me. You've made me realize the importance of love and the value of family."

He pulled the box from his pocket and dropped to his knee beside her chair.

"So I can think of no more fitting way to ask you to share your life with me than in front of the people who matter most to me in the world."

Love, bright and pure, shone from her eyes as she nodded, her hands settling on his chest. "Yes, Liam. I will share my life with you."

He flipped open the lid of the box, prepared to slip the ring on her finger when she pulled him close, her lips pressed to his. Stunned, he murmured against her lips. "Don't you want to see your ring?"

"Later." She pressed her lips to his once more before he pulled back in confusion.

"Isn't that the way men are supposed to seal the deal? With the ring?"

"My love." Her hands rested on his shoulders and her eyes shone with love, bright as the richest emeralds. "Diamonds are nothing but compressed earth. Rare, yes, but still just a pretty rock. It's love that's the rarest of all. Infinitely precious. Far richer than any gem."

As their lips met once more the cheers of his family rose up around them. And as he kissed her with everything he was, Liam knew Isabella had the right of it.

Love was the rarest of all.

And he was a man who had love in abundance.

* * * * *